## WESTWARD DREAMS SERIES

# A Distant Dawn

# Other books by Jane Peart

## The Brides of Montclair Series

*Valiant Bride*
*Ransomed Bride*
*Fortune's Bride*
*Folly's Bride*
*Yankee Bride/Rebel Bride*
*Gallant Bride*
*Shadow Bride*
*Destiny's Bride*
*Jubilee Bride*
*Mirror Bride*
*Hero's Bride*
*Senator's Bride*

## The Westward Dreams Series

*Runaway Heart*
*Promise of the Valley*
*Where Tomorrow Waits*
*A Distant Dawn*

WESTWARD DREAMS SERIES

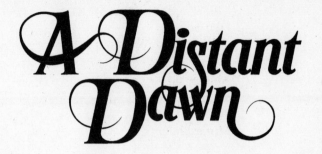

# A Distant Dawn

## JANE PEART

### Book 4

ZondervanPublishingHouse
*Grand Rapids, Michigan*

*A Division of* HarperCollins*Publishers*

*A Distant Dawn*
Copyright © 1995 by Jane Peart

Requests for information should be addressed to:

ZondervanPublishingHouse
*Grand Rapids, Michigan 49530*

---

**Library of Congress Cataloging-in-Publication Data**

Peart. Jane.
    A distant dawn / Jane Peart.
       p.  cm. — (Westward dream series ; bk. 4)
     ISBN: 0-310-41301-X (softcover)
     1. Frontier and pioneer life—West (U.S.)—Fiction. 2. Women pioneers—
West (U.S.)—Fiction.   I. title.  II. Series: Peart, Jane. Westward dreams
series ; bk. 4.
PS3566.E238D57  1995
813'.54—dc20                                   95-35737
                                                      CIP

---

*Edited by Bob Hudson and Robin Schmitt*

*Printed in the United States of America*

---

95 96 97 98 99 00 01 02 /❖ DH / 10 9 8 7 6 5 4 3 2 1

WESTWARD DREAMS SERIES

A Distant Dawn

# Chapter 1

"*L*ook at *that*, Sunny!" the boy exclaimed.

Sunniva Lyndall turned and read the sign to which her sixteen-year-old brother pointed:

WANTED: Young, skinny, wiry fellows, not over eighteen. Must be expert riders, willing to risk life daily. Orphans preferred. Interested persons should apply at the local Pony Express company.

"Well?" she shrugged. Then as she realized why he wanted her to see it she demanded, "Are you out of your mind, Tracy?"

The eagerness on Tracy's freckled face faded.

"Don't even *think* about it!" She held up a warning hand to ward off any further reckless enthusiasm.

"Ah, Sunny—," he protested.

"No! Don't say a word! I won't listen!" His sister's hazel eyes flashed. "You want to get killed before we even get to California?"

She moved away but he grabbed her arm. "Wait just a durn minute, Sunny! We're flat broke, remember? You got a better idea?"

Feeling sick dismay sweep over her at his reminder of their predicament, Sunny spoke more sharply than she

7

intended. "No, I don't have a better idea at the moment, but I'll think of something." As an afterthought, she added, "And you watch your language, young man, you hear?" She walked on. Then, realizing he wasn't following, she stopped and looked back. Her brother was still standing there, hands thrust into his pockets, making a circle in the dusty street with the toe of his boot.

"Come on, Tracy," she called impatiently. For a long moment, Tracy remained staring at the poster. "Come on!" she repeated with increasing irritability.

Reluctantly and slowly her brother moved, mumbling under his breath. Sunny bit her lower lip in irritation. Weren't things bad enough without her having to deal with his childishness? To make matters worse, *she* was to blame for their plight! Blatantly swindled, out of money, stranded in a Missouri border town. Temporarily, at least. Surely when she found the sheriff of this town, explained what had happened . . .

How stupid she had been to trust that blackguard Colin Faraday. The whole sorry scene that had taken place on the train on their way here came back to Sunny in vivid detail.

It had seemed such a good plan, a great adventure, when they had set out from their small Ohio Valley community. Filled with excitement and high hopes, they boarded the train to Independence, Missouri. Even the name was significant to them. It was the "jumping-off place" to the West. There they would join one of the many wagon trains heading to California, where they would homestead and make their fortune.

Sunny remembered how optimistic they were but how hopelessly inexperienced in the ways of the world.

On the train, they encountered an affable fellow traveler. Seated across the aisle from them, he introduced himself as Colin Faraday and soon engaged them in conversation. He seemed so interested in them, asking them many questions about where they were from, where they were going. His pleasant personality, his jolly laugh, and his self-assured manner soon won their confidence. They found themselves telling him their plans, their hopes for the future.

"Well now, if that ain't the best kind of luck. A sure enough example of being in the right place at the right time—and being the right man!" he said with a broad wink. "I don't know how many times I been on this same train and met up with folks like you going west. I have great admiration for people with that kind of dreams"—he leaned closer—"and I'm in the business of making them come true. Leastways, *helpin'* make them come true." He lowered his voice. "But you gotta be careful about gettin' your wagon, your mules or oxen, your supplies. ... The merchants and storekeepers at these towns where the wagon trains set out from are like foxes, ready to devour unsuspecting emigrants like yourselves. Not that you ain't got a good head on your shoulders, no siree bob. I seen that right away. You, young lady, and this here young man, I could tell you know where it's at, but ..." He shook his head. "Heard some sad tales of folks bein'—" a worried look crossed his face—"well, unless you know what you're doin'..."

At his words, Sunny suddenly felt the full weight of what they had done. Buoyed with enthusiasm, she had ignored all the warnings, relatives' dire predictions of the hazards of the undertaking. It was *she* who had read the glowing *Emigrants Handbook* from cover to cover, committing to memory just what they would need to purchase to become part of one of the wagon trains going west. Her hands clutched her small purse, in which was most of the cash they had received from the sale of the house, the furniture, the cow, their three horses. This was the first time since they had left home that she felt she might have taken on more than she could handle. Now the fear that she might not be able to choose wisely, make good assessment of value on buying a wagon, trust the merchants to deal fairly, made her weak with apprehension.

"Isn't there someone we could talk to, someone to consult?" Sunny had asked Faraday in a faltering voice.

"Yes, ma'am, there sure is!" Mr. Faraday laughed heartily. He jabbed his thumb into his chest. "You're looking right at him."

Faraday proceeded to tell them that he was willing to do for them what he'd done for countless others starting out to the new part of the country.

"More than willin'," he assured them. Then he explained how he could procure their "outfit"—wagon, mules, and other necessary equipment—for them and save them from being cheated by unscrupulous suppliers who fed off the ignorant.

"That is very kind of you, Mr. Faraday. But I don't know whether we should impose on your goodwill. Won't that take a great deal of trouble and time for you? From your own business in Fairfax City?" Sunny was torn by her natural reluctance to rely on a stranger. However, the relief of turning over the responsibility to someone more knowledgeable than she to outfit them for the journey west was greater.

"Well, ma'am, I took to you and this young fellow the minute I set eyes on you both. I sez to myself, sez I, now there's a pair of fine, upstanding, ambitious young people ready to face the future and expand this great country of ours. It would be a pleasure—no, let's say a downright honor—to assist such a couple."

He then told them the best way to handle the transaction. He drew a stubby pencil out of his vest pocket, searched in the pocket of his jacket and brought out a crumpled envelope, turned it over and started writing down a list of items to be bought, jotting the possible price in an opposite column. His lips moved as he counted—

audibly but under his breath and therefore unintelligible to them. At last, with pursed mouth and a frown, he gave a sigh and rattled off a sum.

"That's only a by guess and by golly based on the prices the last time I did this for friends. But I'm sure I can do better than this, given a little time." His eyes squinted as he beamed at them both. "And it *might* take time, searching around, comparing prices, gettin' the best deal. So what I suggest is this: When we get to the train stop right before Independence, a place called Cottonwood, you two get off and go to the hotel there, get a room. I'll ride on into town and do my bargain huntin' and finaglin'. Then when I've got your outfit hitched and packed, I'll bring it over so that you can take it on out to the Oakmont; that's where all the wagons assemble for a few days before leaving. They call it the *rondaysvoos* yard."

He handed the envelope over to Sunny.

She drew a sharp breath. The total was more than half of all the money she had. But they wouldn't need much money on the trail, except perhaps at the two army forts, where there were trading posts to replenish their provisions. Naturally, their initial outlay would seem exorbitant. If they had purchased a wagon and supplies at home before they left, it might have been better—but it was too late to worry about that now. She should feel glad they'd met this kind stranger who had so generously offered to help them. She knew she would have been helpless dealing with sharp merchants herself. So with only a few misgivings Sunny counted out the cash into Mr. Faraday's pudgy, outstretched palm.

"I've written to Mr. Lucas Flynt, the wagon master, reserved us a place in his wagon train leaving on the fifteenth of April," Sunny told Faraday.

"Flynt? Yep, know him well. He's top grade. You couldn't put your fate in better hands. Led dozens of wagon trains

11

safely 'crosst country. Heard tell he's had powwows with them Plains Indians."

*"Indians?"* Tracy's eyes lit up.

"Oh, yessir, boy. Some of the trains has run into Indian trouble. 'Cept Flynt's. None 't all." Mr. Faraday folded up the bills, tucked them into the inside pocket of his gaudy plaid coat.

"So then, Mr. Faraday, we'll wait at the hotel for you? And you will bring our wagon, mules or oxen—whichever you decide is the better animal for the long journey—along with our provisions there?"

"That's the ticket, little lady."

"When should we expect you to come?"

"Can't say for sure. These things take time, as I said. But if you don't want to. . ." Faraday made a gesture as if to retrieve the wad of bills and return them to her. But Sunny quickly halted him with a wave of one hand.

"No, no! Mr. Faraday, I just wanted to get some idea of how long we'll be staying at the hotel. I assure you, I appreciate very much what you're doing for us."

As Sunny recalled her words she shuddered. How could she have been so gullible? They had been proverbial lambs led to slaughter.

But he had seemed so nice, so truly concerned about their welfare, so anxious to help. How could she have guessed? She should have been warned by the flamboyant plaid suit, the two-toned shoes, the yellow silk handkerchief, the bowler hat. Now that she thought of it, all of it shouted *beware!* If she had only been smart enough.

At the hotel Sunny was given the only single room available, while Tracy shared a room with four other men on the top floor. Sunny spend a restless night. Noise from the streets of a town that never seemed to sleep, the sound of voices, high-pitched laughter from the saloon downstairs, the rattle of wagon wheels from a stream of seemingly endless traffic outside, made sleep difficult. The second night, worry added to the other things kept her awake. When two days passed with no word from Faraday, the awful possibility that he might not show up at all dawned upon Sunny.

At first Sunny did not confess her growing uneasiness to her brother. On the third morning of their stay, after some cautious questioning, Sunny discovered that no one had ever heard of Mr. Faraday nor of anyone offering that kind of service. Horrified, she came to the conclusion that they had been duped by a professional "con" man. The man had never intended to arrange anything for them; he had simply taken their money and disappeared.

Well, he wasn't going to get away with it. Not if she could help it. She would find some way to bring him to justice and recoup their "nest egg."

When she finally told Tracy, he simply stared at her speechlessly.

"You mean we can't go to California after all?"

"Didn't you understand? That—that *criminal* has stolen our money!"

"You mean like a bank robber?"

"Exactly," she replied grimly.

"What are we going to do?"

"The first thing I'm going to do is try to find Lucas Flynt. We'll go out to Oakmont, the rendezvous yard, and tell him just what's happened. He can probably get the man arrested or—something! I don't know. We've got to do something, Tracy. We're almost out of money."

The hotel desk clerk gave them directions to the livery stable, where they might be able to hire a horse and small wagon or buggy. That's where they were headed when Tracy spotted the sign advertising for Pony Express riders.

Sunny glanced over her shoulder at her brother, who still looked nettled. Her quick rejection of his idea had got his dander up. Realizing that it was only his way of trying to help, Sunny felt contrite. Of course such a job would appeal to him. He rode like someone born on a saddle. They were both excellent horseback riders. Their father had put them both on ponies by the time they were three, taught them to ride. But a job like *that* was out of the question. Even the ad didn't hide the fact that it was dangerous. Said right out, "Must be willing to risk life daily. *Orphans preferred.*" Imagine! Well, they weren't desperate enough to allow Tracy to do *that*! At least, not yet.

# Chapter 2

*S*unny marched determinedly ahead; her brother lagged in her wake at a slower pace. That's the way it had always been. Eight years older than he, Sunny had always been the leader. That's why she felt so horribly responsible now that it was *she* who had landed them in this mess. She was twenty-three and should have known better.

Going to California had been *her* dream. There to find the happiness and independence she longed for, away from her stepmother's nagging relatives. She read all the brochures, all the enthusiastic accounts of how it was a land of opportunity, of untold rewards for those who had the will and vision to work hard. It hadn't taken much to get her brother to become just as eager.

Tracy had been her special charge almost from the time he was born and certainly after their mother died when he was just two years old. Sunny pressed her lips together firmly. Yes, she might have got them into this, but she would get them out!

Even walking through town to get to the livery stable was chancy. Traffic was heavy, the street jammed with the heavy canvas-topped wagons drawn by oxen or mules on their way to Independence some fifteen miles away. Sunny felt a wrenching, indignant sensation as they stood on the wooden sidewalk and waited to cross, watching the wagons pass. *They* would be in one of those—*should* have been— if only she hadn't listened to that smooth-talking crook!

This town seemed to be bursting at its seams, growing, thriving, the gateway to Independence, which was the *real* starting place to the West. There were stores of all kinds— hardware, saddlery—and plenty of saloons! Sunny had noticed that when they walked from the railroad station that first night. The farther they walked, the more congested it got. In the distance, on the outskirts of town, they saw a number of tents. These, they learned, were the camps set up by some of the emigrants waiting for their wagons to be built so they could join up with a wagon train going west. Maybe that's where she and Tracy would have had to stay if they hadn't met up with Faraday, Sunny thought grimly. Maybe that was where they'd end up if—Sunny didn't even finish the thought. As soon as she talked to Lucas Flynt, everything would be straightened out.

At the livery stable all that was for hire was a rickety buckboard and a swaybacked nag who had seen better days and should have been put out to pasture long ago. But convinced that nothing better was available, Sunny paid what she considered to be an unreasonable rental and, after receiving indifferent directions, set out for the rendezvous yard, where Lucas Flynt's wagon train was assembling.

There were a few tense moments as they maneuvered their unreliable vehicle through the crowded thoroughfare until they were out on a rutted country road. Sunny drove while Tracy looked out for the sign with the word *Oakmont,* a name that sounded like a park for a camp meeting or a picnic. They had gone a good distance before Tracy spotted a wooden sign nailed to a fence post and shouted, "There it is, Sis!" He spelled out the crudely printed word. An arrow was painted below it. It was just another bend in the

16

road, an empty spread of stunted pine trees and scrub oaks. Less than ten huge wagons with arched canvas tops were parked at wide intervals. They really did look like sailing ships. No wonder they were called "prairie schooners."

Sunny reigned the spindly horse, who seemed more than willing to stop and nibble at some scraggly grass at the side of the road. So this was the rendezvous yard? The place where their fellow band of adventurers would set off for the great migration across hills, valleys, prairie, and mountains to the golden country of California? Viewing it, Sunny felt a sinking sensation in the pit of her stomach. Somehow she had expected activity, energetic movement, eager preparations being made, talk, laughter, children running about. Instead the only people she saw were a small group of men gathered in front of one of the covered wagons. It wasn't the picture she had held in her imagination all these weeks. Aware of Tracy's anxious eyes upon her, Sunny tried not to show any disappointment, even though it didn't look very promising. She wasn't going to let anything destroy their dream. Inwardly outraged at what had happened and determined to seek justice, Sunny wound the reins over the wooden brake and got down. As she approached them the men turned curious gazes upon her. Sunny took a deep breath, then spoke. "Excuse me, gentlemen, I'm looking for the wagon train leader, a Mr. Lucas Flynt."

In unison three of the men swung their heads to the fourth one, who regarded Sunny with undisguised interest. He tipped the brim of a slouched felt hat back from his forehead with his thumb and took a step forward.

Sunny took his measure. He was slightly under six feet tall, lean—to the point of being lanky—but muscular. His skin, tanned almost as dark as an Indian's, had the look of polished saddle leather, making his eyes startlingly blue. He looked awfully young to be a wagon master. But since

17

he was obviously the one she had to talk to, she said, "Mr. Flynt, we have suffered an outrageous wrong, and—"

Before she could continue, he held up one hand, halting her. "Sorry, ma'am, I'm not Mr. Flynt. I'm Webb Chandler, his scout."

Momentarily taken aback, Sunny said, "Oh, well then, it's Mr. Flynt I must speak to. We were to be a part of your wagon train leaving next week. But a terrible crime has been committed. On the train coming here a man presented himself to be an agent you have used on several occasions to procure proper equipment for the journey"—and here Sunny had to stop to catch her breath and swallow before going on—"and has evidently absconded with our money without purchasing our wagon, our supplies, our . . ." Under his puzzled frown, she came to a stop.

"So? Just what do you want me to do about it, ma'am?" he asked.

"Why—why, help me find him, or go with me to the sheriff and have him arrested if he can be found. He was supposed to meet us here hours ago and then take us to the rendezvous place so that we could join with your caravan . . ." Sunny's voice trailed off as she saw the expression on the man's face.

"Well, ma'am, I'm right sorry for your dilemma—I surely am. But that's not an uncommon occurrence." At her look of dismay his tone softened. "Unless you got somethin' to go on. You know his name?"

"Yes, I certainly do. It's Colin Faraday."

Chandler let out a long, slow whistle, shook his head. "Faraday, eh? Faraday's notorious for spotting—if you'll excuse the term—greenhorns."

Sunny looked shocked. "You mean to say you're not going to do anything to apprehend this thief—who, I

18

might add, used your boss's name quite freely in gaining our confidence?"

A pained expression crossed his lean face. "As I say, I'm sorry as I can be," he drawled, "but don't see as how I can do anything to help. That rascal's probably clear out of the county by now. 'Spect as he left on the next train out."

"With *our* money! And you say there's nothing can be done about it? Where is the law to protect people?"

"People foolish enough to trust strangers? Nowhere, I'm afraid."

Sunny felt a wave of hopelessness mixed with resentment at the condescension in the man's voice. The fact that what he said was the truth only made her feel worse. She didn't need anyone telling her she'd been a fool. She *knew* that. Her throat felt tight, and she felt the stinging sensation of tears at the back of her eyes. She willed them back. Evidently there was no help coming from *this* man. What were they to do? Desperately she groped for some way to rescue herself and Tracy from their dire situation.

"Is there any way we could join up with another wagon? I've still a little money left. Could we possibly pay our way by working? My brother's a champion with horses, and I could take care of children, help the other women in lots of ways."

Chandler looked beyond her as if searching for someone or something to say. Then he looked directly at her. "Ma'am, don't you think this whole matter could be better handled by your husband? Seems to me this is a man's problem."

It may have been spoken with an effort to seem patient, but to Sunny it sounded disdainful. She felt her face burn. Sorry she had revealed her desperation by appealing to his sympathy, she drew herself up and replied coldly, "I have no husband. And I am perfectly capable of handling this myself if you would be kind enough to direct me to the local law enforcement."

A smile tugged at Chandler's mouth, but he replied

solemnly, "The sheriff's office is right next to the Palace Hotel, ma'am. And if you don't get any satisfaction there, might I suggest you try Mr. Flynt himself. Although I doubt he'd tell you much different than I did. As I said, it happens all the time—"

"I don't want to hear about anyone else, thank you!" Sunny snapped. "It's *us* I'm interested in, and seeing justice done." With that she whirled around and started back toward the wagon, almost colliding into Tracy, who had come up and stood behind her during this exchange with the scout. Sunny brushed past him and he had to hurry to keep up with her. She was in the wagon, reins in hand, when he sprang up beside her. He was barely seated before she gave the horse a smart slap with the reins, turned around, and headed back toward town.

Darting a quick glance at his sister, he recognized that set of her jaw, the small, square chin lifted. He knew that look and he knew Sunny. He could almost read her thoughts. After all they'd been through to get here, she wasn't about to give up. She'd think of some way, do something. Tracy didn't know just what.

As the buckboard on its wobbly wheels pulled out onto the road, Webb Chandler looked after the young woman driving it. That lady had spunk and sass, all right. Spirited as they come, she might just be someone to stand up even to Flynt, he reckoned. Of course, she was obviously upset. Her face all flushed, frowning, her eyes sparking fire. Under other circumstances she might be attractive. Dressed too plain though, almost like those women in a painting he'd once seen of the Pilgrims landing on Plymouth Rock. Her high-collared dress was brown—a color Webb couldn't abide—and not a ribbon or bow or flower on her hat, either. While she had been talking she'd impatiently pushed back the untidy wisps of honey-colored hair straggling out from under the shelf of her stiff bonnet. Still, she was one of the prettiest women he had seen in many a day.

# Chapter 3

They returned the horse and wagon to the livery stable, then walked back to the hotel. In the lobby, Sunny went directly up to the counter. The man behind it, bent over a ledger, did not look up at her approach. Sunny drummed her fingers impatiently on the countertop, waiting for him to acknowledge her. Clearing her throat, she said, "Excuse me, sir." The desk clerk still did not move. Was he purposely ignoring her? She tapped the service bell twice. This finally got his attention. He turned, frowning. "Yes, ma'am?" The tone was annoyed but he came forward. Leaning on one elbow, he peered at her with narrowed eyes.

Meeting them, Sunny asked coolly, "I was told I could find a Mr. Lucas Flynt, the wagon master, here. Could you tell me if he is?"

The man jerked his thumb and inclined his head toward the other side of the lobby. "Most likely you'll find him there."

Sunny looked in the direction of his thumb to the far end of the room. Out from louvered doors swirled clouds of smoke, loud voices, laughter against a background of tinny piano music. Obviously the hotel saloon. Could she bring herself to go into a place like that—a "den of iniquity," as her stepmother would judge it? She saw the man behind the counter smirk, and something within her stiffened. Flynt's wagon train was due to pull out in three days. She had to try to convince the wagon master of some way she and Tracy could be on it. Straightening her shoulders, Sunny started toward the swinging doors of the saloon. Tracy caught her arm and said in a low, nervous voice, "Sunny, you don't want to go in there. It's no place for a lady!"

"The kid's right," the desk clerk echoed with a malicious smile.

His comment was like a red flag waving. Sunny's determination hardened. She'd had enough male condescension for one day. Their very future was at stake. Nothing was going to stop her now. Certainly nothing as trivial as something not being *ladylike*. Her fingers pried at Tracy's grip. Between gritted teeth she whispered, "Let go, Tracy. I've got to talk to Mr. Flynt myself. It's our only chance!"

Tracy knew his sister well enough to realize that once her mind was made up, there was no use arguing. Gradually his hold loosened. His expression was one of helpless resignation. "Well, all right, but I'm coming with you."

"It'll be all right. You'll see," Sunny said, wishing she was as confident as she tried to sound. Resolutely she crossed the lobby toward the saloon, Tracy her reluctant escort.

With only a second's hesitation she pushed through the swinging doors. The smoke-filled, stuffy air was sour with the smell of whiskey, and her nostrils quivered with distaste. The noise was almost deafening; loud bursts of raucous laughter mingled with the drone of voices, the din of the piano badly in need of tuning. Standing on the threshold, she took in the scene: men were huddled around tables, others lined up two deep at the long oak bar. She was only dimly aware of a few gaudily dressed women scattered throughout the crowd. Instead her gaze moved slowly around the murky room, eyes searching for Lucas Flynt.

How had the scout described him? Broad as a beam, a mustache red as a fire engine? Tracy's uneasiness mounted. Her own resolve was ebbing when she spotted him. Seated at a round table with a bottle in its center was a hulk of a man with a drooping, rust-colored handlebar mustache, playing cards. A wide-brimmed hat pushed up from his forehead, his shoulders hunched, he studied the cards in his large hands.

She was sure that was the man she wanted to see, to talk to, to persuade.

"There he is," she murmured to Tracy. "Come on."

"Uh, Sunny, I don't think this is a good idea. . .," was Tracy's hesitant response.

Disregarding his last-ditch attempt to stop her, Sunny threaded her way through the room to the table where Lucas Flynt sat. Reaching it, she dragged up her courage. "Mr. Flynt?"

One of the others at the table glanced up, nudged the man next to him, and drawled, "There's a lady wants your attention, Luke."

Still holding his cards, Lucas Flynt slowly lifted his head and pierced her with a look that sent her heart racing, knotted her stomach. The cheroot he held in the corner of his mouth tipped. "I'm Lucas Flynt," he growled. "What do you want with me?"

"I urgently need to speak to you."

The buzz of conversation at nearby tables subsided. Heads turned, chairs scraped back so their occupants could get a better look. This might prove interesting. The primly attired young woman, and the skinny boy standing behind, approaching "Big Luke" was no ordinary occurrence. And while he was playing cards! The possibility of something exciting happening sharpened the curiosity of the saloon patrons.

Flynt moved the cheroot to the other side of his mouth,

24

pulled a card out, tapped it on his chin, then laid it on the table. "You shure it's *me* you want?"

"Yes," Sunny replied firmly. She drew another long breath. "It's business I must discuss. Business of a very serious nature."

He frowned, bushy eyebrows meeting over the big, crooked nose that must have been broken sometime. He raised his steely gray eyes from his cards and gave her a glowering stare that would have intimidated someone less determined.

"This ain't exactly the place, lady."

She was about to stress the importance of her request when a man's voice spoke. "Excuse me, ma'am, but we don't serve ladies in here. You'll have to leave." She turned her head and saw a large, bald man in a striped shirt, with an apron tied over dark trousers—it was the bartender. "And no kids either." He indicated a mortified Tracy, whose face had turned beet red.

"I'm not here to be served. Neither is my brother," Sunny quickly explained. "I've come to talk to Mr. Flynt on business." She turned back to Flynt. "It will only take a few minutes. I implore you—"

"Can't you see I'm in the middle of a game?"

"I'm truly sorry, but if this weren't so very urgent, I—"

"Go ahead, Flynt. Talk to the little lady," one of the other cardplayers urged with a sly cackle.

"Some of your past catchin' up with you, Flynt?" another crony asked with an insinuating wink at Sunny.

Flynt shifted in his chair, breasting his cards, then glared at Sunny. "You'll have to wait till I play this hand. Then I'll meet you out in the lobby."

"Thank you very much," she said tightly. She'd accomplished her object, but now her knees felt weak. Her face aflame, Sunny turned away from the rudely gawking men. Acutely aware of the eyes upon her, the ripple of laughter,

25

the remarks being exchanged among the saloon patrons, Sunny held her head high as she went back out to the lobby, Tracy hot on her heels.

Once outside the saloon, he turned on her furiously. "Dog-gone it, Sunny. You sure done it. Makin' a rare spectacle of yourself in there, and *me* too!" he accused her. "They were all laughin' at us."

She spun around and faced him. "Do you think I care what a bunch of uncouth, beer-guzzling *poker players* think?" she flung back. "This is about *our* money. I'm trying to find some way we can get to California! I'm trying to rescue us, boy! Don't you understand we're stranded here, almost destitute? Instead of being mad at me, you ought to be grateful. I'm doing the best I can."

Tracy got even redder. He lowered his eyes. Sunny's anger melted to understanding. She realized she had embarrassed him. But it hadn't been a Sunday school picnic for her either to go into that awful place. But she'd *had* to. *Somebody* had to. Tracy had just turned sixteen and was hardly more than a child. It *had* to be her, no matter *how* humiliating it was.

"Sorry," he mumbled. She put out her hand and touched his arm.

"It's all right. It's going to work out. It has to," she said. "Let's sit over there in that alcove and wait for Mr. Flynt."

She saw the desk clerk look up as they passed, a snide smile on his smug, pasty face. She would have liked to smack that face, she thought furiously. What if it was *his* mother or sister in the same predicament *she* was in? He wouldn't be grinning like an idiot then. He'd be proud of her. At least, he *should* be.

Glancing at Tracy, Sunny wasn't so sure *he* was. She went over, intending to say a few words to comfort him, reassure him. But when she put her hand on his arm, he shook it off and took a few steps away. His back to her, he stood looking out the hotel window.

His head was down, his chin nearly to his chest, his hands plunged into his jacket pockets. With a shock, she saw his bony wrists protruding. He was growing so fast, that jacket was almost too small for him already! The frightening facts of the situation assaulted her again. Alone in a strange town, money nearly gone. No one willing to help them. *Dear God, please!* was the only prayer Sunny could think of.

Sunny took a seat on one of the stiff, horsehair chairs and glued her eyes on the saloon doors hopefully. She watched every time it opened and men went out, but there was no sign of Lucas Flynt.

Just when Sunny decided Flynt wasn't coming, the slatted doors to the saloon swung open and Lucas Flynt stood there looking annoyed, his gaze sweeping the lobby. Sunny jumped to her feet, and then he strode toward her.

As politely as she could manage, Sunny told him her well-rehearsed story, explaining what had happened and finishing by asking if somehow she and Tracy could work their way to California, hitch up with some other family's wagon.

"We're both strong, both good with horses, and I can do all sorts of things to help the women—" Her voice failed along with her hopes as Flynt shook his head, pursing his lips under the shaggy mustache.

"No way, ma'am. No can do."

"But we signed on. We wrote to your outfitting company. We sent our deposit ... ," she protested.

"I'm sorry as can be, ma'am, but there ain't nothing I can do. It's written in the guidelines set up. Each emigrant has to have their own wagon, team, and supplies."

Shock and disbelief mingled in Sunny's expression. Then her face flushed with indignation. "But I told you. That man—that scoundrel—assured us he would buy everything we needed. He was to meet us here yesterday with—"

"That's a durn shame, ma'am. I cain't tell you how many

27

times I've heard the same sorry tale, but as it says in the Good Book, you gotta be wise as a fox—especially here, as well as in Independence. There's all kinds of scalawags and sharpies out to do in greenhorns."

Sunny bristled at the same term the insufferable scout had used about them.

Flynt shook his head again. "All I can suggest, lady, is you and the kid go back home."

"But we can't—" Sunny began, feeling betraying tears rush into her eyes. She blinked them back, bit her lower lip, which had begun to tremble. She wasn't about to tell this hard-hearted man that they didn't even have enough money for train fare back home. Plus, how could she ever face the "I told you sos" from all the relatives if they did go back?

"You mean there's no way—no possible way—"

"No, ma'am, no way I can see—none at all."

Flynt seemed to be about to say something else, then changed his mind. He was obviously uncomfortable in this situation. He gave the edge of his brim a little tug, then with another doleful shake of his head turned and walked back into the saloon.

Her knees suddenly weak, Sunny sat down. Tracy stood over her, watching her mutely. She felt like crying or screaming—or both. But it was still important to put a good face on disaster. For Tracy's sake. Sunny pressed her lips together. "Well, so much for that. There must be another way."

"Well, there is, but you won't listen," Tracy said, jumping on this moment of indecision.

"If you mean what I think you mean, forget it."

"Doggone it, Sunny, you're so durn stubborn—"

"Keep your voice down, Tracy," she said between clenched teeth. "Don't make a scene. Everybody's staring at us as it is."

Looking around, Tracy saw that her statement was true.

The few people in the lobby evidently witnessed their meeting with Lucas Flynt, perhaps even heard some of the exchange with him. A few had lowered their newspapers unabashedly while it was going on. Tracy shifted from one foot to the other.

Embarrassed, Sunny rose and said in a tense voice, "Let's go up to my room, where we can discuss this *in private*."

"No, I'm going out for a while to cool off," Tracy muttered, and he turned abruptly, stalking across the lobby and out the hotel door, leaving Sunny stunned, standing alone.

# Chapter 4

*C*onscious of the desk clerk's curious eyes, Sunny gathered her shattered dignity like a ragged cloak and turned back to the counter. "My key, please," she said icily. He handed her the key attached to a paper disk on which was printed the number twelve. Ignoring his knowing sneer, she murmured, "Thank you." Then, holding herself very stiff and straight, she went up the stairs. Reaching the top, she went down the dingy corridor to the room she had rented. She opened the door, shut it behind her firmly, then leaned back against it with both hands behind her and closed her eyes for a long moment. What now? What on earth were they to do *now*?

She must pull herself together. She must not give Tracy the slightest cause to suspect that she didn't know exactly what they should do next, what steps to take. First she had to find out just how much money they had. She emptied out her purse, counting the cash out to the last penny. The result was that Sunny felt as if she were staring into an abyss. A dark, bottomless hole without a glimmer of light. She drew a shaky breath, feeling very lonely and very, very frightened.

There had been plenty of times in her life when Sunny had been told she was "unteachable." Her stepmother had often accused her of thinking she "knew everything." Well, this time she didn't. She had refused to listen when everyone tried to talk sense into her. Her stepmother's relatives had been appalled to learn that she had put the house and the valuable farmland up for sale. And when they found out what she intended to do with the money, they had descended on her, cautioning, remonstrating, chastising, even offering to buy the property themselves "to keep it in the family," in trust for Tracy when he came of age. Stubbornly she had rejected all the unsolicited but well-intentioned advice. They had left, shaking their heads. What would they think now if they knew that all their dire predictions had come true?

How could she go home to that kind of reproach? *Home?* There *was* no home to go to, not now, because of her reckless irresponsibility! Reckless. Irresponsible. The very labels *they* had given her.

But how could she have foreseen the possibility of being tricked and robbed?

Sunny put her head in her hands. A picture of Tracy came into her mind, his round, guileless eyes, his freckles, his little-boy grin. He had trusted her. And she had failed him. Swept away by those stories of the glorious opportunities for land and riches in the west she had believed. She had brought all this upon them. It was all *her* fault.

She had always felt hemmed in by the small town where she had grown up; she had always longed for new horizons, to travel and find what was at the end of that mythical rainbow. Going to California had seemed like the ultimate chance to discover it all. Her stepmother had often reprimanded her for daydreaming. California had been her daydream. Now those dreams seemed to have crumbled about her.

Sunny finally raised her head. Enough of this self-pity. She'd have to think of something. Her father had always told them not to complain but to count their blessings. They were both young, healthy, and strong. Surely they could find some kind of work. Both had the skills they had planned to use in homesteading. Tracy knew all about horses. He could probably get a job at a livery stable or maybe a ranch. Sunny could do housework. Although that prospect filled her with despair, she tried to be optimistic. It only meant putting aside their dreams of going to California for a while. She *had* to believe that.

Her stepmother had told her often enough that her tongue was too sharp, her temper too short, and her comments too opinionated, that her attitude in general was unbecoming for a woman. In the future she'd have to be more tactful in dealing with Tracy. She was so used to taking the lead that her manner was sometimes authoritative, and he resented it. Almost always he had gone along with whatever she suggested or decided. Today was the first time he had openly argued with her over a decision. This hint of rebellion in her younger brother had shaken her. Sunny decided she owed Tracy an apology. When he came back, she would lay out her ideas, discuss them with him.

What no one ever gave her credit for was imagination, independence, and courage. If she and her brother were going to survive this major setback, these qualities would have to be employed. She wasn't yet defeated. She'd find a way out of this present dilemma. She *had* to.

Suddenly Sunny felt exhausted, bone-tired, worn out with all the stress of their ordeal. She unbuttoned her shoes, kicked them off, loosened her stays, and stretched out on the lumpy bed. Her eyelids felt heavy, and she shut her eyes. As naturally as breathing she went into prayer. *Dear Lord, don't let this be one of my awful mistakes. I know I'm impulsive, hardheaded, and stubborn, but please, Lord, don't punish Tracy because of me. I got us into this; now please give me the wisdom I need to get us out.*

Outside the hotel Tracy stood looking about glumly. He was furious with his sister and wanted to be away from her worried eyes, her sharp voice, for a little while. He didn't want to admit he was scared too. It was one whopper of a mess. But it wasn't all Sunny's fault. He was just as much to blame. He'd also taken Faraday's bait: hook, line, and sinker. The fella was slippery as an eel. He wished he knew what to do. Wished he had someone to ask. A man. Being too dependent on Sunny wasn't such a good idea. Sunny was smart, all right, but she was still a woman, and there were just some things you needed to discuss with a man. Just then, as though in answer to his wish, Tracy saw a man crossing the muddy street and coming straight toward him. He looked familiar somehow. Why, it was the wagon train scout, Webb Chandler. The man glanced his way, and Tracy saw that he recognized him. Tracy smiled shyly, and the man stopped. A slow grin creased his tanned face.

"Did your wagon and supplies show up yet?" he asked.

Tracy shook his head. "Nope. I guess he's long gone. We sure got took."

"It happens. They should post signs for greenhorns: 'Look out for con men, hold on to your money purse.' Too bad, young fella. But you can probably hitch on to some work—"

"My sister, Sunny, says—," began Tracy.

"Sunny?" Webb Chandler repeated, eyebrows lifted. "Your sister's name is Sunny?"

Tracy's mouth twitched at Chandler's incredulous reaction. "Yes...," he answered hesitantly.

Webb laughed. "Sorry, but she don't strike me as being exactly the sunny type. More like a prickly pear."

Tracy fought an urge to join in the man's chuckles. Serves Sunny right that she gives folks that impression, he thought. She is too durn bossy. Like a burr under a saddle a lot of the time. 'Nuff to make a man downright ornery, with her pickin' *and naggin' at him. . . . But on the other hand, I owe her a lot. Shouldn't join in any joshin' about her behind her back—even if it is in good fun.*

Tracy tried to change the subject instead. "Well, I wuz thinkin' about applyin' for one of them Pony Express rider jobs." He thrust out his chin in an attempt to look self-confident and at the same time tried to gauge what this hardened westerner might say, whether he would encourage or discourage the idea.

"Well, it's a possibility. That is, if you're—" Webb's glance swept over the lanky young man, then he said, half joking and half serious, "It'll make a man of you in a hurry if it don't kill you first!"

Sunny woke with an uneasy feeling. She sat up feeling groggy and disoriented. The room was in shadows. How long had she been asleep? She swung her legs over the side of the bed and padded in her stocking feet to the window and looked out. It was getting dark. Where was Tracy? She hoped he hadn't got into some kind of trouble. She had seen some rough-looking characters out there in those streets. How long had he been gone? Deciding she'd better go out looking for him, Sunny hurriedly thrust her feet into her shoes and was just struggling to get them fastened with her buttonhook, when a tapping came at the door.

"It's Tracy, Sis," came her brother's voice.

With relief Sunny went over, unlocked the door, and flung it open. Glad as she was to see him back safe and sound, her voice was cross when she demanded, "Where have you been? I've been worried sick."

"No need." Tracy came into the room.

"If I'd known what was ahead of us, I'd never have come," she said grimly. "I should never have left our home, left Meadowdale. It was wrong of me. I'm sorry, Tracy."

34

"It's all right, Sunny. Anyway, things are going to work out. You'll see."

Sunny looked at her brother. Tracy's eyes were shining and there was something different about him, a cockiness that she wasn't used to seeing in him. She felt a funny sensation, a premonition that he was about to tell her something she didn't want to hear.

"Listen, Sunny, and don't say nothin' till you hear me out. I've got a job and we can stay here until we have enough money to get us to California."

"What do you mean, you've got a job?"

"Just what I said. I got me a job, so you don't have to worry—"

"Worry? Of course I have to worry. What kind of a job? Where? What do you mean?"

"Now, promise not to get all het up?"

"I won't promise anything of the kind. Not until you tell me what this is all about."

"Well, after I left here, I run into Webb Chandler. You know, the scout with the wagon train—"

"Oh, *him*! That impossible man—"

"Ah, Sunny, you got him all wrong. He's a fine fella. It was him that told me to go apply for the job I got."

Sunny looked at her brother aghast. "And what kind of a job would someone like Webb Chandler suggest?" She felt her stomach tighten in apprehension.

Tracy proceeded cautiously, speaking slowly. "In the first place, it pays a whole lot more than working as a ranch hand or in the livery stable in town. He told me to go to the Express office, that they were hiring"—he halted, still a little hesitant—"riders to carry the mail."

"Oh, no!" Sunny struck her forehead in horror. She remembered very well the wording of the advertisement they'd seen for Pony Express riders. "You *didn't*! You didn't *ever*! *Did* you?"

Tracy nodded. "Yep."

"Well, I won't hear of it! I won't let you."

"I already signed up. Just gotta be sworn in. It's a done deal, Sunny."

Sunny's anger flared. How dare that Webb Chandler take it upon himself to encourage her little brother to apply for such a dangerous job! Furiously she grabbed her jacket, jammed her bonnet on her head, and tied the ribbons under her chin so tight they pinched her skin.

"Well, we'll see if it's a 'done deal' or not! You're underage and you can't sign on to anything without my permission."

"Ah, Sunny, will you listen? If you'd just come and talk to the man who runs the Express office. His name is Mr. Graham, and I told him my sister would—please, Sunny." He threw his hands up in a helpless gesture. "Have you got any other ideas? What else can we do?"

That question stopped Sunny cold. Tracy was right. What else did they have? The fact was, they only had enough money to last them until the end of the week if they stayed at the hotel. Then what? Sunny's fury diminished. Instead she regarded her brother with reluctant admiration. He had the gumption to go investigate the possibility of a way for them to survive. Faced with the reality of their situation, Sunny made a quick decision. The least she could do was go to the Express office and meet this Mr. Graham. "All right, I'll go with you."

# Chapter 5

*I*t was beginning to get dark as they left the hotel. The late-spring afternoon had grown cool and Sunny shivered, as much from nerves as from the chill wind.

As they hurried along the wooden sidewalk there was evidence that the town of Cottonwood was livening up for the evening. Men who had made an early start were already staggering as they pushed through the swinging doors of the saloons that lined both sides of the street. Music blared from the dance halls and taverns. When the doors swung open, Sunny caught glimpses of the garishly lighted interiors and flashily dressed women. Her heart sank. It seemed as if they had somehow stumbled into a kind of Babylon. "Watch it, Sunny," Tracy cautioned, throwing out his arm to keep her from stepping into the street. A wagon with an arched canvas top rumbled past, swaying with the weight of its load. Emigrants on their way to Independence going west. Sunny's heart wrenched. *That's what we should be doing,* she thought. She had dreamed of wide prairies, majestic mountains, and clear, flowing rivers. Instead here they were on their way to talk to a man about Tracy taking some kind of foolhardy job. What had she got her young brother into? Sunny felt weighted with renewed guilt.

"The Express office is right over there," Tracy said, taking her arm as they hurried across the street before another large wagon came looming down on them.

Tracy opened the door into a sparsely furnished outer office. Over a wooden counter, the "infamous" poster advertising for riders was conspicuously displayed. Sunny averted her eyes. She didn't want to see those ominous words again. She suppressed a shudder.

Beyond, a door leading to another room stood ajar. Through it she saw a dark-haired, broad-shouldered man sitting at a desk.

Sunny looked at Tracy questioningly. "Well?"

He moved awkwardly forward, then knocked tentatively at the door. "Mr. Graham, sir? I'm back. I've brought my sister with me. She'd like—*we'd* like to talk to you, sir. That is, if it's convenient."

Tracy was blocking Sunny's view of the man to whom he was speaking. Then she heard the sound of a chair being scraped back, footsteps approaching. The door opened wider, and the Express company manager stepped into the doorway, his height filling it.

Tracy haltingly introduced her. "Mr. Rhys Graham, this is my sister, Sunny Lyndall. Mr. Graham runs the Express company, Sis."

"Good evening, Miss Lyndall."

Sunny was taken completely by surprise. She had not expected anyone like this man—well dressed, impeccably groomed. In the three days she had been in town, the only men she had seen were roughly dressed ranchers, cowboys, wagoners, and emigrants. None dressed like this. Mr. Graham wore a smoke gray broadcloth jacket, white linen shirt, a vest of paisley silk across which hung a gold-link watch chain. What on earth was someone like this doing in this rough-hewn border town?

"Please, won't you come into my office, where we can talk?"

His courteous manner—although it coincided with his appearance—put her on guard. She had the feeling she was being coerced in some way, coerced to allow Tracy to do something that everything within her told her was fraught with danger. Maybe she should turn around, leave before she agreed to something she would regret. But Tracy looked so eager, so hopeful, that she hesitated only for a second. Then as Mr. Graham held the door for her she entered his office.

"Please sit down, won't you both?" He moved two chairs forward in front of his desk, then went behind the desk. He and Tracy remained standing until she had sat down. Once seated she had a better look at Rhys Graham. His thick, dark hair swept back from a high forehead. He might have been considered handsome, except for the thin, white scar that ran diagonally across his forehead, cutting into his left eyebrow, giving him a strangely quizzical expression. His face was thin and clean-shaven, which accentuated the high cheekbones and the deep-set eyes that were regarding her now with interest. Their very intensity made her uncomfortable.

"Now then, what can I tell you about our company, which your brother wants to join as one of our riders?" he asked. His voice was low, well modulated. The term "gentlemanly" described him perfectly. But in spite of his genteel manner, was he someone to be trusted? The image of that sly Faraday—if that was his real name—flashed into Sunny's mind. This man might also be taking advantage of their inexperience. Luring her brother into a situation that was not only dangerous but at worse could be fatal. She must not let Mr. Graham's manners disarm her. She must take charge of this interview, she decided, and state her objections, thank him for the chance to discuss the situation, then leave gracefully. She directed what she hoped was a firm gaze upon him.

"Mr. Graham, as both our parents are deceased, I am my brother's legal guardian. I want to know exactly what he is signing up for as a Pony Express rider."

"I am glad you came, Miss Lyndall, and indeed I appreciate your concern. It is very responsible of you. Let me outline for you our operation here. We appreciate our riders, admire their skill, their courage, their loyalty. They are as interested as we are to give the western territories what they long for and need: news from home, what's happening in the country, the world. We carry the top newspapers and periodicals from back east so that they can keep up with what's going on while they do their own brave bit of exploring, developing our great country. The fact that your brother—and I must say, I have never interviewed a finer applicant for this position than he. Tracy has all the qualities we look for in an employee. I have no doubt he will make an outstanding addition to our roster of excellent riders, high-minded young men we have hired in the past and continue to hire for this special kind of work. He will be part of a select group of young men whom history will remember and future generations will read about and be inspired by."

Slowly all Sunny's resolution crumbled. Rhys Graham's explanation was persuasive. His gaze, riveted upon her as he spoke so movingly, convinced her these were the eyes of an honest man.

Graham got up from his desk, walked over to the window, and looked out for a minute or two as if to give Sunny time to consider. Then he turned back, saying, "We require a strict code of behavior from our riders and maintain close observation upon them to see that these regulations are kept by them to the letter." He pulled open a desk drawer and drew out a paper, handing it to Sunny. "I'd like you to read the statement we have each rider sign before they're hired. It will give you some idea of the caliber of young men we want."

Sunny took the paper and read, "While I am in the employ of this Express company I will under no circumstances use profane language; I will drink no intoxicating liquors; I will not quarrel or fight with any other employee of the firm. So help me God."

Her doubts disappeared. Perhaps this *was,* as Tracy had pointed out, the solution to their problem. At least temporarily. Her brother was an excellent horseman. That should be no problem. And it would provide them some cash, keep them from starving. But they still didn't have a place to live. *She* had to find work. She'd find something, somehow. In the meantime Tracy could do what he did best: ride horses.

Sunny raised her eyes from the printed agreement. "This seems a very good requirement for such a job," she said slowly. Then, after another moment's hesitation and a fervent prayer that she was doing the right thing, Sunny asked, "Where do I sign?"

Graham handed her a pen from his desk and placed his finger on the line for her signature. As she wrote her name he smiled reassuringly at Tracy and said, "Now let's get your brother sworn in."

Sunny held the Bible while Tracy took the oath, and in her astonished eyes her little brother seemed to grow two inches.

She'd hardly had time to absorb her mixed emotions, when she became aware of Graham's gaze regarding her speculatively.

"I was just wondering, Miss Lyndall, if you knew of my other proposal? Did your brother mention that at the Express station there is an important opening we've been trying to fill for some time? One that you might be interested in? After talking to your brother and now having met you, I'm certain it is one that you would be capable of fill-ing." He paused, waiting to see if she showed a spark of interest. When Sunny leaned forward, he continued. "It's managing the station, taking in the mail and packages, sorting and packing the pouches for the riders. This job would mean taking care of the ponies, much the same as you must have done with your own horses on your family farm. Then there'd be cooking meals for Tracy's relief and alternate riders, packing lunches for them to take in their saddlebags. It's not a difficult job but a very responsible one. We need the right person." He paused. "I think *you* might be just the right person."

Sunny could hardly contain herself. Was this the answer to their desperate prayers? It seemed almost too good to be true. *O ye of little faith,* she thought contritely.

"Are you interested?"

"Oh, yes!"

"The Express station is located outside of town. The build-ing is not much more than a bunkhouse, but there's a big kitchen, and two smaller rooms can be used for bedrooms. It's not in too good a condition, but it's livable and your brother and you can stay there rent free. It's been empty since—well, since our last manager left. Our riders have been staying at one of the boardinghouses in town. At the widow McDowell's. That's working out, because she likes the com-pany and they like her cooking." Graham chuckled. "So there'd only be you and your brother occupying the place. I like the idea of having the station manager there, where the mail is brought in and stored until the riders go out. The barn's in good shape, with six stable stalls and a corral. So do you think you can handle it?"

A job, a place to live! All coming at once. Sunny nodded. "Oh yes, I'm sure I can."

"Good! Then it's a done deed." Graham clapped his

hands together. He noticed a slight smile touch her lips; there was yet anxiety in her eyes, but he ignored it.

After their departure Rhys Graham swiveled his chair around from his desk so that it faced the window looking out onto the street. He watched the two figures moving away in the quickly gathering dusk of evening: the tall, lanky boy, the slim, straight young woman. Odd, though, that they should appear so suddenly in his life, just at the point when he was on the brink of making a decision. . . .

The Lyndalls, brother and sister. Tracy and Sunniva. He had been startled when he saw her signature on Tracy's Express rider application. Sunniva. He said it over to himself a couple of times. An unusual name. A theatrical one. It was the sort of name an actress used, or one that was given to the heroine of one of those romantic novels his cousin Emeline used to have her nose in all the time. What kind of parents named a girl child Sunniva? Sunny, Tracy called her. Rhys tried that. He thought he liked that better. It suited her. He smiled to himself. Like a day full of sunshine and blue sky, like a meadow blooming with daisies and lupine. Sunny. He said it a couple of times aloud, the syllables rolling over his tongue. Yes, Sunny was just right for her.

Strange that they should come across his path just now. Lately he had been struggling with his dark cloud: the thick, smothering, foglike depression to which he was subject periodically. Was their arrival chance? Fate? Luck? Or divine coincidence?

The sister of the young man he'd just sworn in as one of his riders had had a disturbing effect on him. Something about her was so reminiscent . . . a memory, a faint echo of something intangible . . . something he had put behind him but which still haunted him . . . that sweetness of what he had lost, irrevocably, through his own actions, his own fault . . . guilt that grew heavier with each passing year . . .

He'd almost forgotten there were women like her—*ladies* like her, he corrected himself. He had noticed all the refined touches: the gloves, the cameo pin at the fluted collar emerging from her neatly fitted jacket, the bonnet framing her face. A natural, unaffected beauty so different from the over-rouged cheeks and kohl-rimmed eyes of the "girls" at saloons like So Long or Trail's End.

Her candid eyes had jolted something within he'd almost forgotten. Rhys closed his eyes, rubbing long, thin fingers across his suddenly aching head.

No, perhaps it was not the right time. He turned back to his desk, to the clutter of papers awaiting his perusal. The past lay upon him like a heavy cloak over his shoulders. The bottle in the lower left drawer of his desk tempted. He resisted. His hand reached for the drawer, then he slammed it shut. "God help me," he groaned between clenched teeth.

On their way back to the hotel, Tracy could hardly contain himself. Relishing his victory, no doubt, Sunny observed wryly. What galled her most was that his rebellion had been encouraged by the advice of that scout, that insufferable Webb Chandler. What right had he to advise *her* brother over all her misgivings and objections?

She prayed that her impression of Rhys Graham was correct. He seemed sincere. She had found herself being swayed as he waxed eloquent about how worthwhile carrying the mail cross-country to California was, how patriotic the riders. But hadn't she been taken in by the apparent honesty of that despicable Faraday? She had thought *he* was honest and reliable, too! And Rhys Graham seemed a man who kept his inner self hidden, protected.

She would just have to trust that it was as it seemed. The pledge Tracy had taken was almost as solemn as one you'd make in church. When Rhys Graham had asked Sunny to hold the Bible while Tracy placed one hand upon it and repeated the promises, it had actually brought tears to Sunny's eyes.

She looked at her brother now and saw how he was bursting with pride. She recognized Tracy's need to prove himself "the man of the family." Actually, it had all turned out much better than she could have hoped. The unexpected offer of a job for her! At least now she could look after Tracy properly. With both of them earning good wages and with no rent to pay, it might not take them long to squirrel away enough money to set out for California again.

They reached the hotel and were just entering the lobby when Chandler came sauntering out from the Gentlemen's Bar and Card Room. The sight of him filled Sunny with resentment. He walked with such self-confident assurance. She turned her head, prepared to ignore him. However, before Sunny could stop him, Tracy brandished his employment certificate and greeted the scout with a wide grin. "I got the job. I'm an Express rider."

"So you signed up, boy! Congratulations," Webb said heartily. Then, his eyes glinting wickedly, he added, "That took a lot of pluck. Seeing as how you had so much opposition."

Sunny gave him a withering glance.

"I hope you are satisfied, Mr. Chandler. Are you in the habit of advising boys to take life-threatening risks?"

"No, ma'am, but I always like to urge a young fellow to stand on his own two feet or sit in his own saddle, as the case may be."

Sunny had not expected such a sharp-edged rebuttal. Webb Chandler seemed to be purposely needling her. She tried to think of something cutting to say in response, but nothing came to mind. Frustrated, Sunny disdainfully drew aside her skirt and attempted to pass. But he was blocking the way. "If you will *excuse* me, Mr. Chandler—," she said coldly.

45

Webb's face twitched with amusement. "Allow me," he said, and stepping to one side, he bowed, battered hat in hand.

Without looking back Sunny, head high, swept past him and crossed the lobby to the stairs, inwardly seething. It irritated her especially that Chandler did not seem to feel the least snubbed. Almost as if he hadn't noticed it. Probably too thick-skinned. To her annoyance his voice followed her. "Not all ladies feel about the Express riders like your sister does. Let me tell you, you're in for some new experiences," he told Tracy, who had lagged behind.

Infuriated, Sunny swung around. Why on earth was he filling Tracy's head with a lot of nonsense! Why didn't he mind his own business?

At that very moment Webb caught her furious glance. A mischievous grin crossed his face. He slapped Tracy on the back and raised his voice. "Well, good luck, fella. Not that you won't need it!" Then he placed his hat back on his head and went out the hotel door, still chuckling.

# Chapter 6

*T*he next morning, Sunny and Tracy rented a wagon and set out for the Express station to see their future living quarters. Tracy was to start his training immediately, taking two trips with a regular rider to learn the route. Meanwhile Sunny would move into the Express station and make it into a "home"—an undertaking that, at her first sight of the place, seemed nearly impossible. She tried to hide her dismay after they unlocked the splintery wooden door and stepped inside, but she was horrified at the condition of the place. It would have discouraged the most optimistic.

From the porch, they entered into a large room divided by a wooden partition. Before the wall of one side there was a high counter on which there was a scale for weighing parcels, packages, and bulk mail. Behind the counter were shelves of various sizes, cubbyholes, and a large, square safe. On the other side of the divider was what might be called an all-purpose room. Down a narrow hall were two rooms that Sunny assumed were the ones to be used for their bedrooms.

The dirt floor sent up little clouds of dust as they walked around. The furnishings were few: a table scarred and stained, a few chairs with missing rungs and broken seats, a stove thick with accumulated grease and food spills. In the two small adjoining rooms, one contained four wooden bunks, the other a rusted iron bed with a lumpy straw mattress covered with dirty, striped ticking.

The place smelled musty, of old dirt, burnt food, a stove that didn't draw, and mildew. Beggars can't be choosers, Sunny reminded herself. Not that they were quite beggars. They were employees. They were going to earn their keep here.

Bleakly Sunny recalled the spotless home they had left. Their "house-proud" stepmother's motto had been "Cleanliness is next to godliness," and she demanded that Sunny see to it that the house was immaculate. Sunny was no stranger to applying "elbow grease" and scrub brush. Knowing that Tracy was anxiously watching her reaction, Sunny tried to overcome the urge to throw up her hands in disgust and leave. She couldn't. There was no turning back.

Tracy had not voiced any second thoughts about *his* decision. In fact, he was almost annoyingly cheerful. Sunny could do no less.

With Tracy's help she could at least get rid of the top layer of dirt and get new mattresses. Their trunks were still at the train station, where they'd left them to be loaded onto their wagon for the trip west. In them Sunny had packed quilts, sheets, blankets, pots, pans, kitchen utensils, and other household items that she'd planned to use on their journey and later in their California home. These could now be put to immediate use in the Express station. No sense thinking of what might have been, she told herself grimly. Crying over spilled milk would be a waste of time. She had more immediate—if not *better*—things to do.

"Well, we've got our work cut out for us here," she declared. "We'll have to stay one more night at the hotel; although I think they're overcharging us terribly, we can't stay here until we get this place cleaned. Come on." She whirled around, motioning her brother to come with her. "We'll find a general store and get some cleaning supplies and at least make a start."

Back in town they again had to fight the heavy traffic of the huge "prairie schooners" lumbering through on their way to Independence. They had to pull over to the side briefly to let one of the big wagons get by. Sunny had to keep herself from saying anything to Tracy about her bitter disappointment. He was so buoyed up by his prospective new career as a Pony Express rider, he did not seem at all downcast that they might be stuck in this backwater town for who knew how long?

Tracy went to pick up their trunks at the station while she was at Ardley's General Store purchasing cleaning supplies and some groceries.

The minute she walked through the door, it seemed to Sunny, all conversation halted and heads turned to look at her curiously. The glances varied, from the veiled ones of curious women shoppers to the boldly appraising ones from the group of men gathered around the potbellied stove. Naturally, a stranger in such a small community was bound to attract attention, she told herself, trying not to feel self-conscious as she went over to the counter. A plump, rosy-cheeked woman in a blue checkered apron, her pewter-colored hair drawn from a middle part to a plait around her head, stood behind it and watched her approach warily.

"Good morning," Sunny said pleasantly, bringing out her list. She needed everything from laundry soap and carbolic disinfectant to baking soda.

Verna Ardley eyed her new customer keenly. Verna prided herself on being a good judge of character. Long experience dealing with the public had given her the ability, and she had rarely been proved wrong, even in a first impression. This young woman presented an interesting challenge. She was about twenty years of age, Verna guessed. Nicely dressed, although too nicely for these parts, where most women were too busy with children and chores to pay much attention to their appearance. A bit on the skinny side, but held herself well. Not so pretty as to spark any jealousy on the part of the womenfolk, married or single, but pleasant-looking enough. Verna always noticed eyes. Like the Scripture said, they were the windows of the soul. This girl's eyes looked directly at a body, with not a speck of cunning or dishonesty, and there was a sweetness to the mouth, even though she was holding it now in a tight line.

Of course, her manner was a little uncertain, yet there was a spunky, independent air about her. That was something Verna recognized and admired in other women, because both were qualities she liked to believe she herself possessed. Still, Verna always maintained a wait-and-see attitude with any newcomer before offering more than service. "Yes, miss, can I help you?"

"Thank you, I hope so. . . ."

For a minute Verna thought she heard a note of appeal in the soft voice. She got a hint of insight that this young woman was not as confident as she appeared and that she needed help, more than simply filling her order—all kinds of help. Maybe even more than Verna could give.

Sunny began to read off her list, and Mrs. Ardley went to fetch each item as it was called until they were all stacked up in a pile on the counter. She then began to add up a column of figures, pausing every once in a while to tap her pencil against her teeth. Finally she announced, "That comes to five dollars and twenty-nine cents."

At the sum Sunny experienced a momentary pang of panic. It had come to more than she expected. Perhaps she could do without some of the items. With a show of calm

Sunny opened her pouch purse to check its contents. Then she made a quick calculation of her remaining cash, hoping she had enough to pay for it all. How embarrassing it would be to ask for some of it to be put back on the shelves. Especially with everybody in the store an audience to her transaction. As she was quickly adding up her money Mrs. Ardley cleared her throat.

"By the way, miss, you're Sunniva Lyndall, ain't you?"

Startled, Sunny nodded.

"You and your brother are the new employees of the Express station out on Hayfork Road?"

Again Sunny nodded.

"Well, I should've mentioned right off that Mr. Graham left instructions that any items purchased for the Express station were to be put on his account."

"Oh!" A wave of surprised gratitude swept over Sunny. "You're sure?"

"That's exactly what he told my husband, miss."

"Well then," Sunny hesitated, "I suppose—since we *are* employees of the Express station—" Then she reached out and separated the baking soda, the sack of flour, the sugar, the eggs, and the tin of molasses from the cleaning supplies and moved them to one side. "Since these items are for our personal use, I'll pay for them myself."

Sunny was too relieved to notice Verna's admiring glance. With Sunny's statement that she would pay separately for the groceries, Verna's estimation of the newcomer had risen.

"So your brother's going to be a rider?" asked Verna as she began bagging Sunny's groceries.

"Yes," Sunny answered.

Some of her anxiety must have crept into her voice, because immediately the other woman said, "Well, if he can ride a horse, he'll do just fine. Mr. Graham takes a personal interest in his riders, I'll say that. Most of them got no families, and he's like a father to them. If one gets hurt

51

or sick, he sees that Doc Hasting takes care of them. Your brother's lucky. Not all the Express companies are that good to their employees." Verna put the cleaning supplies into a box. "There. Now these I'll just ring up on Mr. Graham's account."

It occurred to Sunny that the storekeeper was probably a fund of information about everyone in town and might possibly be able to satisfy her curiosity about Rhys Graham. Hoping to elicit some information about her new employer, she murmured, "That was most generous of Mr. Graham."

"Oh, he's a capital fella, that's for sure. Folks wanted him to run for mayor at one time, but he declined. For all his fine manners and gentlemanly ways, he can handle himself all right. I've seen him take care of some unruly drunks, as well as a couple of gents who had in mind to rob the Express office. He don't tote a gun, but he's someone to be reckoned with. Don't anyone mess with Rhys Graham but once, I'll tell you."

"My brother will come and pick up all these things in a while, Mrs. Ardley, if that's all right. He's gone to the railroad station to get our trunks and other belongings we left there. I'm going to meet him now, then we'll stop back by after that."

"Sure thing. I'll just put them behind the counter here till you all come," Mrs. Ardley assured her.

It had proved providential that Mr. Graham had arranged to pay for the needed cleaning supplies, since their cash was so low. However, it made Sunny feel slightly uncomfortable. Maybe she should stop by the Express office and make sure that this *was* completely satisfactory.

However, just as she stepped outside, she saw Rhys Graham crossing the street, coming directly to the store.

"Why, Miss Lyndall. Good morning." He took off his hat and smiled at her. His greeting was so warm and friendly that Sunny felt suddenly awkward.

52

"Good morning, Mr. Graham. Tracy and I are moving some things to the station today, getting it cleaned. I just had to confirm—I mean, I was told by Mrs. Ardley that any supplies I bought—"

"Yes, of course, everything is to be placed on my account. Business expenses, naturally. I hope you got everything you needed? I must apologize for the state of neglect at the Express station. It's only been used as a temporary bunkhouse up to now. There's never been a woman—it wasn't meant to be a proper dwelling place."

"Oh, it's fine! I mean, it will be. We're very grateful, Mr. Graham. You have been extraordinarily kind. I hope I didn't sound foolish. But I just wanted to make sure. I suppose that since we were so outrageously swindled, I've become suspicious of people offering to do something for us—I mean, it's hard for me to accept the fact that anyone is honest or sincerely wants to help. Or that somehow I won't be taken advantage of—"

Graham's eyes seemed to darken. "I can understand that you might feel that way. But don't let that one bad experience sour you on everyone you meet here, Miss Lyndall." A slight smile softened his expression. "Don't judge too harshly, Miss Lyndall. People are capable of many different kinds of behavior. Most react with fear to something they don't understand or haven't experienced. But I think you'll find—especially out here—that most are both generous and willing to help a stranger."

Somehow his words seemed a reprimand, and again Sunny felt awkward. She felt that she had said too much. Had she somehow offended him? Should she make further explanation? However, Rhys Graham had already replaced his hat and started moving on.

"Well, thank you—I do appreciate all you've done," she stammered.

"Not at all, Miss Lyndall. It is a pleasure to see you again.

53

Have no concern about the bill at the general store. Whatever else you need is to be put on my account. I arranged it."

Feeling flustered and unsettled by this less-than-satisfactory encounter, Sunny walked in the direction of the railroad station. Tracy would have retrieved the belongings they'd left there on the ill-fated day they'd been persuaded to get off the train and wait for Mr. Faraday. Just thinking about that rascal made Sunny's blood boil. Thinking of him also made her recall Mr. Graham's gentle reproach. He had taken her to task subtly for her "tarring everyone with the same stick."

Reaching the railroad station, she found Tracy in a discussion with the freight clerk. It seemed their trunks and other possessions could not be found. Tracy did not have any kind of identification, and the storage room was piled high with an assortment of miscellaneous boxes, barrels, and packages. Quickly Sunny dug into her purse, found the baggage checks they had been given, and the search began in earnest.

The storage room was airless, hot, and dusty. Almost suffocating from the heat and dust, Sunny went out onto the platform to get some air, leaving the clerk and Tracy to continue the search. If, on top of everything else, their luggage had been lost or mistakenly put on a train and shipped out, it would be the last straw! Everything she had in the world had been stuffed into her trunk. There was also the box of cherished keepsakes that had belonged to their mother, to say nothing of Sunny's hatbox containing her best bonnets.

The hoot of a shrill whistle announced a train's arrival. It came chugging down the track, then shrieked to a stop with a loud hissing noise. Abstractedly Sunny watched passengers get off and the station manager hurry out to consult with the conductor. She saw the clerk who had been helping Tracy run down to the end of the train to oversee the loading of some crates. Then the whistle hooted a warning, and the train began slowly moving again. This town was only a proverbial "whistle-stop." Sunny remembered how they had been rushed down the aisle and urged from the train by Faraday. Unknown to them, the real reason was to get them off before they changed their minds, and for him to get away—with *their* money! Seeing the train—on which they should have stayed—begin to pull out brought back all Sunny's anger.

Caught up in that past experience, she watched as the train slid slowly by the platform. Suddenly her mouth opened in a gasp. At first she could not believe her eyes. No! It couldn't be! But it *was*! Faraday! Looking out one of the sooty windows. Then he saw her. Their eyes met in horrified recognition. He ducked his head. Totally losing control, Sunny picked up her skirts and began running alongside the train, waving her arms and shouting at the top of her voice. The wind caught her bonnet, tearing it off. On she ran, screaming, "You! You villain!" But the train was gaining speed. All she could see was the top of the biscuit brown bowler on the crouching Faraday.

"Stop! Stop the train!" Sunny yelled, shaking her fist. But the train rolled on. Gathering momentum, it sped along until it rounded the curve of the tracks and became a tiny speck and finally disappeared.

Breathless from running, standing alone at the end of the platform, her bonnet dangling around her neck by its strings, Sunny wept tears of frustration and fury. Slowly she turned and dejectedly retraced her steps back to the station house, where a small group of people were staring at her. Among them were her brother, the baggage clerk, and the station manager. Tracy looked both bewildered and embarrassed. She realized that *again* she had made a spectacle of herself in his eyes. Well, of course, he didn't know whom she'd seen.

With as much dignity as she could muster, Sunny straightened her bonnet and, in as calm a voice as she could manage, asked the station manager, "Where was that train headed?"

"Kansas City, connections in St. Louis, then New York City," he rattled off.

*It might as well be Timbuktu,* Sunny thought, sighing dismally.

She answered the question in Tracy's eyes with a curt "Tell you later," then asked, "Did you find our trunks?"

"Yep, got 'em in the wagon. 'Fraid your hatbox got mighty badly crushed, Sunny. It was under some wooden crates, and—"

She shook her head and shrugged. "It doesn't matter," she said dully. Nothing mattered except that now she knew there was no hope of bringing that scoundrel to justice, getting back their money, or for that matter getting to California anytime soon.

# Chapter 7

*T*his place was a disgrace. Hardly fit for human habitation! Sunny wrinkled her nose in disgust as she surveyed the Express station. Nothing but hard work would change things. And it was up to her to do it. Tracy had gone on his training run with one of the Express riders and would be away two days.

Swaddled in a muslin "Mother Hubbard" coverall apron, Sunny shoved her hair back under a bandanna handkerchief and dug in. Wielding a broom, she vigorously attacked the accumulated dirt, swooping and brushing out old cobwebs where dried spiders nested. Dust flew everywhere. Sneezing constantly, she swiped at her nose with the back of one hand. Tiny beads of perspiration rolled down her face; tendrils of hair escaped from under the bandanna, which by now was plastered against her damp forehead. Every so often she stopped and, leaning on the broom, marked her progress. After she got all this debris out, the floor would have to be scrubbed. Once the walls were clean, she could whitewash them. The windows still badly needed cleaning. She had done a superficial job on them to let some light in so she could see better, but they would have to be done more thoroughly.

It was hot, dirty work. Nostalgically she thought of the cool, shady porch of their Ohio farmhouse under the trees back home. Why had she ever thought it a good idea to leave? If she had only known she would end up penniless, a pauper...

No, she wouldn't allow herself to think like that. Back there she would still have been under her stepmother's relatives, who would have been checking on her every movement, watching every misstep, criticizing, waiting for her to make a mistake. At least here she was free. Awful as it had been, this was making her own way. She'd learned from her mistakes. This was the way to earn independence. She had to believe it would all work out in the end.

Sunny would never forget the blow of her father's marriage when she was fourteen. She had been so close to him before he brought his second wife home. Matilda Spencer, a milliner with her own thriving business, was not given either to children or domesticity. With her had come a hired girl and a new order in the Lyndall household. Sunny wondered if her father ever realized his mistake. If he had, he never showed it; he just became quieter, more withdrawn, distancing himself both from his new wife and his children. Martin Lyndall died when Sunny was nineteen, and her stepmother spent most of her time thereafter in town or with her own relatives, leaving Sunny in charge of the farm and Tracy.

That was why Sunny felt so protective, so concerned for him. Wasn't it understandable, no matter what Webb Chandler thought? Thinking of Chandler, Sunny felt a thrust of resentment. What business did he have encouraging Tracy to take the rider job?

Sunny drew a long breath. One good thing about hard work: it kept her from worrying too much about Tracy. She filled the bucket and got out the scrub brush and a cake of yellow soap. Down on her knees, she started sloshing the

58

soapy water onto the floor. Her breath came fast as she pushed the brush back and forth on the boards. Soon the grain began to come through. She sat back on her heels for a minute, resting, admiring the results of her labor. Leaving the floor to dry, Sunny went outside. Hands on hips, she scowled at the scroungy exterior. Whitewash was the only answer for the rough, scaly, splintery wood. When she finished cleaning the inside, she'd tackle the outside of the building.

First things first, she thought and went back inside. She had to get rid of this scummy, dirty water, get fresh water from the well, and do a final wash of the floor. Already her back ached. Her wrist pulled as she carried the heavy bucket outside to empty it, so she had to set it down momentarily. Panting from the exertion, she did not hear approaching hoofbeats. She was unaware that she was no longer alone, until she heard a rich, full laugh.

Startled, she jerked around. There, of all people, was Lucas Flynt's scout, Webb Chandler, seated on horseback, grinning at her!

"Afternoon, ma'am," he said, tipping his hat.

This unexpected appearance upset her unreasonably. Seeing him again reminded her of how condescendingly he had treated her at their first meeting and how he had baited her about Tracy. He represented all her own frustration.

She glared at him. He was smiling as though she should welcome him! What conceit! She didn't like the fellow. Never had. Not one bit. Seemed arrogant, full of himself. Who did he think he was, anyway? Dropping by uninvited. Probably had come to gloat and *laugh* at her situation. He also had the air of a man who somehow thought himself a gift to ladies. She would never have admitted it, but she was annoyed that he had found her looking like this. She brushed her hair off her damp forehead with the back of one hand and demanded, "What are *you* doing here?"

"Just riding by. . .then I saw you and thought I'd stop, pass the time of day, ma'am."

"Well, now that you've *passed* it, why don't you just ride on by?" she asked, mimicking his Texas drawl.

Ignoring her sarcasm, Webb dismounted. "You look like you could use some help—if you don't mind me sayin' so."

"I *do* mind, and I don't need any advice, thank you. I repeat, Mr. Chandler, why don't you just go on about your business, *whatever that is,* and leave me to my work."

He made no move to leave. Instead he leaned against his saddle and remarked lazily, "You sure are always ready to pick a fight, Miss Lyndall. Fact is, I know your brother is on his route, and I just thought I might—"

She interrupted. "This Express station has nothing to do with you, Mr. Chandler. What we do here or where my brother happens to be is none of your—"

Webb did not let her finish but went on talking in his casual manner. "Well now, this place is pretty far from town. . .kinda isolated. And it's a well-known fact that sometimes there's money kept out here waiting for pickup or delivery. That might tempt some ornery folks to come out and make. . .trouble. I was just making it my *business*"—here he emphasized his words—"to check and see if everything out here was. . .all right."

"Well, now that you've seen it is, you can be on your way." She deliberately turned her back and started to lift the bucket of dirty, soapy water.

Webb moved quickly, intercepting her and grabbing the handle. "Here, let me," he said. An immediate tug-of-war ensued.

"Let go," she said between clenched teeth.

"Don't be a stubborn little fool. It's heavy. I'll empty it for you."

As they struggled the dirty water sloshed back and forth, spilling water on both of them. Sunny felt it soak through her clothes, onto her feet. The harder she pulled, the more water splashed on her. Angrily she gave a savage jerk of the handle and suddenly, swearing, Webb let go. As he did she lost her balance, staggered backwards, and fell, dumping the contents of the bucket on top of her. Drenched and enraged, she sputtered in helpless fury while Webb doubled up with his eyes shut and laughed uncontrollably.

She could have killed him! He was insufferable. As he continued to laugh she scrambled to her feet, tripping over the wet hem of her dress, and rushed toward him, fists doubled, ready to pound him.

"Beast!" she screamed. "You're no gentleman. You're the worst, crudest, most despicable ...," she ranted helplessly, running out of enough names to call him. Webb made a grab for her flaying arms, his grip like steel, holding her off.

"Now, now, little lady. There's no cause to take on like this. If you'd allowed me to do what I wanted—that is, do a heavy job for you—this wouldn't have happened." He paused a minute while she continued to try to wrest herself from his grasp. "Just take it easy. I don't want to hurt you. I'll let you go if you'll just calm down—"

Seeing an advantage in doing that, Sunny went slack. Webb's hands loosened. She stepped back, then before he could move, she swung around and grabbed up the half-empty bucket, and with all her strength she slung the remains of the dirty, soapy water at him.

Instead of being angry, he started laughing again. He casually brushed the front of his fringed leather shirt where the water had splashed upon it, and gave her a small salute.

"Now I think we're even, miss. So I'll take your earlier suggestion and be on my way." With another tip of his hat brim, Webb swung himself up onto his horse, picked up the reins, and turned his horse's head.

It was only then that, to her absolute horror, Sunny saw Rhys Graham on his gleaming roan horse, standing at the gate to the Express yard. How long had he been there? How much had he witnessed? She thought she might die of humiliation.

Rhys dismounted and walked toward her. He was as immaculately groomed as ever, although more casually dressed in a beige linen riding coat, his boots polished. He removed his hat and acknowledged Webb with a nod.

If Rhys noticed Sunny's sodden skirt, her generally disheveled appearance, he gave no hint of that nor made any comment. She might have been perfectly groomed, dressed for a tea party. Right then and there, Sunny *knew* Rhys Graham was *the* perfect gentleman. Not like some she could mention . . . She threw Webb a poison look.

"Good day, Miss Lyndall," Rhys said. "Sorry to drop by unannounced. But I've been concerned about how you're settlin' in out here. I knew the place was in bad shape. We took it over in a hurry, and the boys used it as a bunkhouse without too much fixing." He included Webb in an ironic smile. "Cowboys are used to sleeping on the ground with only a bedroll and don't expect very much in creature comforts when they become riders. But a lady's different. . .and I've wondered if we shouldn't make some other arrangements for you."

Sunny made an ineffectual swipe at her hair with both hands and smoothed her skirt, knowing neither action helped much. "Oh, I'm fine, truly, Mr. Graham. And we've done quite a lot to improve things. Do come in and see." Pointedly ignoring Webb, Sunny moved to the front door and opened it so that Rhys could walk in and look the place over.

To her annoyance Webb dismounted and followed them inside. Even her daggerlike glance did not intimidate him.

Rhys walked into the middle of the room, looking slowly around without making a comment. However, Webb let out a slow whistle. "Lady, you've done some magic. It isn't the same place."

Sunny followed his glance with a feeling of satisfaction. She had thoroughly cleaned, brushing the ceiling and walls with a stiff broom, sweeping and scrubbing the floor until the wood grain of the planks was now plainly visible. The strong smell of lye soap had replaced the odor of accumulated dirt. Clean windows allowed sunlight in through the once-grimy panes. Sunny had to keep her mouth prim to keep from smiling at Webb's obvious surprise and approval. But even a compliment from *him* was some reward for all her hard work.

"Yes indeed, Miss Lyndall, you've done wonders in a very short time," Rhys nodded. "If there's anything you need in the way of additional furniture, equipment, cooking utensils, or whatever, do feel free to order from Ardley's and, of course, put it on the Express company account."

"Thank you," Sunny murmured, feeling both grateful and a little discomfited to have Webb overhear Mr. Graham's offer. She felt sure that this kind of generosity wasn't usually extended to *employees*. She hoped he would not get the wrong idea. An awkward few minutes followed; both men remained standing there, glancing around as if still examining the interior. Sunny wasn't sure whether or not she should offer them some refreshment. But that might appear to be turning a business visit into a social occasion. Before she could decide, Rhys spoke.

"Well, I'll be on my way now. You too, Webb? If you're going back to town, why not ride along with me? I have a few things I'd like to discuss with you."

Whatever had been Webb's original intention, there was not anything else he could do but accept Rhys' suggestion, and they left together.

Watching them ride out the gate, Sunny thought how different the two men were. Rhys Graham seemed oddly out of place in this frontier town, while Webb Chandler somehow belonged with the hills, the sagebrush, and the spectacular skies.

Webb and Rhys parted company at the fork in the road, and Rhys rode back into town alone. This morning's visit out to the Express station had again opened a window of memory in his mind. One he had kept closed for a long time, one he had thought locked. The Lyndall girl had first pried it open when she had walked into his office the day before.

Both her vulnerability and her strength had attracted and interested him. He admired the way she had tried to hide the fear and the panic he had seen in her eyes and the way she had eventually accepted the inevitable and signed the papers of permission for her brother to become a rider.

Rhys winced. He always had a twinge of conscience when he signed up one of these kids. That's what most of them were—as young as some of the drummer boys who'd run away from home to join up during the war. Foolhardy youngsters bent on adventure—never mind the risk—who learned too soon what war was really like: not a glory road but hell. . . .

Rhys shuddered, thrusting the horror back. He couldn't waste time worrying about boys whose families didn't seem to. Of course, most of them had no families—as the want ad said, "Orphans preferred." He was in business, wasn't he? The mail was important. Someone had to take it—through storms, sleet, and narrow mountain passes, over ledges and canyons, and trails sometimes blocked with rock slides and snow. He tried to see that they were well rewarded—those that survived.

Rhys shook his head as if to clear it. He was in town now and reined his horse in front of his office, dismounted, and hitched the horse to the railing. He went inside and into his private room, then slumped down on the oak swivel chair behind the massive desk. Staring out the window onto the main street, he let his mind wander.

In Rhys' memory was lodged a place where he some-times allowed himself to visit, not often but once in a while, where there was a rambling clapboard house with dark green shutters and a wide porch overlooking a well-kept garden. Beyond that was an orchard, always—in this mental picture—blooming, with pale pink apple blossoms perfuming the soft air. A breeze was forever causing the leaves on the tree-shaded lawn to move gently. It was a world far distant from the looming blue ribbon of hills that rimmed this dusty little town.

Somewhere in this picture was the shadowy figure of a young woman, slim as a willow wand, with a cloud of sun-glossed hair. The features were indistinct, but Rhys imag-ined there would be softly curved cheeks, a delicately formed mouth tipped up at the corners in a gentle smile, and intelligence and wit in her thickly lashed eyes—not unlike Sunny Lyndall's hazel ones . . . .

With an effort Rhys pushed the thought of Sunniva Lyn-dall from his mind. She had awakened memories best not recalled, had stirred a longing to revisit that place he had relinquished and dared not enter again.

# Chapter 8

*S*unny woke up with a start, shivering from a bad dream. She hadn't had one of those in a long time. Not since that first night Tracy had taken the mail run alone, after having only twice accompanied another rider. She had hardly slept at all that night; her imagination had run wild, picturing all sorts of horrors happening to her brother on his first trip. Rising before dawn, she apprehensively waited for his return.

To her utter amazement, instead of coming in haggard, exhausted, and discouraged by the hazards of his new job, Tracy had returned jubilant. She had listened in disbelief as he enthusiastically described the excitement of the job, regaling her with stories told by other riders. Finally, reluctantly succumbing to her suggestion that he get some sleep, he had flopped on his bunk bed and slept for the next ten hours.

Now it had only been three weeks since they began running the Express station, yet sometimes it felt as if they'd been here forever. Although Sunny was proud of how well, how responsibly, Tracy was doing his job, she saw him changing before her eyes, becoming self-confident and even cocky as he became a seasoned rider. Maybe it was selfish, but she missed that special place she had always had with Tracy. Daily he was becoming more of a man.

Sunny had to face an unexpected reality. Tracy actually *liked* the job. He had taken to being a rider like the proverbial duck to water. What if he liked it *too* much? That thought haunted her. What if, when the time came and they had saved enough money to finance it, Tracy didn't want to go to California?

That possibility nagged at her as she lay there. He didn't talk about California anymore. Not that they talked much about anything. He was too tired when he came in from his route, and on the days he was off, other chores kept him busy. It troubled her a great deal, but she decided not to say anything to her brother. For the time being she would have to put up with Tracy's boyish pride in taking on a challenging job and proving he could do it. Being a Pony Express rider was the peak experience of his life so far. Gradually the glow would dim. Eventually he would burn out with the long, hard rides, the rough terrain, the winds of winter, the ravages of the trail. She had to believe that. Otherwise she might have to resign herself to staying in this town for the rest of her life. It seemed almost symbolic. Just as Cottonwood was on the border of Independence, the "jumping-off place," remaining here would be like remaining on the brink of adventure, independence, freedom—all that going west had signified to her. No! Sunny threw back the covers and jumped out of bed. Nothing was going to make her give up that dream.

Fighting the mingled emotions of depression and hopelessness, Sunny got to work. It hadn't taken her long to learn how to manage the Express station. She was smart and quick, and she soon caught on to sorting and marking the mail and writing receipts for the payroll pouches and banknotes packed into the riders' saddlebags each day. Doing her job well gave her much satisfaction. However, the more organized and better at it she became, the more time she had to think. The more time she had to think, the more she fretted over their situation.

Today all morning long she felt restless. She got the indoor chores out of the way, quickly deciding that the more vigorous work of taking care of the ponies would take her mind off her problems and keep her from dwelling so much on her own discontent. She had started wearing a pair of Tracy's worn jeans, which she had cut off at the knees, under her skirt when working in the corral or barn. It made bending, stooping, mucking out the stalls, and pitching hay easier. She pulled them on now and tucked the hem of her dress into sturdy boots. Then she went outside.

When Tracy and the other riders were out on their routes, the Express ponies were her responsibility. The fact that her father had taught Sunny to care for her own horse when Sunny was much younger stood her in good stead in this job. But currying and brushing these "critters" was trickier by far than tending to her gentle mare back home. The ponies had a wild streak, were stubborn and resistant to being handled. It took patience—not one of Sunny's strongest traits—and a lot of concentration.

She was doing just that sort of concentrating, keeping a firm hold on a pony's haunches to brush his hind legs, when he suddenly pricked up his ears and whinnied. "Easy, Bramble," she said. Turning around to see what had spooked him, she was chagrined to see Webb Chandler. Leaning his folded arms on the top rail of the corral and placing one booted foot on the lower one, he grinned at her.

"Howdy, Miss Lyndall."

Sunny gave him a cool look. "What are you doing still around? I thought Flynt's wagon train had taken off a couple of weeks ago." She frowned; the idea that she and Tracy *should* have been on it, on their way to California, still rankled.

"Decided not to go this trip. Too much infightin' and wranglin' between the Iowans and the Tenessans who'd joined up to travel west together. Couldn't see nuthin' but trouble with all that brewin' before they even got started."

"What do you want *here*?" she demanded ungraciously.

"Good golly, Miss Lyndall." He gave a long, low whistle. "I declare, I never met a lady who was always so cross and mad at the world, frowning and working." He shook his head.

"There's a lot of work to be done, and my disposition is my own business, Mr. Chandler," she snapped. "Not that you help it by your constant coming around and bothering me." She went back to brushing the pony's shanks.

A few seconds of silence followed. She felt self-conscious working with him staring at her. Why didn't he leave? But he kept standing there, making no move to go.

"Your brother out on his route?"

She didn't bother to answer. If the man had any sense, he'd *know* this was the riders' work she was doing. She started brushing the pony's haunches.

"How does he like the job by now?" Webb asked.

"What business is that of yours, whether he likes it or not?"

"Well now, mebbe I feel a mite responsible. As you pointed out, I did encourage him some."

All Sunny's smoldering resentment resurfaced. She spun around, hands on hips, and confronted him. "Don't you have something better to do? Other folks have work to do, even if *you* don't!"

He gave her a scrutinizing look. "Don't like to see little brother grow up, do you? Mebbe this is the time to cut the apron strings, let him go."

His words stung like a wasp's bite. Sunny felt her cheeks burn. "Who asked you for advice?"

"I'm jest sayin' that doing a man's job seems to prove he don't need no mother-henning. Only mentioned it 'cause womenfolk don't understand how it is with a young fella trying his durndest to prove himself—"

Suddenly she'd had enough of Webb Chandler. She wasn't going to take any more of his nonsense. She'd tell him off once and for all and make sure he understood. Who did he think he was, coming out here uninvited, handing out advice? "Listen, Webb Chandler, and listen good. I don't like repeating myself. I don't need your advice or your help. Why don't you just go about doing whatever it was you were doing before you came out here?" She grabbed Bramble's bridle, pushed open the corral gate, and started toward the barn.

Webb followed. He stood at the door while she took the pitchfork and shifted some hay into the feeding box. "Sorry. No offense meant."

She didn't turn around or acknowledge his awkward apology, just went on pitching. When she finished, Webb was gone. Still, what he'd said about Tracy had hit a sore spot, and she couldn't forget it.

For some reason, for the next few days Sunny felt lonelier than ever. She felt almost *homesick*. She hadn't realized she would miss some of the things she had grown bored with back home. School friends she had grown up with, gone with to choir practice, ice-cream socials, quilting bees, and taffy pulls. Here there was nothing, no one. No one her age, not one woman in town, had given her more than a curious glance or a cool nod.

Tracy was no company at all. Gone four out of seven days a week, sleeping half the time he was home. The rest of the time, he was busy doing his chores, sharing the barn work and the care of the ponies with the other riders.

One morning Sunny was feeling especially lonesome and sorry for herself when she went to Ardley's General Store to do her shopping. Coming inside, she noticed a box in the corner. In it was the cat she had sometimes seen sunning

70

herself in one of the store windows. Now the cat had kittens. One tiny black face raised itself over the edge of the box and seemed to stare at Sunny with great blue eyes. There had always been cats at home. Oddly enough, their old long-haired gray "Pommy," whom they'd had since he was a kitten, died only a few weeks before they left. Cats were cozy; cats were good company. Sunny suddenly wished she had one. Just its presence in the Express station building would provide another living thing on those long, dark nights when Tracy was gone.

As Clem Ardley stacked her supplies on the counter and bagged them for her Sunny asked tentatively, "Have you found homes for all the kittens?"

With twinkling eyes, he shot her a speculative glance. "You interested in having a cat?"

"Well yes, if—"

"Far as I'm concerned, you can have 'em all, the whole kit and caboodle!" He laughed heartily at his own joke.

"Just one would be fine. Are you sure?"

"Take any one you want."

"I think I'd like the little black one."

Mr. Ardley came around from behind the counter, scooped up the fuzzy black kitty and handed it to Sunny. It was all squeaks, shrieks, and sharp little claws. Sunny juggled it, then stuck it under her jacket, close to her bosom, and refastened the buttons. It quieted at once. Sunny and Mr. Ardley exchanged a smile, then he carried her bundles out to the Express company wagon for her. She kept the kitten snuggled against her inside the jacket as she climbed in, picked up the reins, turned the horse around, and started home.

As soon as she reached the Express station Sunny, still cradling the kitty, jumped out of the wagon and hurried inside. There was a fire in the stove, and she put down the scrap of black fur in front on the hearth where the heat

71

had made it warm. She filled a saucer with milk, which he quickly began to lap up. She found an old, soft, torn shirt that belonged to Tracy but was too tattered to mend and bundled it up into a little nest. When the kitten had finished the milk, she picked him up gently and settled him in his makeshift bed. From that day on the kitten was a joy. Watching him skitter, jump, and play provided entertainment and amusement. Whenever Sunny sat down, he hopped into her lap, twirled around a couple of times, then curled up and went to sleep. He followed her around the house, always at her heels, so much so that she often almost stepped on him or tripped over him. It seemed natural to give him the name Shadow.

# Chapter 9

*A* few weeks later spring seemed to burst into full bloom. The days were so lovely that more and more Sunny was drawn outside. It was too nice for the chores usually done inside. One May morning she carried her metal washtub outdoors. Placing it on wooden sawhorses, she started doing her laundry. Soapsuds were flying and she was scrubbing vigorously on her tin washboard when a familiar voice greeted her.

"Good mornin', Miss Lyndall. Hard at it as usual, eh?"

Sunny inwardly groaned. Not that pesky Webb Chandler *again*? Couldn't the man take a hint?

"Seems like every time I ride by, there you are workin' your head off. Don't you ever take a day of rest? Matter of fact," he drawled with a hint of laughter in his voice, "don't think I've ever seen you lately but with a broom or a horse."

She straightened up, flicked the suds on her hands back into the tub, and glared at him. "What do you want this time?"

"Well, Miss Lyndall, I've been thinkin'. You and me— well, we got off on the wrong foot somehow. I'd like to make amends—"

"Not necessary," she replied curtly.

"Well yes, ma'am, it is. My Aunt Pem, who raised me, always taught me that if you've offended someone—even *unintentionally*—you should try to make things right." With that Webb whipped a bunch of bright yellow daffodils out from behind his back and held them out to her.

Sunny was taken aback by the unexpected gesture. Suddenly she felt a little guilty about the rude way she had treated Webb Chandler. Tracy often accused her of being too quick-tempered, ready to fly off the handle, as well as being "too durned bossy." She knew she had blamed Webb unfairly for their not being allowed to go on Flynt's wagon train. Mostly she had resented his comments about Tracy. Maybe because she suspected he was right.

She wiped her soapy hands on her apron and accepted the bouquet a trifle sheepishly. "Thank you. They're very pretty."

"They're out of Verna Ardley's garden," he told her. At her raised eyebrows he hastened to say, "Oh, she told me to go ahead and pick as many as I liked! She has dozens of 'em. Said they shouldn't go to waste."

Sunny suppressed a smile. Obviously Webb Chandler wasn't an experienced flower giver.

"The Ardleys—well, they're like a second family to me," he explained. "Anyway, the real reason I come out here this morning is—" He paused. "Seeing tomorrow's the Sabbath and they say even the Lord took one day a week off, I thought you might like to ride into the hills where it's cool and have a picnic."

"With *you*?"

"Yes! Why *not* me?" He looked affronted.

Probably never been turned down by a girl before, Sunny guessed. A mischievous idea popped into her head. Taking a moment as if to consider the invitation, Sunny said, "Well . . ."—she dragged the word out—"to answer your question, Mr. Chandler, I most certainly *do* take a day off. I plan to do so tomorrow. And since you pointed out tomorrow *is* Sunday, I will be attending church. If you also plan to go . . . ?" she let the supposition dangle.

*Church?* Webb gulped, nearly letting out a yelp of surprise. *Church?* He hadn't been inside one since he'd run away from his Aunt Pem when he was fourteen. One of the reasons being that she'd insisted on dragging him to church three times a week, twice on Sunday. Not that he didn't believe in the Almighty. He did. On more than one occasion he'd had to call upon him for help, and he'd usually come through. Or given him the idea of how to get out of whatever mess he'd got himself into. But church . . . Somehow that didn't suit his style.

Seeing Webb's reaction, Sunny knew she had hit the mark. At the same moment, she realized she had been, as Proverbs 6:2 said, "ensnared by the words of your mouth." Until just then she had not had the slightest intention of going to church. She had disliked the thought of going to a strange church where she knew no one. Just as her stepmother had always warned her, her wicked tongue had got her into trouble. Now she had no choice but to do what she had told Webb she was going to do.

Webb recovered himself quickly. He had not missed the swift change of expression on Sunny's face. He suspected she had spoken on the spur of the moment. Two could play at that game, he decided. He nodded solemnly. "What a high-minded suggestion, Miss Lyndall. My Aunt Pem would be so pleased that you have reminded me of something I have lately been so lax about: church attendance."

Sunny glanced at him sharply. His tone was sanctimonious in the extreme, and she suspected he was up to something. While she was trying to decide what Webb continued, his drawl pronounced. "Of course, being on the trail as much as I am, Sunday services are a kind of happenstance event, depending on whose wagon train you're with. One time it's the Baptists, the next it might be the Methodists. But then it's

75

all God's Word, as I'm sure you'd agree. Well then, I'll be on my way. And looking forward very much to seeing you tomorrow."

With that Webb swung into his saddle and, smiling to himself, turned his horse around and went through the gate.

*Well, we'll just see about that, Mr. Chandler!* Sunny said to herself as he rode off.

The next morning broke hot at seven. Getting up and looking out the window at the brilliant sunshine, Sunny regretted her impulsive declaration to Webb Chandler the day before. She dreaded the thought of getting into proper Sunday attire, bonnet, and gloves and driving into town in the heat. *Serves me right!* she thought. She hadn't worn anything but a denim skirt and muslin blouse for weeks. Bemoaning the state of her hands, which were reddened and roughened by all her recent hard work, she slipped a pair of crocheted lace gloves into her handbag to replace the leather driving gloves when she got into town. Finally she put on a blue Irish linen dress and her straw bonnet with daisies, which she had hoped to wear for the first time in sunny California. Satisfied with her image reflected in the wavy little mirror over the kitchen sink, she hitched up the horse and wagon and set off for church.

She was some time finding the town's one little church, which was almost hidden behind the row of stores, taverns, dance halls, and saloons on the main street. Its bell was already tolling as she hurried up the steps. She found a seat in the back pew and sat down. Feeling a little flustered and warm, she wondered why she had made the effort. To impress Webb Chandler? She should be ashamed of herself. Sitting in the small, airless wooden building, Sunny did not feel the least bit spiritual. Why had she even bothered to come? After a few heads had turned for that first curious stare when she entered, no one had deigned to speak or even so much as nod to her. She might as well have been invisible. She felt increasingly uncomfortable, miserable. At *that* thought, the small voice of her conscience nudged, *So you come to church to be seen?* Almost visibly shrinking, she tried protesting, *But my intentions were good.* But *were* they, *really*? Next she was struck by the old question: what was paved with good intentions?

After three hymns were sung, Sunny started to sit down, when a fourth was begun. Hastily she reopened her hymnal and flipped through the pages to find the right one and join in a rousing "We Shall Gather at the River." When it was concluded, she waited to be sure the singing was over and the rest of the congregation was seating itself before she took her seat.

"I'm atakin' my text from Matthew twenty-four, beginning at verse eleven," a voice bellowed so loudly that Sunny jumped. Startled, she glanced at the man behind the pulpit. His stature was such that his head of wiry gray hair was just visible above the lectern. With that loud voice, he could have won a hog-calling contest back home. His delivery was dramatic; he rolled his r's and trilled his syllables as he pronounced words like *tribulation.* He accompanied this by waving his Bible aloft with one hand so that its pages fluttered while he pounded his other hand in a fist upon the edge of the pulpit.

Sunny was so fascinated watching him that unfortunately some of the content of the sermon was lost to her. Despite all those scriptural warnings and threats, Reverend Billings beamed beatifically on his flock as he closed his message. Then he moved down the middle aisle, placing himself at the door to shake hands with members of the congregation as they left the church.

No one seemed unduly upset by the dire predictions enumerated in the morning's sermon. All looked cheerful as they shook their pastor's hand and went out into the sunshine. Over and over she heard the comments, "That's preachin'. Amen," "Mighty fine service, Pastor," and "Good sermon, Reverend."

Feeling at a loss as to what to say to him, Sunny waited until he was deep in conversation with an elderly couple, then she slipped past him and down the steps.

Small groups of people stood chatting in clusters in the churchyard. Webb Chandler was nowhere in sight, she saw with both satisfaction and a tiny nagging regret. So he hadn't shown up after all. Not that she was surprised.

She started walking to where she had hitched the horse and wagon, when she heard a familiar male voice greeting her.

"Good morning, Miss Lyndall."

Sunny turned to see Rhys Graham across the street from the church. She stopped and replied, "Good morning, Mr. Graham." As he approached she noticed he was as impeccably turned out as usual.

"Lovely spring morning, isn't it?" he asked, taking off his hat.

"Indeed," she agreed, noting his pearl stickpin in the silk cravat, and the pleated shirt.

From the top of the church steps, Webb saw Sunny talking with Rhys Graham. She was smiling up at him. And Graham looked as if he were enjoying it.

Could anything be going on there? Nah, probably not. Rhys was years older than Sunny. Had always kept to himself. Webb had never heard a hint or rumor of him being involved with any woman. But then, Sunny Lyndall was different.

Webb was even baffled by his own feelings about her. She was a puzzlement to him, and a challenge. His taste in women usually ran to another type entirely. Redheads often, with curvaceous figures, or exotic brunettes, Spanish-looking. She was slender, almost too slender. Didn't look like any of the ladies pictured in some of the gazettes he'd seen. Not really beautiful either. Her nose was too short, her cheekbones too high, her mouth too wide. But in spite of its width, it was a mouth he'd sure like to kiss. He found her mighty attractive.

Webb guessed he'd better wait till they finished talking before he approached her. He wondered impatiently what they were talking about.

Graham smiled down at Sunny. "Attending church, I see."

"Well, yes. My first time here." She was about to make some reference to the rousing sermon, when *his* comment showed he had some acquaintance with the fiery preacher.

"Did you get a good scare or an exhortation?" Rhys asked dryly, a look of amusement in his deep-set eyes.

"A little of both, I think." She smiled. "Although to be truthful, I'm ashamed to say I was so fascinated by his theatrics that I missed most of his message."

"You couldn't know this, of course, but Reverend Billings has quite a testimony. He was a carnival barker before he got the call, you see. Old habits are hard to break. Even after you're saved."

"I take it you didn't hear him this morning?"

Rhys shook his head. "I rarely attend Reverend Billings' services."

"Then you've missed quite a performance."

Suddenly all the humor Sunny imagined she had seen in Rhys' face disappeared.

"Actually, I should have said I don't attend church regularly. I didn't mean to poke fun at Reverend Billings. He is a completely sincere and totally dedicated man of God." He paused, then said, "After all, it doesn't matter *how* as long as the gospel is being preached, does it?"

With that statement Rhys Graham tipped his hat, said, "Good day, Miss Lyndall," and walked away without another word.

Sunny was bewildered by Graham's abrupt change of

manner. Maybe it had been in poor taste to mention the way Reverend Billings conducted his service. But Graham had brought up the subject. Sunny shrugged. It seemed to her that Reverend Billings was not the only person in this town with an unusual history. She had thought from the first that there was something strange and mysterious about Rhys Graham himself. She was standing there looking after his departing figure when she saw Webb Chandler coming toward her, a wide grin on his face.

"Miss Lyndall, wait." He came up to her, and as she started toward the wagon he fell into step beside her. "I saw you in church, and afterwards I was trying to get over to speak with you, but the reverend pulled me aside—" He laughed, straightening his jacket lapels. "I *should* say yanked me by the coat. I've been trying to get away ever since."

"Spotted you as a sinner, no doubt!" Sunny said flippantly.

Webb's grin widened. "Well, he was trying to talk me into getting baptized. Big doings down at the river this afternoon." He laughed. "I finally convinced him I'd been baptized when I was ten and it took."

"Not so anyone could notice," Sunny said archly.

Webb made a show of wincing. "You've got a mean streak, Miss Lyndall." Then he went on. "It kinda spoiled my plans to take you on a picnic at the river this afternoon. I mean the place will be packed." His look of disappointment quickly changed to one of possibility. "Of course, there are other places we could picnic. I know some dandy ones."

"I am just sure you do." They had reached the wagon, and Sunny opened her handbag to exchange her lace gloves for the leather ones. "But it's of no importance to me anyway. I never agreed to go anywhere with you, Mr. Chandler."

His face registered disappointment. "But I thought we'd buried the hatchet! I thought—"

"You thought wrong, Mr. Chandler," she replied sweetly,

taking perverse pleasure in deflating his assumption that she had accepted the invitation.

Suddenly Webb's eager smile disappeared. His eyes narrowed speculatively.

"Well, maybe it wasn't such a good idea anyway. Maybe it wouldn't have been much fun no matter where we went or what we did." He paused and Sunny suddenly felt exposed by the way he was looking at her—*through* her. Then he said slowly, "You know, Miss Lyndall, when I first met you, I was surprised you weren't married. I thought sure it wasn't for lack of chances. But now I think I've got it figured out. It's your tongue. You use it like a weapon, and no man could take that for long." He turned and without a backward glance sauntered away.

His words cut her like the stinging flick of a riding whip. She climbed into the wagon and sat there for a minute, the reins slack in her hands. She wanted to be angry, but the urge to cry was stronger.

She bit her lip. How dare he talk to her like that? And why should she care what Webb Chandler thought? Why had it hurt so much? She answered her own question: because the *truth* always hurts.

# Chapter 10

The short-lived spring turned into summer. And hot. Sunny missed the long, cool spring of her native Ohio Valley. Here it seemed that spring had come and gone like the snap of a finger.

Even if it had, Sunny was suffering from "spring fever" or some kind of similar ailment. She found herself depressed. Just woke up that way. She couldn't figure out why or find a remedy for it. From the time she dragged herself out of bed, dressed, awakened her brother, cooked breakfast, and packed his saddlebags to send him off on his route, it was an effort. The minute Tracy left, all the dismal thoughts she held at bay fell on her like a sack of potatoes. She could hardly find the energy to do her chores.

It seemed to have started after that Sunday she'd attended church. It wasn't the service, she knew that; going to church was supposed to uplift and inspire you, not pull you down. It might have been the odd conversation with Rhys Graham afterward or the abrasive encounter with Webb Chandler. Whichever it was, she hadn't seen either man since.

She'd half expected Webb to show up, like the proverbial "bad penny," in spite of his telling her off when she turned him down on his picnic invitation. But he hadn't been around. And Graham had sent another rider out to pick up the weekly receipts instead of doing it himself and staying as he usually did for a few minutes' pleasant visit.

Suddenly her aloneness and isolation hit Sunny. She had never felt quite this lonely in her entire life. Better get busy doing something, she told herself firmly. That way she wouldn't have so much time to think, to feel sorry for herself.

She got started on tasks she'd been avoiding, so that she wouldn't be able to dwell on how miserable she felt. Still, her mind was whirling with uncomfortable thoughts.

The confrontation with Webb Chandler preyed on her mind. Why did the fact that he hadn't been around bother her? Hadn't she purposefully discouraged him? To be truthful, she'd been rude. She'd overdone it. He'd had every right to say the things he had to her that Sunday. Now that she'd had time to reconsider, she would have apologized. Not that she'd had a chance. Almost every day, she'd thought he might appear nonchalantly, the old assured grin on his face, his eyes filled with merriment. She almost *missed* him.

And Mr. Graham. She hoped she hadn't offended *him* in some way. After all, she and Tracy were dependent on him for their jobs. She'd gone over and over their conversation but hadn't been able to figure out what she might have said wrong. Sunny frowned and rubbed harder.

*I can't stand this place! Can't stand the loneliness. I wish I'd never left Lyman Corners*—She stopped short. What was she thinking about? Hadn't she been dying to get away from there? Hadn't she felt trapped in that small-town community? Hadn't she longed for change and adventure?

*I'm as bad as the Israelites longing for the leeks and onions of Egypt,* she accused herself. So what was she *really* missing? If she only had someone to talk to! Another woman, a *friend!*

By twelve o'clock she was worn out. She still had a long,

lonely afternoon to fill. She washed up, took off her grimy apron, put on a clean one, then plopped down at the kitchen table, chin in hand, and stared out the window, sighing impatiently, "If only something would *happen*—"

The words were hardly out of her mouth when she saw a small buckboard turn into the gate. A woman was driving. Sunny jumped up and rushed to the kitchen window to see who it was. As the woman got down from the wagon and started up to the porch Sunny recognized her. Verna Ardley.

It was Verna, but not the everyday Verna behind the counter at the store. This Verna had on a ruffled sunbonnet and a crisp, flowered calico dress, and she was carrying a basket covered with a checkered cloth.

Sunny was immediately aware of her own appearance. Her first visitor *would* have to be the wife of the storekeeper! Sunny had been here just long enough to know that Ardley's General Store was the hub of the town, the center where all information was passed back and forth, discussed, chewed over, repeated dozens of times. She gave a quick look around. At least the place was clean, as neat and tidy as she could make it. There was no time. She'd have to answer the peremptory knock sounding at the door.

"Why, Mrs. Ardley. What a nice surprise," Sunny smilingly understated. "I'm afraid I'm not fit for company."

Verna held up one hand to stop her apology. "Can't stay to visit. Jest came to ask you and your brother to come for dinner after services Sunday."

"Why, how kind of you. Well yes, I'd love to. I mean, *we'd* love to. He's off on his mail run, but I'm sure he'll be pleased. Thank you very much."

Verna shook her head. "It's nuthin' fancy. I'd have asked you sooner but knew as how you was gettin' settled and all. Well, we'll expect you around one. Come right on over after church." She thrust the basket forward. "I thought you could use some of my strawberry jelly and apricot jam.

84

Know you haven't had time to put in a garden or do any canning yet."

"Why, thank you, Mrs. Ardley."

"If you'll jest take the jars out and set them down, I'll be taking my basket on home."

"Yes, of course," Sunny said. "Won't you come in?"

"You've done right smart fixin' up this place," Mrs. Ardley commented approvingly as she followed Sunny inside. She stood looking around while Sunny emptied the basket of a half dozen glass jars of glistening fruit preserves. "When I heard a young woman was goin' to be livin' here—well, I said to Clem that place ain't fit for anyone to live in, let alone a *lady* from back east. But then Webb told us—"

At the scout's name Sunny stiffened. She felt herself blush at the idea that Webb Chandler might have been talking about her, giving his opinion to those fellows gathered around the potbellied stove at the general store. It was almost too much to bear. However, Mrs. Ardley seemed to think nothing of the fact that other people's business was discussed openly.

"Yes indeedy, you've made it right homey, seeing as what you must've started from." Mrs. Ardley was beaming. She gave Sunny a nod. "And you such a slip of a gal! Who'd have thought it?"

Handing the basket back to her, Sunny walked with her caller out onto the porch. Mrs. Ardley went down the steps, saying over her shoulder, "Well then, we'll see you on Sunday."

"Yes, and thank you again for the invitation."

Sunny watched from the porch as Mrs. Ardley got back into the little wagon, picked up the reins, and trotted out through the gate.

Sunny went back inside feeling more cheerful. What a nice gesture of friendship. And from Mrs. Ardley, of all people. Sunny had never thought the woman to be very warm or friendly when she had gone into the store. It was Mrs. Ardley's husband who joshed with the customers, greeted everyone with a smile and friendly hello. Well, you couldn't always judge right off, Sunny had at least learned that much. She was reminded of the jovial Faraday, with a rush of anger. She would never have guessed him a crook!

When Tracy returned from his ride, Sunny relayed the Ardleys' dinner invitation to him. He gave an exaggerated cheer. "Hey, that's good news! A real, honest-ta-gosh, home-cooked dinner!"

"What do you mean by *that* remark?" Sunny demanded, placing one hand on her hip as she turned around from the stove, where she was frying steak and potatoes.

"No offense, Sis. But our meals *have* been pretty much ... well, the same old stuff—"

She reached for a dishtowel and flung it at him.

Tracy put up both hands and ducked.

"Better watch those complaints, brother, or you'll find yourself cooking your own supper," she warned, but she was smiling. To herself she had to admit that their menu had consisted pretty regularly of fried steaks, thick flap-jacks, gravy, and one disastrous, dried peach cobbler. But that was because she'd been so busy trying to get this place clean and because she wasn't used to baking in this poor clunk of a stove.

Tracy was right, though: it would be nice to sit down at a table and be served somebody else's cooking for a change. Sunny found she was looking forward to next Sunday.

This was the first time for Tracy to attend church, since he was either out on his route or sleeping Sunday mornings. Anxious that they make a good impression, Sunny washed and ironed a white shirt for him and insisted he wear a dark blue string tie. She put a new lace collar on her best dress and pinned it with her mother's cameo brooch.

With her daisy-trimmed straw bonnet in place, she was finally satisfied with how both she and Tracy looked.

Because of all their unusual fussing with appearance, they were a little late arriving at church. At the door, one of the ushers stepped forward, shook Tracy's hand, then smilingly showed them to a pew. This friendliness that had not been extended to her on her first visit to church puzzled Sunny. Slowly it dawned on her that everyone in town knew the Express riders. They were recognized and admired for their work in carrying the mail. This was something she had not realized before. It *was* a dangerous job, and people appreciated their willingness to take it on. Glancing sideways at her brother, Sunny felt a warm glow of pride. Much as she had resisted his decision, she saw now that his work was important.

Spontaneously the proverb "A man's gift makes room for him" came into Sunny's mind. Tracy's gift certainly was horsemanship, a kind of reckless courage, and indifference to physical hardship. As a Pony Express rider, all those qualitites were fully utilized. Yes, Tracy had established himself in the community. Yet she had not found her place here.

Coincidentally, it seemed to Sunny, the sermon was taken from James 1:17: "Every good and perfect gift is from above, coming down from the Father." Reverend Billings took this theme further with many scriptural references in rapid sequence, too many for Sunny to keep track of. She did remember the one from 1 Corinthians 7:7, "Each one has his own gift from God," and that it was necessary for each "to stir up the gift of God that is in you." Sunny wasn't sure if she had a gift. If she did, she wasn't sure what it was.

At the conclusion of the service, the Ardleys came up to them right away outside and began introducing them right and left to others exiting the church building. As they walked to their separate wagons Mr. Ardley gave Tracy directions out to their house, and they parted company.

Sunny urged Tracy to drive slowly. "You're not racing to keep your schedule," she reminded him, "and we ought to give Mrs. Ardley time to get home and at least take off her bonnet before we pile in on her. Why don't we take some side roads and look around a little?"

The hotel where they had stayed those first anxiety-filled nights was located at the lower end of Main Street, which was lined with saloons and dance halls. That had been Sunny's first impression of the town. Since then she had been too busy making the Express building livable to explore farther than between it and Ardley's General Store. Now as Tracy drove leisurely along they saw that there were tree-lined streets with pleasant frame houses and neatly fenced flowering gardens. Sunny was chastened. Now she was seeing a whole other side of the town she had decided to dislike. People with families lived here, went to church; their children attended school. These people led lives not too unlike the people back home. More and more Sunny was finding out that first impressions can be very wrong.

"Think we've dillydallied long enough?" Tracy asked. "I'm sure getting hungry." He glanced at her slyly. "That wasn't much of a breakfast you gave me."

"*You!*" she exclaimed indignantly, pursing her lips to keep from smiling. "All right, you can turn around right here. Do you remember Mr. Ardley's directions?"

"Yes, big sister," Tracy droned with exaggerated patience.

"Sorry!" Sunny replied with just as exaggerated meekness. "Just thought I might refresh your memory in case—"

Tracy laughed and they went the rest of the way with their old, easy good-humored camaraderie.

The Ardleys' two-story frame house was set in a grove of aspen trees. It was painted lemon yellow and had dark green shutters. As they drove up front Sunny saw two men sitting on rush-back rockers on the shady porch. They got to their feet as Tracy helped her down from the wagon. To her astonishment she saw that the man standing beside Clem Ardley was Rhys Graham. Sunny was taken aback. Mrs. Ardley had not mentioned she was having other guests. Before she could feel flustered, remembering the odd encounter with him, she returned his courteous greeting along with Clem Ardley's warm welcome.

"Howdy, Miss Lyndall, and you too, young fellow."

Just then Verna appeared at the front door. "Hello there. Come inside, won't you, Miss Lyndall?" she invited. "We'll let the menfolk stay on the porch till everything's ready."

Stepping inside, Sunny looked around appreciatively. The Ardleys' front room had none of the stiffness of most city parlors. Instead it was comfortably cozy. Flowered cretonne curtains at the windows, hand-hooked rugs on the polished floor, comfortable, old-fashioned furniture piled with lots of embroidered pillows that Sunny was sure were also Mrs. Ardley's handiwork. It was a room where a man could be at his ease after a hard day and yet showed the caring touch of a home-loving woman.

"Take off your bonnet, won't you?" Mrs. Ardley suggested. "Then we'll go out to the kitchen. I like company while I finish up the last-minute things. I've just got to mash my potatoes, so come along and we'll have a good jaw while I do."

The pin-neat kitchen was large, bright with sunlight. Copper utensils hanging on pegs glistened. Cabinets were painted a glossy yellow, and there was a big rocker near the shiny black stove.

Mrs. Ardley closed the door to the hall quietly and took Sunny's arm and whispered, "I know you wasn't expecting there'd be more'n just us, a chance to get acquainted. But my Clem, well, he's alyus askin' people out. Most of the time without a 'by your leave.' Not that I mind a bit. I cook more than for two anyhow. So—" She looked anxious. "I hope you don't mind?"

"Of course not, Mrs. Ardley."

"Oh, call me Verna, please!"

"Well then, Verna, not at all."

"Good!" Verna went to the stove, lifted a deep two-handled pan off and took it over to the soapstone sink. She put a colander into the sink, then poured the water out, letting the boiled potatoes tumble into it. She turned them into a big bowl and moved to the square table in the middle of the kitchen and began to vigorously pound them as she went on talking. "I'm surprised Webb didn't come."

At the mention of the scout's name, Sunny started.

"Webb's like family, we don't pay him much mind. He drops in all the time. When he's in town, that is. Mostly at mealtimes." Verna went on, chuckling softly. "But now Mr. Graham—well, it seemed a shame not to include him. He come up to me after church and spoke so pleasant and all, it just popped into my head and out of my mouth to invite him. He being a bachelor and alone and all."

Sunny did not respond to that.

"Funny about Webb not showin' up. He knew you two was comin'. Clem said he overheard Tracy tellin' him at the store yesterday."

Secretly Sunny wondered if *that* might be the reason Webb hadn't shown up. Maybe he didn't want to see *her*! Her cheeks got warm at the probability. Why else would Webb pass it up?

"Mr. Graham thinks the world of your brother. He told Clem he'd never had a fella take to being a rider so easy." Verna turned and gave Sunny a knowing look. "He had some nice words to say about how well you was managing the station, too."

Sunny smiled and said nothing. Of course Rhys Graham would do and say the gentlemanly thing. Webb

Chandler was another kettle of fish. If he didn't want to see her, he'd make that plain. At least she could give him credit for being honest.

Even if it meant missing a delicious meal, Sunny thought ironically as they sat down to dinner. Verna was a marvelous cook. The dinner table practically groaned with platters of fried chicken, a pot of savory baked beans, applesauce, cornbread, buttered turnips, and two kinds of pie—rhubarb and plum.

The conversation was conducted mainly between Clem Ardley and Rhys Graham, with Verna occasionally urging second helpings on everyone. As it turned out, Clem was a great reader, newspapers mainly. He and Graham had much to discuss: national current events, local politics, the settling of the western territories, as well as the progress of plans to build a transcontinental railway across the plains.

"When that happens, of course, that will be the end of the Pony Express," Rhys said. "Cars on steel rails can travel faster and carry more mail." He looked at Tracy reassuringly. "Of course, that won't be for quite a while. Your job's safe for some time."

*Safe?* Sunny thought. She realized Rhys was using the word in another context, because by no stretch of the imagination could a Pony Express rider's job be called safe. It was risky, hazardous, dangerous. So far Tracy had been lucky. There'd been no accidents, not even a loose stirrup or a pony tripping and falling. The weather remained good. He hadn't been caught in a sudden storm or a flash flood. Nor had he been attacked by Indians. None of the other horrors Sunny imagined when Tracy was gone, the nightmares from which she awoke shuddering with fear some nights, had happened. She just hoped that soon they could accumulate enough money to make new plans to go to California.

"Don't you agree, Miss Lyndall?"

91

The question jerked her back to the dinner table. She had to beg their pardon and ask for it to please be repeated.

Soon after dinner Mr. Graham took his leave, and since Tracy had to start early the next morning on his route, he and Sunny also said their good-byes, with thanks for such a pleasant day. Verna insisted they take an extra pie she'd baked, then walked with them out to the wagon.

"Now don't be a stranger, you hear?" Verna said to Sunny. "I only work at the store four mornings a week. The rest of the time I'm right here at home. So don't get lonely over there at the Express station when your brother's on his route. I love having company."

Driving back to the Express station, Sunny felt warmed by the older woman's genuineness. It was almost as if her prayer for a friendship had been answered.

Still, there was the small, niggling question of why Webb Chandler had turned down his usual dinner. Was it *really* because he knew *she* had been invited? Did he find her *that* unpleasant to be around? Truthfully, she knew she had been.

# *Chapter 11*

*D*ays passed, then weeks, and the hot, dry summer set in. Sunny was still plagued with the empty restlessness she'd felt in the spring. Their "grubstake" for California was growing slowly. Would they ever have enough? Or would she be forever stuck on the brink of the exciting life she had envisioned for them? Tracy seemed to have found being a rider the most natural thing in the world, as if he had been doing it all his life. He never even talked about California anymore.

One sweltering June day when Sunny rode into town for supplies, she saw a banner of red, white, and blue bunting draped across Main Street, with a sign in foot-high letters:

INDEPENDENCE DAY BARBECUE—EVERYONE,
COME ONE COME ALL
FOURTH OF JULY, TOWN PARK

It was probably intended to whip up enthusiasm in folks to celebrate the nation's birthday. But it did just the opposite for Sunny. A wave of nostalgia for her hometown's annual Independence Day celebration rushed up within her. The firemen's band playing stirring marches from the stand by the lake, families gathering with picnic baskets, happily getting ready to watch the fireworks scheduled to start at dark. Afterward there would be music for dancing in the open-air pavilion. Sunny could almost see how it had been the first year she'd been allowed to go to that part of the celebration—the fireflies dancing in the azalea bushes that surrounded the pavilion, a full moon shimmering on the surface of the lake. Remembering it now, everything seemed better than it really was. Even Billy Taylor—her escort, who had seemed dreadfully dull at the time—was imbued with looks and charm.

Well, she certainly had no plans to attend. It would be just another working day at the Express station, packing the mail pouches for the riders. Tracy was probably scheduled to ride that night as well.

However, Sunny hadn't counted on Verna's insistence. "Of course you're going to come! Nobody misses the Fourth of July here! Even the Express station is closed. The riders don't ride. Of course you and Tracy will be there."

But when the day of the barbecue came, she still lacked much enthusiasm about going. All the previous week she had avoided looking at the July fourth date on the calendar. It was a melancholy reminder that if things had not worked out so disastrously for them, she and Tracy would have been at the halfway point on the trail to California.

Webb tethered his horse to the fence, then with a nonchalant air, thumbs in belt, sauntered unconcernedly to the edge of the crowd. The air was thick with the tantalizing smells coming from the barbecue pit, where a huge steer was roasting on the spit. Nearby underneath the trees, a group of men was gathered. Women in brightly colored dresses were fluttering around the long table that had been set up a little way from the pit. They were chattering and carrying on like a flock of birds as they set out bowls and dishes and large pitchers of lemonade and ice tea. His eyes searched the crowd for a glimpse of Sunny among them, but he didn't see her.

Reckon she wasn't here? Disappointment flooded over

him. Suddenly he spotted her, and his heart tripped a mite. She had on a blue dress and was wearing a wide-brimmed straw hat. Relief and excitement spread all through him. He started to go over, then saw she was talking to Rhys Graham. Webb decided to wait awhile.

A couple of men standing in a huddle under one of the shade trees hailed him. Knowing he would immediately become the butt of some rough joshing if he looked too eager to join a lady, he walked over to them. Besides, hadn't he learned his lesson about Sunny Lyndall? Her tongue was like a razor, always at the ready, its blade sharpened to cut deep into a man's very heart—if he let it.

Seeming in no hurry, he traded trail stories for a while but kept occasionally glancing in Sunny's direction. When he noticed Rhys leaving for the refreshment table, Webb saw his chance. With a great display of casualness, Webb left the group of men and sauntered over to Sunny.

Close up she looked even prettier than at a distance, the brim of her hat dipped over the fringe of curls framing her face. It wouldn't do to let her know what a picture she made. She'd most likely turn a compliment into an insult. The way her chin was tilted, she already had her guard up. She had seen him approaching.

Webb took off his hat, smoothed back his hair, and said, "Hello, Miss Lyndall."

She nodded coolly.

"I see you took my advice," he drawled.

"And what advice was that, Mr. Chandler?"

"You know that old saw about all work and no play, don't you? Getting out, mixing with folks, enjoying yourself, being sociable."

Was he deliberately trying to provoke her? It had been weeks since she'd seen him—actually since that day at church when he had told her off so rudely. But she had already decided that if she saw him at the barbecue, she

95

would be civil and polite. So she simply replied, "It's a very nice picnic."

"Yep, folks always told me it was. Most years I've missed it, been on the trail, celebrating Independence Day in the middle of the prairie. Watchin' out for hostile Indians isn't exactly my idea of a picnic."

When Sunny made no response, Webb glanced around and then remarked casually, "I see you're lettin' your brother off his lead for a change?"

Turning to look in the direction Webb had jerked his head, Sunny saw Tracy talking to a very pretty girl. She was tossing her curls saucily and flirting outrageously with him. Tracy, who was usually shy and became beet red and tongue-tied if a girl even glanced his way, seemed to be enjoying it thoroughly.

When Tracy had told her he was going to pick up a friend and wanted to take the wagon, Sunny assumed he was going to meet one of the other riders, so she accepted when Verna offered to come by and give her a ride into town with them. So that's why he'd wanted to use the wagon!

Peeved that Webb had pointed out what she hadn't known, Sunny struggled to conceal her dismay. But her shock must have been apparent to Webb, who was watching her. "Gotta cut the apron strings, or sooner or later he'll bust loose anyway, tearing the apron as he goes," he commented quietly.

At his words all her good resolutions not to rise to his bait vanished. "Don't you have anything better to do with your time but give *unsolicited* advice?"

"Just trying to be helpful—"

"Well, *don't*!"

"Yes, ma'am." He shrugged. Doggone if he hadn't gone and put his foot in it again!

Just then Rhys returned. As he handed Sunny her cup of strawberry lemonade he nodded to Webb and said, "Good turnout today. Best one yet, I'd say. Planning to stay for the barbecue?"

"Don't look like that's goin' to happen anytime soon."

"After the speeches usually. There are dignitaries from back east here today. So I guess it won't be served till after dark, most likely."

"Not much in the mood for political speechifying. Most of it don't ring true, somehow." A slight edge was in Webb's voice. "Don't many seem to remember us after they get back to Washington."

"Guess we have to give them the benefit of the doubt."

Sunny, cheeks burning, sipped her lemonade. She could feel Webb's wary glance, but she wouldn't look at him. Instead she studied the contents of her cup, allowing herself a darting look to where her brother still hovered over the girl.

Tracy *had* changed since he'd become a rider. He was growing up. That remark of Webb's she'd overheard the day Tracy signed up came back into her mind now: *Not all ladies feel about the Express riders like your sister does. You're in for some new experiences.* It had annoyed her at the time, but now she knew it was true, and that smarted even worse. Riders were sort of celebrities in Cottonwood. They were admired for their derring-do, and they all thrived on the adulation. Especially from the young girls.

She came back to the present when she heard Webb say, "Well, I'll be moving along."

Rhys asked, "You're not staying for the watermelon-eating contest or the barbecue then?"

Webb just shook his head. "Kinda lost the mood," he said, then he tipped his hat. "Good day to you both."

Rhys watched Webb amble back to the group of men still laughing and talking under the trees. "Splendid chap, Webb. Never met a more honest, good-hearted fellow," he remarked. "A *real* Christian. Not like the 'whited sepulchres' who call themselves Christians."

Still smarting from Webb's outspokenness, Sunny was surprised at Graham's comment. It certainly wasn't *her* impression of the man! She felt the twinge of possibility. She had often been too quick to make judgments about people. Could she be wrong about Webb Chandler?

The rest of the afternoon Sunny was too distracted to thoroughly enjoy it. She found herself constantly seeking out her brother and the evident object of his new interest. By early evening she felt as fizzled out as some of the Roman candles that hadn't worked.

After the fireworks display, she sought out Tracy, saying she was tired and would like to leave. Rhys, who was standing nearby, immediately offered to drive her back to the Express station.

"Oh, I don't want to take you away!"

"I wouldn't stay for the square dance anyhow. And I can see Tracy wants to. Please, Miss Lyndall, it would be my pleasure."

Tracy seemed relieved, and there really was nothing else Sunny could do but accept his offer. On the way Sunny was quiet, while inwardly her emotions were churning. Why hadn't Tracy just told her he wanted to spend the day and evening with this girl? He had introduced her as Betty Brownlee. Why had he never mentioned her before? Where had he met her? How long had this been going on? Sunny felt hurt, left out, betrayed in some way. She and her brother had always been so close, but now . . .

Rhys glanced over at her and said, "You're so quiet. Is anything wrong?"

"No," she assured him.

But when they reached the station, Rhys asked again. "You're sure nothing's wrong?"

"No, really."

"You're probably tired."

"Actually, I'm wide awake. Besides, I'll wait up for Tracy."

"You might have a long wait. The last I saw him, he was promenading with that pretty girl, Betty. He'll probably see her home." Sounding amused, he added, "The long way 'round."

"Yes, I suppose that's true." Sunny sounded unsure.

"It's sometimes hard to see people close to us changing." There was a slight pause, then Rhys said seriously, "Younger brothers more than most, I would imagine. I think you have to realize that Tracy is doing a man's job, Miss Lyndall, and doing it well. He's feeling sure of himself, wants to be independent, be his own man. I'm sure that's hard to accept. You've probably heard the saying 'The tighter you hold the reins, the more a horse bucks'?" When she did not respond, Rhys said, "I'm sorry, I spoke out of turn, didn't I? I shouldn't have said that."

"You needn't apologize, Mr. Graham."

"I think I should. Please forgive me?"

"Of course," she murmured.

They came to a stop in front of the Express station. Rhys got out of his buggy, came around, helped Sunny down, and they walked onto the porch. At the doorway, they stood almost shoulder to shoulder—for Sunny was tall for a girl—while she unlocked the door. Then as she turned to say good night and thank him for the ride home, Rhys said, "There's something I'd like to say, if I may. You and your brother have come to mean a great deal to me. I'd like to think we've become friends. Friends out here use each other's first names. Could you—would you—call me Rhys?"

"Oh, I don't know. You are, after all, our employer. It would hardly be proper. . ." Sunny felt awkward, not having expected such a request. She hesitated. "Let me think about it—"

"Well then, perhaps at least in private? I guess what

I'm really asking is—I'd like very much to call *you* Sunny." A moment passed, then he said, "Never mind. I won't press you."

Rhys started down the steps, then halted, saying over his shoulder, "Be sure to lock and bolt the door until your brother comes home. Some of those cowboys were celebrating pretty hard, and you don't want some of them seeing your light and wandering in off the road, thinking they've made it home." He went down the rest of the steps. Without turning around, he said, "Good night, Miss Lyndall."

Sunny was thoughtful after she closed the door. It had been an eventful evening on several counts. She had so much to think about. Tracy. Strange that such different men as Rhys Graham and Webb Chandler had given her the same advice about her brother.

Let him grow up, let him be himself. She knew she was afraid to let go, afraid he would wander too far away, go too far, like a colt she was trying to train.

She knew they were both right and that the advice had been given with the best intentions. Why did she accept one's counsel and resent the other's?

She felt uncomfortable about the incident that had taken place at the door. Rhys' request that they call each other by first names troubled her. That and worrying about Tracy kept Sunny wakeful most of the night.

Back in town Rhys Graham was also sleepless. His feelings for Sunny Lyndall had almost taken over his good sense. Standing in the doorway, he had wanted to kiss her. From the first he had behaved out of character where she was concerned. Acting on impulse—something he rarely did—he had offered her the management of the Express station, not even being sure she would accept it. Her courage, strength, resourcefulness, and determination had won his respect. And more. Rhys knew that gradually his feelings had changed, grown deeper. However, knowing where those feelings might lead, he knew he must check them. He did not have the right, not with his background, not with his past . . .

# Chapter 12

*S*unny woke feeling cross. She yanked the covers. Her blanket and quilt had got twisted with all her turning and tossing throughout the restless night. She didn't remember when she had finally fallen asleep. But she did know that gray light was creeping in the windows when she heard Tracy come in at dawn.

Foolish boy! Staying out till who knows what time, when he had to go out on his route this morning. She just hoped that in his desperate race to prove himself a man, he wasn't thinking of falling in love! But what could she do about it? Gloomily she recalled the advice given her by both Webb and Rhys. Everything seemed to have been taken out of her hands. Sunny sighed, got out of bed, and went to wake up Tracy.

Half dead from lack of sleep, he stumbled out of the bunk room, gulped down a mug of coffee she had brewed. He shook his head sullenly when she urged a bowl of oatmeal and some toasted cornbread. There was no conversation between them. Just as well, Sunny thought, or she might have gone into a tirade about his staying out so late. Finally he shouldered the mail pouches and with a gruff good-bye went out to saddle his pony and leave.

Sunny ranted mentally at that stupid Betty Brownlee. Tracy had probably lingered on her family's porch half the night, trying to work up enough courage to kiss her before saying good night, instead of sensibly coming back to the station and getting a good night's sleep.

*Cut the apron strings. Quit mother-henning. Let the boy grow up.* These comments echoed hollowly in her mind as she stood at the window, watching him disappear in the morning mist.

It was easy enough for Webb Chandler and even Rhys Graham to give her advice about letting Tracy go; they didn't understand how close she felt to her brother. She remembered the day he was born! The little scrap of a baby bundled in a blanket. "This is your little brother, Sunny. He's going to be *your* special charge from now on," their mother had whispered to her.

No matter how tall or how big or how independent he got, that's how she'd always think of Tracy. She couldn't help it. He was the baby she'd diapered and bathed, the little boy whose neck she'd scrubbed, whose hair she'd washed and cut for so many years. How *could* she not care what he did, what he thought, what happened to him? Their lives were linked—past, present, and future.

Sunny tried to keep busy all that day. She didn't want to think about Tracy. She didn't want to think about Rhys Graham. She certainly didn't want to think about Webb Chandler.

Late the following evening she heard the whinnying of the ponies, and the sound of hoofbeats for which she had been anxiously listening the last few hours. She rushed to the window. Just as she reached it and was peering out, a dirty, disheveled Tracy stumbled into the room. Wearily he staggered over to the bench by the table and flung himself down. He folded his arms on top of the table, and his head sagged onto them. He was too tired to even speak.

"Hard trip?" she asked anxiously.

A muffled groan was her answer.

She hurried to boil water, dragging in the tin tub from the shed and filling it in front of the stove. She unwrapped a new cake of soap and placed it, along with a large sponge, on the bench alongside the tub. Then she turned to her brother. "Tracy, your bathwater's ready. Come get in 'fore it cools off."

Tracy stood, still looking sleepy.

"Here, take off your clothes. They're filthy."

Tracy stared at her.

"Give them to me. They'll have to be soaked before they're washed."

He just stood there.

"Hurry up," Sunny urged impatiently. "Your water's getting cold."

Tracy scowled. "You can git 'em later."

Quickly she turned her back, saying over her shoulder as she left the room, "Well, just drop them on the floor beside the tub. I'll get them when I empty the bathwater."

To her chagrin she again recalled Webb Chandler's words, which had been reinforced by Rhys Graham's sage remarks. Both men had seen what she had been blind to: her brother was growing up. She couldn't treat him like a child any longer. She would have to think of him as— what? An equal partner?

Sunny realized she had come to a crossroads in her relationship with Tracy. She would not be able to make arbitrary decisions as she had in the past. Together they would make the journey that lay ahead, or else their lives would take different directions.

Goodness, there was such a lot to think about! Once life had seemed so simple. Sunny's goal had been clear. To get to California. Then everything would fall in place for them. Had she ever been *that* naive?

# Chapter 13

*W*ith so many things on her mind, Sunny longed for someone to discuss her new problems with— someone older, wiser. This struck her as ironic. Hadn't she always resented other people's advice?

Almost as an answer to her need, after church on the Sunday following the Fourth of July barbecue, Verna invited her to come for a visit.

"Tuesday's my day off from the store," she told Sunny. "We can have a nice visit to ourselves with no menfolk around." Verna's eyes twinkled.

Sunny accepted gladly. Maybe she could tactfully bring the subject around to Rhys Graham's interest in her. It was a situation Sunny was finding increasingly hard to handle. One she had not anticipated and one that she felt she certainly had not encouraged. Maybe Verna could give her some sage advice.

That afternoon, after tidying up and finishing her chores, Sunny rode over to Verna's. She tethered the pony under a shady tree on the cool side of the house. As she came up on the porch Verna looked out the kitchen window and called, "Hot enough for you?" then came to the door and held it open for her. "Come on in out of that heat."

Stepping inside, Sunny untied her bonnet strings, drew off her straw hat, and fanned herself with it, saying, "Whew, there's not a breeze stirring out there."

"I made lemonade," Verna told her. "I put it in the springhouse. I'll just go get it, then I'll pour you a nice, cool glass. I'm doin' my berries, making jam, so I'll have to keep at it while we have our chat."

A few minutes later Sunny was seated in the rocking chair, sipping the tangy chilled drink while Verna busied herself at the stove. After a bit Verna looked over, surveyed her guest with sharp eyes, then commented, "You look kinda peaked. Anything wrong? Not got the summer complaint, have you? If you do, I've got jest the thing for it—"

"No, no, Verna. It isn't that. It's . . . well, I think I have a problem."

"If you *think* you've got one, you most likely have. Anything I can do? Help with?"

"I don't know." Sunny sighed. "It's about . . . well, Mr. Graham."

Verna didn't look surprised. "Uh-huh."

"You see, I thought he had always been most generous to us, very kind. It actually was a godsend when he offered me the job of managing the Express station. But now—" Sunny hesitated, debating how much she should tell Verna about the incident on her doorstep after the barbecue. "Well, he seems to have changed. I don't know if it's something I've done or said."

Verna looked amazed. "Don't you see how the land lies, gal?"

Sunny shook her head.

"You'd have to be blind as a bat not to see it!" Verna declared, her hands on her hips. She turned back to the stove and gave the boiling berries a few quick stirs before facing Sunny again. "You should have heard how he jumped at the chance to have dinner with us that first Sun-

106

day you and your brother came." She pursed her mouth and looked over her spectacles at Sunny.

Sunny didn't say anything, just gazed back at Verna. After a while she said, "I wish you hadn't told me. Now I'll feel uncomfortable around him."

"Well, like I said, you'd have to be a bat not to have seen it," was Verna's tart response.

"But it's impossible." Sunny jumped out of the chair, almost spilling her lemonade. She shook her head vigorously. "It's out of the question. Soon Tracy and I will be going on to California, and—" She took a few steps back and forth across the kitchen, paused, then turned back to Verna and said, "Please, don't say anything to anyone else. Especially not to Tracy. We talked of nothing else but California for nearly a year before we came here. I don't want anything to spoil Tracy's dream."

Verna's glance was skeptical. "No dreams of your own, Sunny? No heart's longing for a home, a husband, children?" She pulled a long face and asked, "Are you your brother's keeper?"

Sunny shook her finger playfully. "Don't misquote Scripture, Verna."

Verna went back to stirring, and Sunny picked up her bonnet, put it on, and looped the ribbons into a bow. "Besides, going to California was *my* idea first." She started for the door, then turned back. "I know you have my best interests at heart, Verna, but—"

Verna half turned from the stove, waggling the wooden stirring spoon at Sunny like a teacher's pointer. "Needn't concern yourself about *that*. Just don't come crying to me when it's too late. When you've missed your chance."

Sunny smiled. She realized her friend's tart rejoinder was not an intentional reprimand. She suspected that Verna was beginning to think of her as the daughter she'd never had, wanting the best for her. Rhys Graham, in Verna's opinion, *was* the best any mother could imagine in a suitor.

Outside Sunny untied Bramble and got into the wagon and headed to the Express station. Verna's statement had stunned her. Rhys Graham *in love* with her? Why hadn't she been aware of it or suspected it? She'd never guessed. She had been too self-absorbed maybe, too preoccupied with her new life, her new responsibilities. When she thought of him at all, it was as their employer, actually their benefactor. That's why his impulsive behavior the night he brought her home from the barbecue had been such a surprise.

*No dreams of your own, Sunny? No heart's longing for a home, a husband, children?* Verna's question brought up something Sunny hadn't thought about much recently. Up until now *her* dreams were Tracy's. The dream of going to California *together,* homesteading, living a new, adventurous life.

Of course, like any girl growing up, she'd had secret dreams of a someday romance. But not lately. And not about Rhys Graham.

He might possess some of the qualities—good looks, status in the community, manners—that might *once* have seemed ideal in the man of her dreams. But her dreams had changed. Out here in Missouri, certainly in California, a woman looked for different qualities in a man. Suddenly Sunny asked herself: When had her romantic dreams changed? What had changed them? Or more importantly, *who?*

# Chapter 14

*S*unny was outside hanging out a week's laundry. Even this early in the day it was hot. The sun beat on her back as she pinned up Tracy's heavy, coarse, cotton work shirts and his soaking wet jeans. It was hot, tiring work. Finished, she went back inside and poured herself a glass of the sun tea she had made earlier, and sat down at the kitchen table to drink it.

Tracy had left at dawn on his route. Two long days alone stretched before her. It was too hot to work in the garden or to ride into town or over to Verna's. But Verna would be at the store today anyway, Sunny remembered, sighing.

As often happened when she had time on her hands, unwelcome thoughts came. Was California a far-off dream? One that might never come true? Would she be stranded here forever? If only she and Tracy had gone with the wagon train, they would have been reaching the Sierra Mountains by now. Sunny's thoughts were like ripples from pebbles tossed into a lake: one circle led to the next and the next. Finally she brought herself up short. It was pointless to dwell on this. It only made her unhappy. She should get busy, stop thinking.

So Sunny began straightening out cabinets, rearranging

kitchen shelves. Thus occupied, the hours passed quickly. Suddenly she realized that the sun had moved and her clothes must be dry. She went back outside to bring them in.

It was past noon and the sun was high, glaring. Squinting into it, she unpinned the clothes, piling them into the willow clothes basket as she moved down the line.

Something—some movement—alerted her, and she turned just as two men on horseback rode in through the gate. From that distance she couldn't recognize them. She wasn't expecting anyone. She watched them slow their horses to a walk as they passed the corral, giving the sleek Express ponies the once-over. They halted, leaning forward, pointing, nodding their heads as if discussing the animals fenced there. Who were they? What did they want? They didn't look at all familiar. From her vantage point, shadowed by the side of the building, Sunny observed them with a vague feeling of uneasiness. What were they doing here? They looked as if they might have been riding a long time. Their horses were shaggy, had matted manes, and moved as if weary.

The men didn't see Sunny at first. As they moved slowly toward the Express station building they were talking to each other in low voices. What were they discussing? Sunny stepped out into the sunlight, holding her willow basket in front of her like a shield. The men seemed startled at her sudden appearance.

One of the men nodded to her, muttering something to his companion, who then stared at her. They both reined their horses only a few feet from where Sunny stood. She took a step back. The bigger of the two pushed his sweat-stained hat back from his forehead, pulled the red bandanna from around his neck, mopped his darkly stubbled face. Then he spoke to Sunny. "Afternoon, ma'am. We been travelin' a mighty long way. We'd be obliged iffen we could bother you for some water for ourselves and our horses."

110

She did not want to sound too friendly, as though welcoming neighbors. Cautiously Sunny replied, "There's the well and a trough. Help yourself."

"That's right kind of you, ma'am." He gave what passed for a smile, although there was no real pleasantness in it. He jerked his head to the other man. "You see to it, Jake." They dismounted and he tossed his reins to Jake, who took both horses by their reins and led them over to the trough. The man who had spoken got out a small pouch of tobacco, slowly rolled himself a cigarette. With his thumbnail he flicked the end of a match into flame, lit it. As a swirl of smoke spiraled up in front of his face he squinted, his eyes staring at Sunny. Then he asked casually, "This your spread, ma'am?"

"This is the Express station."

"Your husband run it?"

Something in the man's voice sent a sliver of fear down her spine. Instinctively she knew she must not show it. Nor let them know she was here by herself. For a minute she hesitated. "No, my brother and I do."

His scraggly eyebrows lifted. "Do tell? You look mighty young to be in charge of an Express station."

She didn't answer. Her fingers tightened on the handles of her basket. She wished they would get their water and go. She didn't want to put the basket down or go inside, leaving these suspicious-looking strangers out here.

She saw him look toward the building and the barn. Checking for any sign of someone else around? Under most circumstances if a man were on the premises, by now he would have appeared to check out who had come.

The stranger probably guessed she was alone. Sweat gathered into her palms. The man looked back at her, his narrowed gaze intimidating. Sunny looked away, over to the trough, where the horses drank thirstily. They must have been ridden a long way. Hard and fast, from the look of them. Were these men running from something? The law?

She felt a fluttering in her stomach like a covey of quail coming out of the brush. An inner warning came: *Don't act afraid. Act confident.* Inwardly she was teetering on the brink of panic. The urge to run into the building and bolt the door was strong. She took a few steps in that direction. As she did the man's voice stopped her.

"We're a sight hungry, ma'am. Could use some grub. If you could spare some, we'd be mighty grateful."

Let these two in the house? In sight of the safe, the mail shelves? While she was here alone? She wasn't about to do that. But the man's eyes were boring into her, allowing her no escape.

The other man was returning, leading the horses up to the hitching post in front of the building. The man who had been doing all the talking shifted his body slightly, and his free hand smoothed the gun holster on his hip, remaining there provocatively.

Her heart banged and she could hardly breathe. Should she offer to fix them some food? She felt confused, dizzy with fright and indecision. As she hesitated the other man walked over to stand beside his partner. They both stood there at the bottom of the porch steps, blocking her way into the building. She had to either think quickly of something to say or allow them to come in with her.

Before she could think of anything, the man spoke again. "Well, ma'am. We come a long way. Sure are hungry. So's our horses. Reckon you've got a good supply of feed for all them ponies you got. Jake'll jest take a look down at that barn yonder. Mebbe you and me kin go inside and rustle up some food?"

Go inside alone with *him*? Sunny's breath was coming so fast it almost choked her.

The men exchanged a look, then both looked back

boldly at her. The taller man's mouth twisted into a humorless smile. The other one gave a harsh laugh, more of a snort.

If only Tracy were here! Should she lie and say her brother would be back any minute? The threatening gleam in the men's eyes convinced her that they'd see through any such ploy. What could she do? Pray! *Oh my God, an ever present help in times of danger, protect me.* The clothes basket was getting heavy; its handles were cutting into her hands. Impulsively she acted. With all her strength she threw the basket toward them, hitting them hard on their knees, momentarily unsteadying them. She made a dash for the steps, running into the building, slamming the door behind her, and shoving the wooden bolt into place. She fell against it, breathing hard. Next she ran to the window and saw that they were both stumbling about, cussing and snarling. Realizing that because of the heat she had opened all the windows, she rushed through the house, banging them down. From the front window she saw that the big man had drawn his gun and was sneaking around the side of the house. *Oh, dear God!* She clutched her hands to her breast and shuddered. She was alone here, helpless against two men. *Please, help.* They could break down the door. Now that they were angered, there was no telling what they would do! She sagged against the wall, closed her eyes, and prayed.

Never before in her life had a prayer been answered so swiftly. Almost at once she heard the sound of other horse hooves. She opened her eyes, rushed to the window, and looked out. Of all people, Webb Chandler was cantering up to the building. Sunny went weak with thankfulness. The two men had whirled around at Webb's approach. On a horse he looked taller than he actually was. Sunny noticed with some astonishment that his expression was stern, fiercely belligerent. He must have taken in the situation at once. He brought his horse to a skidding halt and the animal reared. Then he spun around, facing the two strangers, his hand resting on the rifle in its holder behind him.

Her ear pressed to the door, Sunny heard Webb demand, "You fellas here on Express company business?"

Jake shifted uncomfortably, glanced at his partner. The other man seemed to take Webb's measure before answering, "Nah, jest stopped to give our horses a little rest and water."

Webb's hand stroked his rifle. "Looks like that's been done, so I suggest you all git movin'."

"Come on, Tanner," Jake urged as he swung himself up into his saddle, holding out the other man's reins toward him.

Tanner took his time walking over to his horse, still watching Webb. He grabbed the reins and mounted, then gave Webb a malevolent look before swiveling his horse around. Both men rode out the gate, stirring up clouds of dust in their wake.

Sunny flung open the door and rushed out onto the porch. "Oh, thank God you came when you did, Webb!" she exclaimed breathlessly. "I've never been so glad to see anyone in my life!"

"Well, that's a nice change from the way I'm usually greeted out here," he grinned. He got off his horse and began picking up the assorted clothing scattered all about, now soiled with dirty hoofprints where the intruders' horses had trampled them in the dust. Holding one item up with a quizzical expression, Webb remarked, "I think you're going to have to do another wash, Miss Lyndall." He chuckled as he gathered the laundry into the empty willow basket.

"Oh, never mind about that!" Sunny retorted impatiently. "How in the world did you happen to come out here just now? I don't know what I'd have done. I was so scared—" Her voice broke. In spite of her attempt to appear brave and unshaken by the incident, to her dismay Sunny suddenly felt limp, sick, and faint. Her knees went weak, and she grabbed hold of the porch post. Clinging to it, she pressed her face against the wood, and tears began to fill her eyes. Shaking with sobs, she was unable to stop crying.

The next thing she knew, Webb was beside her. Strong hands on her shoulders gently pulled her close, holding her firmly. She heard the murmur of his voice soothing, as if to a hurt child, "It's all over now." She felt the roughness of his jacket, the buttons pressing into her cheeks as she leaned against him.

"They didn't *do* anything to you, did they?" Webb asked fiercely.

Choking back sobs, she shook her head. "But who knows what would have happened if you hadn't come."

Something in her longed to remain held in this reassuring embrace. But the independent woman she was trying to be would not allow her. She pulled away and stepped back. Unable to completely stem the tears, she burst out, "Those awful men! This awful place. I wish we'd never come here. I wish I could just up and leave and never see this whole terrible place again." She knew she was making a fool of herself, and in front of Webb Chandler, of all people!

"Aw now, come on. You just had a bad scare, that's all."

She shook her head. "No, I mean it. I can't handle it. I give up."

"Not *you*! Never. You're strong, like a willow. . . .You might bend, but you won't break," Webb assured her. He dug a clean, folded red bandanna handkerchief out of his pocket and handed it to her.

"Well, maybe not. But if it weren't for Tracy, I wouldn't stay." She took the handkerchief.

Webb studied Sunny while she dabbed at her eyes. Even now, with the end of her small nose reddened, her wet eyelashes stuck in little points over the wide hazel eyes, she

115

was doggone pretty. But there was more to her than just that. This little lady had something else he hadn't encountered often. Something he admired. Watching her get ahold of herself, Webb drawled, "By the way, just how did that basketful of clothes get strewed all over the place?"

"I threw it at them!"

"You *what*?" Webb began to laugh.

Sunny smiled somewhat sheepishly through her tears. "I threw it at them so I could make a run for it into the house."

Webb began to roar with laughter. "My oh my, Miss Lyndall, I gotta hand it to you. You're one lady with a lot of spunk! I'll say that for you."

For a minute Sunny basked in his admiring glance. "It didn't help much," she shrugged. "Only made them mad, I'm afraid. That man pulled a gun, you know."

Webb's face got serious. "You know, you ought to learn how to handle a shotgun."

She looked at him in alarm. "Oh, no!"

"You might never need it or have to shoot it, 'cept maybe as a warning. But it's a good thing to know. It's the knowing *how* that's important, should somethin' ever come up you had to."

With surprise she realized Webb was too much of a gentleman to say, "For instance, like today, if *I* hadn't shown up." She also realized she had not thanked him, shown him how truly grateful she was.

"I'll take it on myself to bring one out, show you how to clean and care for it, how to load, and how to shoot."

"Thank you," she said humbly. Then, "The least I can do is offer you something to drink. I have some sun tea made. Will you have some?"

The old teasing grin was back. "Why, I'd be pleased to do just that."

She brought their glasses out onto the porch. They sipped it in silence. Sunny was still recovering from the frightening incident, and Webb seemed completely comfortable not forcing conversation. Before he went, he made it a point to check the barn and suggested she leave the ponies in the corral overnight so she would be sure to be alerted if any intruders came on the property.

"Tracy will be home tomorrow," Sunny told him.

Webb nodded, then promised, "I'll be out first thing to teach you to shoot."

Feeling suddenly shy, Sunny said, "Thank you very much. For everything."

"Don't mention it." He smiled, adding with a grin, "My pleasure."

After Webb left, Sunny couldn't remember much of what they had talked about while they had their tea. She *did* remember the surge of relief at seeing him ride in the Express station gate. The gratitude for the way he had sent those characters packing. Her cheeks grew warm as she remembered how comforting it had felt to be in the protective circle of his arms, so close she could hear his heart against hers.

That night it was a long time before Sunny could sleep. Every creak, every cricket, every faint snort or whinny from the corral, brought her to quivering wakefulness. Webb was right. Having a gun and knowing how to use it would give her some security when she was here alone.

Thoughts of Webb also kept her awake.

She had seen a whole new side of Webb Chandler this day. Strength and tenderness. She recalled Rhys Graham's comment about him: *A real Christian*? What other traits might he have that she had never given him credit for? He had certainly seemed a knight in shining armor riding to her rescue today. An unlikely image to have of the scout.

True to his word, bright and early the next day Webb showed up. Sunny came out on the porch to greet him

"Ready for a shooting lesson?" he asked her as he dismounted.

"I'm not sure. I've always been afraid of guns."

"I'm going to teach you to use one so that other people'll be afraid of *you*. Knowing how takes the fear away. Like I said, you may never have to use it. But *knowing how* is the thing. A woman pointing the barrel of one of *these*"—he unbuckled a double-barreled twenty-gauge shotgun from behind his saddle and held it up—"at you, and seeing she knows how to pull the trigger, will scare any sane fella right out of his boots."

"I'm still not sure," she said doubtfully.

"You'll catch on quick. I guarantee you'll be glad you did."

"Would you like some coffee?" Sunny asked tentatively, hoping to delay the lesson a little longer.

"Sure. Thanks."

Sunny went into the kitchen and poured two mugs of the coffee she had freshly brewed. When she came out, Webb was sitting on the porch steps. She handed him his mug, and as their fingers brushed she felt a little quiver go through her. For a second their gaze met, then Sunny looked away quickly. She sat, thinking it was funny how since yesterday everything about Webb seemed different. Nicer, gentler, sweeter even. Of course, that was nonsense. Her imagination. She was just so grateful he'd come when he had—which reminded her of something she'd wondered about. "By the way, how did you happen to come along out here just when you did yesterday?"

Webb took a long sip of his coffee before answering. There was mischief in his eyes when he did. "Oh, just riding by to pass the time of day," he teased, jogging her memory of the first time he'd done just that and they'd had their disastrous tug-of-war.

She blushed but just said, "Well, I'm awfully glad you did."

Webb finished his coffee and put down his cup, then held out his hand and pulled Sunny to her feet.

"Come on, time for your lesson."

Webb was a patient teacher. He demonstrated to Sunny how to unlock the catch of the shotgun, open the chamber, slip two shells in, cock it, rest it securely against her shoulder, aim, and squeeze the trigger.

With infinite patience he went through the procedure several times, making sure she understood how to load the gun safely. Then he placed a half dozen empty tin cans along the top rail of the fence, behind the barn so as not to frighten the ponies in the front corral.

"Those will be your targets. Let's see how many you can knock off." He showed her how to place her feet, take a position, and focus where she wanted to shoot.

As Webb came and stood behind her he gently helped her prop the gun against her shoulder. At first Sunny was too much aware of him to concentrate. Aware of the sun-smell of his skin, the scent of his leather vest, his muscular shoulder pressing against her back, his fingers on the nape of her neck as he gently moved her head to the right angle to aim . . . Then Webb's steady voice matter-of-factly coaching her quieted the flurry of her emotional response to his nearness. She began listening carefully to his instructions, and before long all her attention was on learning how to use this powerful weapon.

After several times going through the routine of shooting, reloading, and shooting, Sunny's aim improved and a number of her shots sent tin cans rattling off the fence. This brought a low whistle from Webb. Sunny felt inordinately pleased by his "Well done!"

"I told you you'd catch on quick. You'll be a crack shot in no time flat, Miss Lyndall." He gave her a nod of approval. "We better quit for now. Your arm and shoulder'll probably be kinda sore. But the idea is to practice. Keep practicin' and the better you get. Just line up the cans over and over till you can puncture them one after the other, knock 'em all off."

He took the gun from her, unloaded it, and swung it around, shouldering it. "For a first time, you did real good, Miss Lyndall."

Webb was regarding her with unabashed approval. And something more. She sensed it, saw it in his eyes, felt something so strong flowing between them it made her almost dizzy.

*I must be getting light-headed from the sun!* Quickly Sunny reminded herself of Verna's telling her that Webb had a "way with women." With a chuckle, Verna had told Sunny that many of the local girls had their caps set for him, to say nothing of some of the dance hall "ladies." "He's the kind that grannies want to mother and younger women would like to march down the aisle with, but Webb—well, he's like a wild horse who likes running free on the range and don't want to be tamed. He gets skittish when anyone gets marriage in their eyes. Some men are born bachelors. And I reckon Webb's one of them."

Well, *she* certainly didn't have her cap set for him! And going down the aisle with anyone was a long way off in her future. Certainly not until she got to California. Certainly not with a "rolling stone" like Webb Chandler. With an effort, Sunny dragged her gaze from the blue eyes looking into hers so intently and turned away. She started walking back up toward the building, and Webb fell into step beside her. When they got back to where Webb had hitched his horse, he said, "I suggest you practice every day for a while till you feel at ease with handlin' the gun. You'll do fine. I can see you're a fast learner, Miss Lyndall."

"Thank you for coming—and for teaching me and all."

Webb set his wide-brimmed hat on his head, tightened

the leather strap under his chin, then tugged the brim. "No thanks necessary." He mounted. "So long, Miss Lyndall," he said, turning his horse and riding off.

Following Webb's suggestion, Sunny had a daily practice session. She made a target outside, away from the barn and corral. In two weeks time she felt confident that come any emergency, she could handle herself and the gun. As he had also predicted, "knowing how" had given her a sense of security she did not have before. She had not liked the way she felt after that awful day with those two men. Until she really knew how to use the shotgun, she was jumpy, looking over her shoulder, thinking she saw things. When Tracy was gone and none of the other riders were around, she had to work up courage to go out to the barn, lead the ponies into the corral. All things she had learned to do well and had taken pride in doing. One of the things she had been especially proud of was how she had adapted to life alone at the station. After that one frightening episode, her hard-won independence had been shaken. Now she felt it had been restored. Thanks to Webb.

When Tracy came home the day of her shooting lesson, she'd explained what happened and why she planned to start target practicing every day. He thought it was a good idea, although he seemed worried about her being alone, in case something else happened. While Sunny was regaining her confidence as the days passed, he kept suggesting they should mention the incident to Rhys Graham.

Sunny eventually dissuaded him. "I'm getting real good, Tracy. Webb says just the sight of one of these is enough to run off most anyone who'd come out here with any ideas."

"Well, if Webb says so . . ."

That seemed to satisfy her brother, who admired Webb greatly. Sunny had never understood why—until now.

Nor did she mention the incident to Verna. She didn't

want word to get back to Rhys Graham. He might decide they needed a man to run the station. To lose her job at this point, and the money it brought in, the nest egg they were building up for when they could leave for California, would be a disaster.

# Chapter 15

*A* scorching August led into a September in which the dregs of summer lingered. Everything was dusty, dry. Grass turned brown, sunflowers wilted along fences, the midday sun beat down relentlessly. Sunny felt as listless as the weather as she entered Ardley's General Store one day. She found Verna putting up a poster announcing the upcoming harvest ball.

Sunny glanced at it indifferently, then remarked to Verna, "I've come for some material."

Verna beamed. "Goin' to make yourself a new dress for the dance, I wager?" She finished hammering the last nail to the sign, then hurried to the counter, behind which were bolts of cloth on the shelves. "I've just got in some lovely yardage that'll make up real fine."

Sunny shook her head. "It's curtain material I want, Verna. Calico. Besides, I'm not going to the dance."

Verna looked shocked. "Not going? What do you mean, not going? Of course you will. You *can't* miss it! It's the biggest social event of the year."

"Somehow it doesn't seem much like fall or weather for dancing, Verna—," Sunny began but was immediately cut off by Verna.

"That's just it! It'll get everybody out of the doldrums! It's a great time," Verna said positively. "You'll enjoy it, trust me."

"Oh, I don't know ..." Sunny sounded reluctant.

"Nonsense! You've been working hard all these weeks, looking after that brother of yours, besides minding the station. You deserve a little fun. Everybody'll be there."

Then Sunny plaintively asked the eternal feminine question, "But what on earth would I wear? I haven't been to a party or a dance in—months." Actually, it seemed like forever. Her workday life at the Express station precluded any sort of dress-up clothes. Mostly she wore a clean shirtwaist and cotton skirt—and sometimes, of course, Tracy's old jeans underneath, which not even Verna knew about.

"Didn't you bring a party dress along in your trunk?" Verna demanded, raising a quizzical eyebrow. "Didn't think they danced in California, eh?"

Sunny had to laugh at her friend's satirical question. "I had other things on my mind when I thought about California."

"Well, be that as it may, you've got to have something pretty to wear to the harvest dance. It's the one time in the year all the ladies wear their finest. And I've got some yardage at the store I want you to see. Matter of fact, had you in mind when it came in."

She would not take no for an answer.

Verna Ardley had taken a great interest in Sunny. Since her first wariness, she had come to admire the young woman. Her lack of whining and complaining over a situation that might have caused others of her kind to go into mild hysterics and take the next train home had won Verna's staunch support. "That gal has gumption," Verna had told her husband. "She needs a hand up, a listening ear and a strong shoulder to lean on if need be." Clem nodded and wisely didn't put in his two cents worth. His private opinion—"The Lyndall gal is pretty as a picture and twice as

124

smart"—he'd expressed to Rhys Graham and Webb Chandler and some others, all of whom seemed to share it.

"Now, here it is, Sunny," Verna said, bringing out a bolt of cloth from under the shelf and placing it on the counter for Sunny to see. Verna lowered her voice confidentially. "I've not shown it to anyone else. But it'd be just right for you. Your colors and all. Wouldn't it make up into the sweetest dancing dress?"

Sunny shook her head regretfully. Their budget and the amount she was trying to save each week didn't allow for extras.

"No thanks, Verna. I've decided I'm not going."

"Land sakes! What are you talking about?" Verna asked incredulously. "Nobody misses the harvest dance!" Then her face softened as she realized what the problem might be. "This is specially priced, 'cause I knew there wouldn't be much call for it. There'd just be about enough for someone the size of you. Just look at how pretty it is," she coaxed.

"Oh, Verna, don't tempt me . . . ," Sunny pleaded. But it was too late, as Verna held out a length for her examination. It was periwinkle blue lawn printed overall with tiny clusters of daisies and buttercups tied with trailing ribbons of deeper blue. Sunny weakened. Lightly her fingers traced the delicate pattern.

Watching her, Verna knew she had made a sale. "See, it can be trimmed with this," she suggested, laying a roll of Swiss eyelet ruffle beside the material.

"I really shouldn't," Sunny sighed. "But—"

"Now, no buts. You're going and that's the end of it. I'll put it on next month's account," beamed Verna, quickly measuring out several yards, adding the trim and lace, placing both on top of the curtain calico, wrapping it all together in brown paper, and tying it with a string. Verna turned to one of the shelves behind her and brought out a wheel of ribbon. "What color ribbon for your hair?" she asked, pulling her fabric scissors out of her apron pocket.

Sunny laughed helplessly. "Violet, I guess."

"There you are. And you'll thank me when it's done." Verna smiled.

In spite of some guilty pangs, Sunny left the store with the wrapped parcel of dress material, trim, and lace. She found she was even looking forward to making herself a new dress and attending the harvest dance.

Back at the Express station she dragged the battered, leather humpbacked trunk from the corner and opened it. Lifting off the shallow top tray, she searched the contents for some of the things she had almost forgotten she had brought with her. Tucked into tissue paper at the bottom were dancing shoes, lace mitts, and a fan. Perfect accessories for the dress she planned. It might really be fun, and it would certainly be a break from her monotonous routine.

With Verna's help the dress was cut out, sewn, and ready for her to wear to the harvest dance. Sunny was thrilled with the result. It had tiny pink and blue flowers scattered all over a lavender background, a frill of lace at the neckline and at the elbow-length puffed sleeves.

The dance was being held at the town hall. Tracy would be back in time to take her. For once Tracy didn't seem to object to the prospect of wearing a white ruffled shirt and a string tie.

Life had been so humdrum, so hard, these past months that the closer the time came to the night of the dance, the more excited Sunny got. *You'd think it was a ball at the governor's mansion,* she chided herself, but that didn't stem her excitement.

That afternoon she washed her hair in the water from the rain barrel first, then boiled water for the tub. Sunny bathed, lathering lavishly with the special scented soap she had experimented making. All they had at Ardley's General Store were the big blocks of harsh, yellow soap. This, of course, was sufficient to clean off the dust, grime, and grit of the trail for Tracy when he got home, but it was very hard on delicate skin. Sunny had saved all the grease she could manage, melting the accumulated fat from bacon rinds, tallow, and drippings. Then she poured it into the lye water leached from woodstove ashes simmered in a huge kettle for hours. Into this she stirred a mixture of crushed clover and some dried lilac petals from a bouquet Verna had cut for her from a bush in her yard. The result had not been perfect. But at least she had been able to mold several small cakes for her own personal use.

By the time Tracy got home, had his bath, and dressed, Sunny was ready and waiting. Tracy didn't so much as mumble one complaint when Sunny insisted on trimming his hair. She was so preoccupied with her own appearance, she never discerned the reason for his unusual compliance. That is, until they arrived at the dance and he made a bee-line to the side of Betty Brownlee.

Deserted on the threshold of the dance floor, her foot spontaneously tapping to the sound of fiddle music, Sunny glanced around, not admitting to herself for whom she was looking. When she saw him, her heart gave an astonishing little flutter. He looked all slicked down, hair dark and smooth, crisp white shirt, flowing tie, boots polished to a high gloss. Seeing her, he smiled and made a move as if to cross the room to her. At the very same moment Sunny heard a voice beside her say, "Good evening, Miss Lyndall," and there was Rhys Graham. "May I have the pleasure of the first dance?"

Reacting spontaneously, she accepted the invitation. The minute she did, she wished she'd waited for Webb, but it was too late. Rhys was holding out his arm to lead her onto the dance floor, which had been freshly sanded and waxed for dancing. As she reached for the loop on the side of her skirt to lift it she caught a glimpse of Webb's disappointed expression before he turned away.

Rhys held her rather stiffly as they circled the floor, saying, "You'll have to forgive my awkwardness, Miss Lyndall. I've not had much opportunity for this sort of thing. I was brought up by a Quaker grandmother, and dancing was considered—" He smiled ironically. "Well, it wasn't included in the rest of my education."

For all of his deprecating, Rhys was a smooth dancer. Sunny was also somewhat out of practice, she discovered, but they managed to complete the set reasonably in step. Again Sunny wondered about this man. Little by little Rhys dropped hints about himself, like mentioning a Quaker background. Still, he seemed to cloak himself in shadows, only at rare moments revealing bits and pieces of what made up his personality. He still seemed out of place here in this "gateway to the West" town, remaining an enigma.

Sunny soon found out it was the custom here for everybody to get a chance to dance. There were no wallflowers. All it took was a tap on a dancer's shoulder and an "if you please," and away that dancer went with another partner. Sunny circled the floor with two or three before the music stopped and Rhys was at her side again, suggesting they get some cooling punch. He took Sunny to one of the chairs at the side of the room, then excused himself to get the drinks. Left alone, Sunny looked around interestedly at the roomful of people. It was quite a mix. As Verna had forewarned her, *everyone* came to the harvest dance. She recognized some of the ladies she'd seen at church, along with the schoolmarm, Miss Eddy, who Verna had introduced her to one day at the store. All ages were represented. She saw the church organist, a lady nearing seventy if a day, young women holding babies that they bounced in their laps in time with the tunes, middle-aged "grannies" who gossiped on the sidelines and watched the dancers, and children of all ages dancing together. Evidently no one was excluded. With amazed disbelief, Sunny spotted some extravagantly gowned and "painted" ladies, obviously girls from the dance halls. They would've been hard to miss. Their brightly colored dresses were in sharp contrast to the "best" calicos and cottons of the other women in attendance. However, tonight they were a little less flamboyantly attired and less rouged than they probably were when "at work." But they did not act the least ill at ease, hobnobbing this once with the more conservative citizens. Neither were they being snubbed or ostracized.

Sunny was just wondering where Webb had disappeared to when suddenly he was standing right in front of her. He smiled down at her, his teeth very white against his sun-bronzed skin. "Howdy, Miss Lyndall. If you don't look a picture tonight."

"And so do you!" she retorted. "I hardly recognized you!"

He *did* look handsome as could be.

"Would you like to dance?" he asked.

Remembering how she felt before in his arms, Sunny wondered if she should risk being that close again. She flicked open her fan, fluttering it to cool her suddenly-flushing face.

"I'm surprised, Mr. Chandler. I didn't know dancing was among your many accomplishments."

"Oh yes, ma'am. Some do say I'm quite a *terpsichorean*." Webb drawled the word elaborately, looking pleased at being able to roll it out so grandly.

"Oh, my! Is it catching?" Sunny asked in mock horror.

He laughed and held out both hands. "Try me and I'll prove it."

The band was playing what sounded like a waltz, and Webb whirled her into its rhythm with a sure, strong lead. Over his shoulder she saw Rhys return to where he had left her. Holding two punch cups in either hand, he stood glancing around until he saw them. His puzzled look turned into one of disappointment. Sunny felt guilty. That soon vanished when Webb drew her closer, whispering, "You smell like lilacs." For a moment she shut her eyes, a sensation of delight sweeping through her. It was such an unexpected, romantic thing for him to say. Flattered but a little flustered, she felt the need to regain their old adversarial rapport.

"My apologies for doubting your word, Mr. Chandler. You're every bit as graceful on a dance floor as on a horse."

"What kind of compliment is that?"

"The only kind I know to give. Just an honest opinion."

"That's one thing I can sure say about you, Miss Lyndall: you're nothing if not flat-out honest about your opinions." His eyes were laughing as he looked at her. "An unusual thing in a woman!" he added mischievously. "Most lead you on till you think you've made some headway, then *wham*—"

"You sound very experienced in the ways of women, Mr. Chandler."

Just then the music came to an end as Milton Beemis, in charge of the dance, climbed onto the band platform, held up both hands, and announced, "Comin' up next is the Cinderella."

"Ah, doggone it, they always do that!" Webb said.

"What on earth is it?" Sunny asked.

"You'll see."

Milton Beemis' voice rang out. "Ladies, take off your left shoe and, holding it in your hand, start moving in a big circle to the music. Gents, form a circle outside the ladies. When the music stops, ladies, toss your shoe into the middle and make way for the gents to scramble in for a shoe. Gents, when you grab a lady's shoe, it's up to you to find the lady it belongs to—and *she's* your partner for the next set."

Webb relinquished her as the circles began to form. "What kind of shoe are you wearing?" he asked. She didn't have a chance to reply, because Webb was jostled out of the way by a large, burly cowboy and pushed as others crowded in, and they were separated.

Amid much laughter, little shrieks, and exclamations, the ladies began untying, unbuckling, unbuttoning, the shoe from their left foot. Hobbling a little on her one stocking-clad foot, Sunny joined the circle of ladies. The music began again and everyone started moving. The band entered into the fun by slowing down as if they were going to stop and then picking up the melody again, and the circling continued. When it finally came to an abrupt stop, there was a wild tossing of shoes. A mad scramble followed as the men dashed through the ladies' circle, searching for the shoe whose lady they wanted to dance with next.

Holding her breath, Sunny stood waiting excitedly to see who her partner would be. She was taken completely by surprise when a red-faced, broad-shouldered fellow with muttonchop whiskers, holding her small kid slipper in the palm of his beefy hand, turned up. He introduced himself as Harper Nelson, a cowboy at the Bigelow ranch. Before he swung her practically off her feet as the music started for the next set, Sunny saw Webb still standing in the middle of the circle. In his hand was a red satin slipper, its curved French heel studded with rhinestones.

Sunny lost track of him after that. The dance became a free-for-all. It seemed all a man had to do was tap another man on the shoulder to exchange dance partners. Sunny did not lack partners. She was whisked from one to the other. She danced with a hefty rancher who pumped her arm so energetically as they two-stepped around the floor that some of her hairpins fell out. Grateful for an excuse to catch her breath, she excused herself to repair the damage. She went to find the "refreshing" room set aside for the ladies.

As she left the dance floor Sunny saw Webb dancing with

the girl she'd heard someone call Juanita. She was an exotic-looking dance hall girl with dark hair swirled into a loose knot, curls tumbled randomly down on white shoulders. She wore ruffled black lace on a crimson gown with a flounced skirt short enough to reveal slender ankles. Curiously Sunny glanced at her feet. She was wearing red satin shoes with heels that sparkled. With a jolt she realized Webb was *still* dancing with the girl whose slipper he'd found. Most people had changed partners a dozen times since the ladies' shoe toss. To Sunny's discomfort, they looked as though they were enjoying each other's company enormously. Sunny's mouth tightened. All her easy acceptance of the dance hall ladies being made welcome at the community dance disappeared. With a sharp jab something else replaced it: jealousy.

She hurried outside, around the back of the building. The path leading to the refreshing room skirted the long wooden porch that circled the dance hall. Couples taking the air between dances strolled there, and small clusters of people chatted in low voices, their figures indistinguishable in the darkness unless they were touched by the glow of the lighted windows.

The ladies' room was empty at the moment, and Sunny was glad. She needed time to collect herself. She felt upset. Impatiently she took out the rest of her hairpins and began to rearrange her hair. The mirror was chipped and mottled and so her image was somewhat distorted, yet it revealed her petulant expression. That irritated her more. What did it matter to her who Webb danced with? Why should she care anyway? Reluctantly she answered her own question. Something had happened tonight while they were dancing. All her old animosity toward him had faded. She had felt pleasurably lighthearted, light-footed, light-headed . . .

Ever since the day he rescued her, something had changed between them. She was too honest not to admit she was strongly attracted. It was more than just gratitude toward him for teaching her to shoot. She recognized the feeling. She had felt it twice before in her life. Once, when she was fourteen and in love with her piano teacher. The other time, with the young assistant minister that had come one summer to help Reverend Dorsey, their regular minister, who had fallen from a ladder while cleaning the bell tower of the church, breaking his arm and several ribs. Sunny had spent hours gathering flowers to take over to the church, making all kinds of excuses to go by there. She had suddenly become a regular attender at the Wednesday night prayer meetings. After he returned in September to the seminary in Louisville where he was a student, Sunny had pined all winter. She had written letters she never mailed, written poetry she tore up, daydreamed constantly about being a parson's wife.

Had she unconsciously been drifting into the same kind of thoughts about Webb Chandler? She must be out of her mind. A man—a man's man—a wagon train scout! A man with no roots, reckless, irresponsible. To feel the same way about someone like him as she had about a teacher and a preacher? Impossible!

The trouble was, her feeling toward Webb was stronger. Lately she had felt a kind of underlying purpose in all that had happened. Could it have been more than coincidence for she and Tracy to be stranded in this town on the edge of Independence? Could they have been delayed here for a reason somehow, so that . . .? So that they could meet certain people, fall in love? Was there *really* a kind of destiny that overruled people's plans?

There was, *if* you believed all those silly romantic books. Which of course she didn't. Sunny slammed down her brush, shoved it into her reticule. She wanted to get back to the dance. It was getting late. There was still time to dance with Webb again, to see . . . She gave a final pat to her hair and hurried out.

Outside a delightfully cool breeze was blowing. Sunny stopped for a minute to breathe deeply of it before going back into the warm dance hall. As she stood there she heard a woman's low, soft laugh. Something made her turn her head. There against one of the supporting porch posts she saw two figures, male and female, silhouetted against the light from the windows. The woman's head was thrown back, tossing a mass of curls as her full-throated, seductive laughter came again. The man, one arm stretched over her head, leaned toward her. He was speaking in a low, teasing voice Sunny recognized, even though she could not make out the words. It was that Texas drawl she had teased Webb unmercifully about. It was Webb, and the girl must be the enchanting Juanita.

Sunny's cheeks grew hot. It was shaming. Her heart felt bruised, hurting painfully. She didn't want to feel this way—not for someone like Webb Chandler. She clenched her hands. She didn't want to go back in to the dance, but she couldn't stand out here. She shivered. The cool wind had begun to make her feel cold. On the verge of tears, she hated the idea of walking back into the lighted room filled with music, the sound of dancing feet, the laughing voices and gaiety. But she had to. She could never let him know what she'd seen or how it made her feel. Straightening her shoulders, she took a deep breath and went back inside.

Intermission over, the band struck up again. This time a familiar melody she particularly loved. She had just successfully got her emotions under control when she saw Webb strolling toward her, and she panicked. Suddenly she couldn't move but stood there at the edge of the dance floor as if her feet were frozen.

"I've been lookin' for you," he smiled, holding out his hand to her. "My dance, little lady?"

Something cold hardened Sunny's longing to move into his arms and dance with him again. "I'm afraid not,

134

Mr. Chandler," she said icily. "I've already promised the next set. But I'm sure you can find another partner without any trouble."

Webb's eyes narrowed. He looked bewildered, almost stunned. Sunny took perverse satisfaction in the hope that she might have hurt him a little. At least punctured his ego. Over his shoulder she saw Rhys coming across the hall. She smiled and waved with her unfurled fan. Webb turned to see to whom she was directing this flirtatious gesture, and when he saw Rhys, he gave Sunny a long, knowing look, then stalked away. Rhys hurried to her side.

Sunny couldn't remember much of the rest of the evening. She talked, laughed, and danced, but it was all forced. She kept seeing that silhouette against the windows, the sound of low voices, the intimate position of the two figures. Why had she allowed herself to be caught up by the slow-talking charm of that Texan—that "lady-killer," as Clem Ardley jokingly called him?

The night she had looked forward to so happily was ending for her on a sour note. She wanted to go, to escape. Impulsively she said, "Oh, Mr. Graham, could I ask you to take me home? I have a slight headache, and I'm afraid Tracy isn't yet ready to leave."

"Of course. It would be my pleasure."

Immediately Sunny wished she hadn't given in to the impulse. Rhys seemed almost delighted at the opportunity. After what Verna had told her, she had purposely avoided doing anything to invite Rhys' personal attention. Now he might think she was making an occasion to be alone with him. Irrationally she blamed Webb. If she hadn't been so upset about seeing him with Juanita . . . But it was done now. She would just have to be completely impersonal, talk about Express business on the way home.

When she came back from getting her shawl, Rhys was waiting for her. She couldn't resist the urge to take a last look to see if Webb was dancing. But he was nowhere in sight. Probably out on the verandah again with Juanita! Sunny was glad that in the darkness her burning cheeks could not be seen.

On the ride out from town, Sunny tried to still her churning emotions, to carry on some kind of conversation. She didn't succeed in doing either very well. Anything that came to mind to say seemed too banal or artificial, so she decided to remain quiet. He too was silent until they reached the Express station, then he asked casually, "Did you enjoy yourself tonight?"

When she didn't answer at once, Rhys glanced over at her. "Did something happen to make you unhappy? I thought I saw an expression on your face that—" He hesitated. "Don't answer if you don't want to."

Astonished, Sunny said, "You're very observant."

"Not always. Not unless . . . well, I noticed, that's all." When she didn't offer any explanation, he got down, came around, and helped her out of the buggy. A pale moon shed a milky light over everything, softening the harsh outlines of the building.

Sunny felt again the rise of humiliated anger. She was still smarting from seeing Webb flirting with someone else. Well, she'd just have to get over it. He wasn't worth her giving him another thought! Her foolish feelings were probably brought on by the frustration of being trapped here and lonely . . .

With a start she realized Rhys was talking to her, and she had to ask him to repeat himself.

"I just said it was a lovely night, the moon and all—you weren't listening, were you? It's been a long evening, and you're probably tired. I noticed you didn't miss a dance."

"Yes, it *was* quite an evening."

They walked slowly over to the building. When they reached the porch, Sunny put out her hand to thank him.

Instead he captured it in both of his, holding it. "You know, I searched for *your* shoe! I blamed myself for not checking what kind you were wearing. I didn't get a chance to dance enough with you."

Sunny tried to withdraw her hand, but he held it fast.

"I've grown very fond of you, you know," Rhys went on. "You *and* your brother. He's growing into a fine young man. Dependable, serious. You should be proud of him."

"Oh, I am," Sunny replied, wondering where all this was leading.

"He's intelligent too. Not just a rider. I think I could train him to be a very good station manager, to take on more responsibility if and when he tires of riding."

"But you know we're going to California."

"I thought maybe you'd changed your plans." Rhys' voice was hopeful. "I know Tracy is quite interested in one of the local girls, Brownlee's daughter. He has a huge spread, lots of cattle. He'd probably welcome a son-in-law with Tracy's qualities."

Sunny tugged gently at her hand. "Tracy's still very young, Mr. Graham—"

"*Rhys*, please."

"I don't think he has settling down or marriage on his mind."

"You sure about that?"

She drew in her breath. "Well, he hasn't said anything to me."

"Maybe I spoke out of turn," Rhys said. "It's just that your and your brother's plans are important to me. *You* are important to me, Sunny."

Sunny felt a little dart of alarm. Rhys had called her Sunny! The use of a first name of someone of the opposite sex, except to a close relative, assumed intimacy. Between a young woman and man it meant an affectionate relationship. Rhys had spoken it so naturally, Sunny realized he must think of her in these terms. Now it had inadvertently slipped out. He didn't even seem to realize what he'd done, because he went on speaking. "Have you any idea of how much you have come to mean to me?"

His hands tightened on hers, his voice grew intense. He leaned toward her, and for a minute she thought he was going to kiss her. She stepped back, and reluctantly he let go of her hands.

"I'm sorry. I've offended you, haven't I? I spoke too frankly. I think I've frightened you. I didn't mean . . ."

"No, no, of course not," Sunny said breathlessly. But she drew away, opening her purse, fumbling for her keys. "Thank you for bringing me home."

He seemed chastened. "It was my pleasure. And if—" He started to say something more, then stopped.

"I'll say good night now," she said, opening the door.

"Good night," Rhys said. Then softly, "Sweet dreams, Sunny."

Sunny went inside. She leaned against the closed door, listening to the sound of Rhys' buggy wheels gradually fading as he went out through the gate.

What an evening it had been! It was all too bewildering. Sunny slipped off her dancing shoes and folded her shawl. She sighed deeply. Tracy had better get home soon. Not keep her waiting up.

She was suddenly weary. She wanted to go to bed, go to sleep. She didn't want to worry about what Rhys Graham had hinted or what was happening to all her plans—most of all she wanted to stop thinking about Webb Chandler.

# Chapter 16

The day after the harvest dance, Sunny set to work cleaning the stove. *Just like Cinderella after the prince's ball. Back to ashes and cinders,* she thought grimly, remembering the ladies' shoe toss. At least her mind was taken up with the grubby job rather than her humiliation at seeing Webb Chandler with the dark-eyed Juanita. Sunny brushed harder, faster. Why should she care? Still, the memory caused resentment to tighten inside her. Whatever amused him so that he threw back his head and laughed set Sunny's teeth on edge. The whole intimacy of the scene bothered her most.

Only a half hour before, he had danced with *her,* had whispered, his lips against her hair—then he was out in the moonlight with Juanita! Sunny gritted her teeth and shoveled out the ashes with a vengeance. She wished she'd let him know she had seen them, shown him how tacky she thought they were being. However, if she had done *that*, he might have assumed she *cared* . . . Oh, figs and apples! What possible difference could it make? None whatsoever!

Then why did she feel so betrayed? Before last night

hadn't she discouraged Webb? Why now should she feel rejected? Why this grating sensation of jealousy?

The truth was that ever since that terrible day when he had come to her rescue, something unspoken but very real, something she couldn't explain away, had happened between them. Even that day she realized her feelings about Webb had changed.

She had been excited when she went to the dance, expecting to see him, anticipating his reaction when he saw her in her new dress, hoping—well, Sunny wasn't sure just what she'd been hoping. For a brief time it seemed as if everything would turn out happily, just as she had imagined. Until . . .

No use going over all that again. Sunny got up from her knees, emptied the ashes into a bucket to take outside. She was not going to waste another minute thinking about the incident. It was stupid and childish and she was going to forget it.

At one time she might have fretted about such things. But not anymore. She had changed, grown up! Everything that had happened had changed her. She had plenty of better things to think of. Decisively Sunny went out to her garden to pull weeds.

She weeded two rows, priding herself on how strong she had become. Her slender body had toughened; there were muscles in her slim arms and wrists now. Working with the ponies had increased other skills as well. She felt she could handle them better, that she had more patience. She was capable of so much more than she had ever thought possible. Coping with the Express company business, keeping up with daily chores, unexpected tasks. She could do lots of things as well as Tracy—hammer a nail, shoot a rifle . . . *That* thought naturally made her think of who had taught her. She quickly thrust it away. She'd given Mr. Chandler enough of her thoughts today!

As if thought could produce reality, she heard the sound of hoofbeats. She turned around just as the very subject of her inner turmoil cantered through the gate. In sudden confusion she went back to yanking the stubborn weeds out of her carrot patch.

"Mornin', Miss Lyndall," he greeted her cheerfully. Her mouth straightened into a hard line. *Just as if nothing had happened!* she thought indignantly. She was torn between two urges: one to ignore him, the other to confront him about Juanita. Neither was a good idea, she decided.

She leaned back on her heels and lifted her curls off her neck, securing them with her bandanna handkerchief. Why was it he always came when she looked her worst? And why should that bother her? Putting up one hand to shield her eyes from the sun's glare, she watched him saunter over. It galled her to find pleasure in his trim, muscular frame, his oddly graceful stride, as he walked toward her with his usual confidence.

"Had a good time last night, did you?" he asked casually. "You got away so quick, I didn't get a chance to say—"

"*You* seemed to be enjoying yourself," Sunny retorted crossly, then she could have bitten her tongue. She shouldn't let him know she noticed. Without intending to, she blurted out, "Having too good a time to even notice when we left."

"Oh, I saw you leave, all right. You and Rhys." There was insinuation in his tone of voice.

Sunny's eyes widened. "Well, you could've said good night."

"I was just trying to tell you I didn't have the chance to say *good-bye*. That's what I come out for today. To say good-bye."

"Good-bye?" Her surprise was genuine.

"Yep. Signed on with a wagon train leaving day after tomorrow."

His announcement hit her like a stone landing on her

chest. She dropped her trowel, straightened up, and looked at him in surprise before managing to say, "Isn't this awfully sudden?"

"I would've told you last night. But like I say, I didn't have the chance."

"You through with scouting?" she asked, surprised.

"Nah! Jest wanted a change. As a matter of fact, I've been hankering for a change of sorts. And this was too good to turn down. Pays good. Actually, it's as escort to a group of English *gentlemen*." He emphasized the word with a trace of sarcasm. "They're on a hunting expedition. Want to actually *see* the buffalo they've read about. They need an escort to Fort Laramie."

"Huh!" Sunny swallowed this added bit of information, then said, "I thought you hated the way men were hunting buffalo! I believe the word you used was *slaughtering*."

He shrugged. "They're paying me a heck of a lot of money."

"Oh? Well then, I suppose *that* would be enough to make *you* change your principles," Sunny snapped.

He gave her an odd look that made her wish she hadn't said it.

"Money's not the reason. Besides, I never said I *approved* of it. They just need someone who knows the territory, buffalo country. You see, they're a new breed of hunter. They've got a lot of newfangled *photographic* equipment. Want to take pictures more than to shoot. Seems like back in England people are interested in slide shows of the American wilderness. One of them plans to write a book to go along with the pictures."

Sunny felt chastened. As usual she had spoken too quickly, had jumped to conclusions. She started to get to her feet, and Webb stretched out a hand to help her, then quickly plunged his hands in his pockets instead.

"Anyway, the main reason I rode out before I left was to

142

see—" He broke off, glancing around. "Haven't had any unwelcome visitors, have you?"

Sunny was ashamed. Had she been wrong about him? *Again?* Maybe he really cared about her, was concerned about her safety. She shook her head.

"Well anyway, I was jest thinkin' it might be a good idea for you to have a dog out here. With your brother gone so much and all." Webb looked around, not meeting her eyes directly, and said almost indifferently, "So I wondered if you might want to keep my dog, Dandy, for me while I'm gone. He's a great watchdog. 'Course, his bark is a whole lot worse than his bite. He's a real good companion. I got him when he was a pup, but I can't take him along on my scouting trips. I've sometimes left him with the Ardleys, but their dog's just had pups, and Verna has her hands full. There's other places I could leave him, I reckon—" He paused. "He gets lonesome. Figured you might get a tad lonely, too. Reckon you two could keep each other company?"

Taken aback by the offer, Sunny stared at him for a moment. This man was always putting her off balance. Blowing hot and cold with her. Showing interest one time, indifference the next.

"He's a real nice dog—gets lonely when he's left, that's all."

At Webb's affectionate tone of voice, something softened within her. Her impulse was, of course, to keep the dog. She loved animals. Then just as quickly Sunny remembered the scene she had inadvertently witnessed the night before. If she agreed too quickly, he might get the idea—

"Well ...," she dragged it out as though she were considering it. Then perversely she decided to put it on the basis that *she* was doing *him* a favor, not the other way around. "Why, I suppose—if you can't find someone else to keep him for you, I'd be glad to."

A knowing smile briefly touched Webb's mouth. His eyes

seemed to say, "I'm on to you," but all he said was, "Good. I'll bring him out later on so's you two can get acquainted."

With that he turned and strolled back to where he'd hitched his horse. He mounted and without looking back rode out the gate.

Sunny stood motionless, looking after him with a mingling of regret and wishful thinking. He hadn't mentioned last night, as if *their* three dances had never happened!

Sunny felt confused, unsettled, unhappy. She felt as if she were caught in another tug-of-war. Her heart was pulled one way, then another. She was attracted to Webb yet suspicious of that attraction. He was so hard to figure out. She recalled something Rhys Graham had once said about him: *Webb likes to put on a tough front. He's like a chestnut—hard on the outside, soft and mellow inside. Keeps his good deeds to himself. But he's done plenty of 'em that I know of personally. He really cares about people.*

He certainly seemed to care about her and her safety, Sunny conceded. The question was, how much? And dare she allow herself to care about him?

Later that afternoon Webb arrived with his dog, a brown and white spaniel-cross. When Sunny saw Webb ride through the open gate, the dog was running alongside him. Sunny came out on the porch to meet them. Webb walked over, stopping at the bottom of the steps. He squatted down, sitting on his heels, stroking the dog's head, saying in a low voice, "This here's Dandy. And this is Miss Lyndall, fella. You're to watch out for her, protect this place, y'hear?" He looked up at Sunny. "Maybe you should come down, put out your hand, let him get your scent. Let him get the idea that you're takin' my place for now."

Sunny came down the steps, tucked her skirts around her, sat down, and held out one hand to the dog's muzzle. Velvety brown eyes turned questioningly to Webb. "It's all right, fella," Webb said soothingly, fondling the silky ears.

The dog made small whining sounds of pleasure. "He'll do all right here. He's got a mighty good bark. He'll keep you safe, won't you, boy?"

Sunny hadn't meant to say it, but she'd been puzzling over it all day, so it just popped out. "What's the real reason you're going off like this—taking this job with the hunters?"

Webb looked up at her again. His expression held mockery and something else indefinable. Under his steady gaze, she felt her cheeks flush. "There's reason enough," was all he said, and she was silenced. Then Webb stood up. "Well, I think you two'll do fine. I'll be takin' off."

The dog moved, too, running to the side of the horse, quivering in anticipation that they were starting the familiar race back to town or wherever his master led. But Webb whistled him back to his side.

"No, fella. You're to stay here. Stay." The command was firm. For a split second the dog seemed to hesitate, then he came, whimpering low in his throat. "Take your place." Webb gestured with a downward movement of his hand. The dog did as he was told. Webb glanced at Sunny. "He knows. He minds well. Just speak quietly, firm."

"When will you be back?"

"Can't say for sure. Maybe a month, maybe more. Maybe I might even stay out west, if I've a mind to. Might even give up scouting after all, settle down!" He smiled wickedly. "If I don't come back, Dandy's yours. If you don't want him, I have someone else who does." He took off his hat and made her a sweeping bow. "You were my first choice, Miss Lyndall, being you're so *sweet-tempered* and all. Thought Dandy'd have a right good home till I get back." He walked over to his horse and mounted. He tipped his hat, swung his horse around, smiled, and said, "So long." To Sunny there seemed an awful finality in his words. As she stood watching him until he disappeared in the clouds of dust raised by his horse's hooves old feelings of being forsaken, of losing something important to her, washed over her.

Just then Dandy threw his head back and gave a mournful howl. It was as if the dog knew Webb's leaving might be for good. An instant empathy for the animal prompted Sunny. She leaned down to pat his head comfortingly. But Dandy moved away from her and with a sigh flopped down in the corner of the porch, putting his nose onto his paws.

That night, emotions Sunny thought she had long ago put behind her surfaced. She discovered that the old wounds of losing her father when he married Matilda had never really healed. To her utter surprise they were somehow now mixed with Webb Chandler's leaving. Seeing him ride off had brought an instant sadness, a soreness to her heart, a loneliness to her spirit. Almost the same way she had felt seeing her father ride off from the church, newly married. She had promised herself then that she was never going to love someone so much again. Her father's remarriage had broken Sunny's heart, because it excluded her, changed her life. Even at that tender age, she'd decided that loving someone gave them the power to hurt, and she would never let it happen to her again. Being vulnerable was a weakness. Sunny had determined to be strong. That night she wept, not knowing exactly why or what it had to do with Webb Chandler.

# Chapter 17

*S*unny missed Webb. More than she cared to admit. Missed those impromptu visits, those teasing remarks, the provocative look in his eyes. Dandy missed him, too.

Webb's dog proved both a comfort and a challenge to Sunny. Master and dog were a strange pair, she often thought. Why Webb had brought the dog here Sunny could never quite decide. Although obedient, Dandy maintained an aloofness, seeming only to suffer her attentions.

It puzzled and hurt Sunny a little that the dog kept his distance. Eventually he allowed her to pat him or talk to him when she fed him or placed a pan of cool water by his dish. But for the most part Dandy kept up a wall that no amount of coaxing or petting overcame. Dandy daily took his place on the station porch, facing the gate as if waiting hopefully for his *real* master's return.

At first Shadow showed his indignation at the arrival of a new animal into the household by scurrying on top of the table, the hutch, or the rocker, arching his back and hissing. Soon, however, a truce was reached between the kitten and the visiting dog. In fact, one day Sunny found her black cat curled up back-to-back with Dandy, both asleep in a patch of sunshine.

A week after Webb's departure, Rhys came out to the Express station. At the sound of Dandy's barking, Sunny went out onto the porch just in time to see Rhys leaning over and patting Dandy, whose tail was wagging. Rhys looked up at Sunny and remarked, "Nice dog, isn't he? Belongs to Webb Chandler, right?"

Feeling as though she should explain, Sunny said, "Yes. We're keeping him for Webb while he's away." She purposely said *we* to give the impression it was Tracy's friendship with Webb that had resulted in Dandy's stay.

"Good idea," Rhys nodded. "*I* should have thought of giving you a dog of your own. For protection when you're here by yourself, as well as for company. We'll have to see about that when Webb comes home and wants Dandy back." He came toward the porch steps. "So is everything going all right out here? You need anything?"

"No, thank you. We're fine. I don't have last week's receipts yet, but it won't take long, if you want to wait. Or I can have them for you tomorrow."

"Whichever is best. I might as well wait."

"Come in then, and I'll get them together."

"How's Tracy?" Rhys asked as he followed her into the front of the building, where the office was.

"Fine, I guess." She gave a rueful smile. "I hardly see him, though. When he's in town, he's either sleeping or doing chores or with his rider friends."

Sunny went behind the divider and unlocked the safe. Rhys, on the other side, leaned his elbow on the counter and asked, "Does it bother you that your brother is finding other interests? Friends of his own?"

"Oh, maybe a little. It's not his fault, and it's only natural. I suppose it's just that I've always kinda looked after him, especially after both our parents died. I have to keep reminding myself he's growing up. He's not my little brother anymore."

A smile touched Rhys' mouth, but his eyes weren't smiling. "It happens like that sometimes," he said. "Overnight, boys become men. It happens often in the West. Life moves faster out here. Too fast sometimes. Differences that should be settled by discussion and debate are taken care of by guns." Sunny saw something flicker in Rhys' eye, glint there for a single second, then vanish. What was it? Anger? Bitterness? She could not guess. "I've seen it happen too often," he continued. "Small disagreements escalate into violence. Out here, without the constraints of a more settled kind of life, family reputation, church, the law—all the influences that keep society civilized—are sometimes forgotten. Men seem to elevate recklessness more than honor, hatred more than tolerance or compassion. Hatred is demonic. It turns men into brutal beasts. It robs them of their humanity."

Rhys' face suddenly underwent a change as if he were remembering something vividly. Then just as quickly he said, "How did we get on this subject? Forgive me. The only reason I mentioned it was I thought maybe it might help you understand about circumstances causing people to change. Like your brother is doing with his new responsibilities. It has nothing to do with you, his feelings for you. He's growing up, that's all. Don't take it personally."

"You're right, of course," Sunny agreed, wondering why it was so much easier to accept Rhys' comments about Tracy than Webb's. "And I am glad Tracy is happy, is making friends."

"This isn't a bad place to put down roots, you know. It's a good community, good people. Not growing too fast like a cattle town, nor does it draw riffraff like a gold strike would. Not even too close to Independence, for that matter. It'll develop at its own speed. Be a fine place to settle down, raise a family."

Suddenly conscious that their conversation might

become too personal and remembering Verna's warning, she quickly changed the subject. "Well, this is everything. All the receipts, dated received." She stacked them and slid them across the counter.

"Thanks. You're doing a fine job, Sunny. I appreciate it," Rhys said, opening a leather packet and putting the receipts inside. But he made no move to leave.

Sunny felt awkward. She was uncertain of how to treat this visit, as business or social. Usually when Rhys came on business, he maintained a very formal manner. Especially since the harvest dance and what happened after, she could no longer treat him as simply an employer. She would have to be blind as a bat, as Verna put it, to not see Rhys had more than a passing interest in her. How to handle it?

Trying to seem natural, Sunny came out from behind the office enclosure and moved toward the kitchen. At the stove, she lifted the still half-full coffeepot questioningly.

"Yes, thanks," Rhys nodded and walked over to accept the cup she handed him. Dandy had trotted after them into the building and remained by Rhys, his tail wagging hopefully. When Rhys sat down, Dandy went over to him and rested his head against Rhys' knee. For a minute Rhys silently caressed the dog's head, then he looked over at Sunny and picked up the thread of conversation he had been pursuing. "For myself, the longer I was here, the more I felt like staying. I suppose there comes a time in a man's life when he wants to settle down, put down roots, establish a home—wouldn't you agree?"

"I really couldn't say. Tracy and I have talked of nothing else but going to California for over a year—since our stepmother died. Coming here was to be the start of the great adventure of our lives."

"I understand. But you don't think maybe Tracy has changed his mind? Especially since he's been courting rancher Brownlee's daughter? I heard he's been talking about buying some land *here*—"

Jolted, Sunny turned wide-eyed to Rhys.

"I didn't know that! I mean, I knew he often rode out to the Brownlee ranch on his days off, but about buying land, no—" The conviction in her tone faded. "At least, he hasn't said anything like that to *me*."

"I'm sorry if I've spoken out of turn, Sunny. I like your brother very much. He's smart, bright, got a good head on his shoulders. He's becoming a man capable of a lot more than riding the Pony Express. He's got a future, and it may be here." He paused. "Any chance *you* would change *your* mind? Or be willing to?"

Sunny bit her lip, shook her head.

"I've not even thought about it. We—or at least I—have always thought . . ." She lifted her chin a little. "As far as I'm concerned, nothing's changed. We plan to move to California as soon as possible."

What Rhys said about Tracy's plans shook her badly. How could Tracy go behind her back, talking about things he never discussed with her? She felt left out, betrayed. After all she had done for him! For Tracy not to have shared something so important was a hard pill to swallow. She struggled not to show her hurt. To cover up her emotional reaction, she scooped up Shadow from the pillow on the rocking chair, cradling him in her arms.

She wished Rhys would leave, give her a chance to sort out her thoughts. But he kept sitting there, regarding her thoughtfully. Then he said, "About California—I guess it has a lure for everyone. I had in mind to keep going on to the coast myself. But now somehow I feel different. I'm not running away anymore. I think I've found what I want, what would make me happy."

Sunny felt a vague uneasiness. She had the feeling they were heading into dangerous territory.

He seemed to notice her discomfort. "I'm afraid I might have said something to upset you. If I have, please forgive me. I value our friendship too much to ever do anything that might offend you."

"I know that."

"You must know what a high regard and respect I have for you. I will never bring up any subject that might cause you distress under any circumstances, unless—unless you give me reason to believe that it would be acceptable to you."

The more he said, the more uncomfortable Sunny became. She wanted to bring this conversation to an end.

Taking the hint, Rhys got up, placed his empty coffee mug on the table, picked up his hat, and moved toward the door. Sunny followed him out onto the porch, still holding Shadow in her arms as if for a shield.

At the edge of the porch, Rhys gazed into the distance, and Sunny again was struck by the nobility of his profile, the almost classically Greek structure of his high-bridged nose, his strong chin. He pointed toward the rim of blue hills beyond the gate, saying, "Someday I'd like to take you up into the hills not far from here. I want you to see a remarkable view. It's where I plan to build my house."

Without thinking, Sunny asked, "To live in by yourself?"

Immediately she was sorry. Her question posed an answer she might not want to hear. Even though the brim of his hat shaded his eyes, Sunny felt their thoughtful speculation as he turned to look at her. Then he said slowly, "I hope not. I sincerely hope not, Sunny."

Watching him ride out, Sunny had the feeling that their relationship had crossed some line and that nothing would ever be quite the same between them again.

Back in town at the Express office, Rhys had questions of his own to confront. Had he said too much? Gone too far? Had he dared to hope again? Was it possible to recapture all he had abandoned? To find in this woman the tenderness, the passion, the beauty, of a life he had lost? The constant loneliness had its source—a source he had to keep hidden, but it could not be denied. He had forsaken his right to the sweetest part of life, had kept its possibility locked away at a distance.

Did he have the right? *That* was the final question. If she knew—

Rhys moved his hand to the lower left drawer of the desk, then drew it back as if it contained a poisonous snake. No! Never that again. The only chance for true happiness was honesty. A picture of Sunny's eyes came into his vision—their candor, their innocence, their trust.

Forming a fist, Rhys banged it on the desk. Until he knew, until he asked Sunny outright, he could not decide what to do. He had to risk her rejection before he could seek her understanding.

During the next two days, Sunny could think of little else except what Rhys had said about Tracy. She did not risk bringing the subject into the open. But her inner resentment grew day by day, building a barrier of unspoken tension that had never existed before between brother and sister.

Maybe it was mostly rumor; after all, Rhys had only hearsay evidence. Yet rumors always seemed to have a germ of truth. Certainly Tracy hotfooted out to the Brownlee ranch every time he could. So what if it was all true? What if he *had* fallen in love with Betty Brownlee? What if he *did* want to settle down here and become a rancher? What then was *she* to do? There was no way as a single woman Sunny could go to California by herself. Lucas Flynt had made that clear enough before.

Thoughts of California—of the snowcapped mountains, the golden poppies, the oranges as big as melons, the constant sunshine—were what had kept her going all these dreary months. Were they all doomed to be just idle day-dreams, unfulfilled fantasies?

Simultaneously Rhys Graham's feelings for her began to have some unexpected impact. The fact that he had originally planned to go to California himself came into her mind at odd moments. Several times he had mentioned that in a few years, after the transcontinental railroad was completed, the trains would carry the mail, and then the Pony Express would be obsolete, his business gone. Would he *then* be content to build a house on a hillside here? Alone? Or might he again consider going west?

She still hadn't dared ask Tracy about his possible change of heart or his intentions. She knew she was avoiding learning something that just might break her own heart.

Fall was in the air. Although the days remained sunny and warm, the afternoon sun departed sooner and the evenings became cool. Sunny felt a strange melancholy that had nothing to do with the change of seasons. Or at least she didn't think it did. Yet a pervasive feeling of sadness hovered.

One particular evening Sunny was alone and fighting this creeping self-pity. Tracy had gone out. After coming in from his route and grabbing a few hours' sleep, he'd washed up and changed clothes. Then, mumbling some excuse to Sunny about going into town, he'd saddled one of the ponies and left. Sunny was sure whatever errand he might drum up in town, he was headed out to the Brownlee ranch to visit Betty.

Resolutely determined to be cheerful, Sunny lighted the fire and got out her mending basket. She had just started darning one of Tracy's socks when there was a knock at the door. Dandy's head rose, a rumble of a growl deep in his throat. He got to his feet with hackles quivering and approached the door, where he braced his back legs and stiffened, awaiting a word from Sunny in case it was necessary to attack an intruder.

She placed a hand on the dog's head and called, "Who is it?"

"Rhys, Sunny." She immediately threw back the bolt, opened the door, and he stepped inside. It had been almost two weeks since she had last seen him.

"I hope I'm not disturbing you, Sunny. I haven't the excuse that I was just riding by and decided to stop. I've come for a special reason."

"Of course." Her heart gave a queer little thump. She remembered some of the things he had *not* said, and at the same time she recalled the things Verna *had* said. "Come in."

He declined the cup of coffee she offered and pulled up a chair on the opposite side of the stove. He sat forward, leaning his arms on his knees, his hands clenched.

"Sunny, I'm sure you've sensed that I've grown to care for you a great deal. More than care—" He halted. "Do you know what I'm trying to say?"

Sunny shook her head, her heart uneasy. "That would be presuming—no, but I have a feeling it might be better left unsaid."

"If you don't want me to, of course, I won't."

Not knowing what to say, Sunny said nothing, and Rhys continued.

"I don't think I've done a very good job of keeping my feelings for you secret, Sunny. I've stayed away, trying to think things through. I understood that you did not wish me to go further the other afternoon. Why I was not sure. Perhaps duty to your brother? Reluctance to give up your original plans? And I respected your wishes. However, since then I've come to the conclusion that to withhold speaking frankly of my intentions is not forthright. I should do so and let *you* have a chance to consider my proposal. May I?"

Knowing she could not deny him that privilege, Sunny said, "Of course."

"Since you have no older male relative, at least none that I know of, and Tracy is not legal age, I must ask you directly. Would you do me the great honor of marrying me?"

Sunny chose her words carefully. "I'm flattered Rhys, but really—"

"Wait!" He held up one hand to keep her from interrupting. "As I mentioned the other day, when I started west some years ago, I planned to go on to California. But when I got to Independence—well, several unexpected things happened to delay me. Not unlike you and your brother. Although my experiences weren't as devastating as yours. Still, they were of the kind to make me stop, rethink my plans. Challenges, opportunities. The Express company seemed a stroke of good luck at the time I bought it. The thought of California began to fade somewhat. I grew to like it here, the town, the people—but what I wanted to tell you is this: if you would do me the great honor of marrying me, I would certainly consider the possibility of heading west again."

When Rhys left, a light rain was falling. They had talked for over an hour. He got back in his buggy and, sighing heavily, picked up the reins and headed back toward town. He felt inordinately let down. The fragile hope he'd had earlier was replaced by the old despair. At one time this disappointment might have led him to seek solace in drink. At least he felt no temptation to do that now.

What had he expected? Sunny had not rejected him out of hand. Neither had she seemed completely surprised by his proposal. Maybe he should have pressed for an answer once he'd fully explained his intentions. He hadn't dared to risk that. It was so recently that he'd allowed himself to imagine what it might be like to love and have someone love him in return.

At least she had not turned him down or refused to consider it. He had been quick to tell her to take all the time she needed, that he was willing to wait. He had lived long enough to know that nothing worthwhile in life comes easily. As he entered town Rhys felt a stirring of new hope rise in his heart. He felt more than ever that Sunny Lyndall had come into his life for a purpose. Was that purpose to give him a second chance? Hadn't he paid his penalty? Served his term? Suffered regret, remorse, repentance?

Night after night he had awakened from a nightmare—reliving the act that had brought him to this place, this moment in time. . . . The terrible loneliness, the scalding shame, would sweep over him. Then he knew he could not bury the past. His mind, his conscience, his soul, would not allow him that release.

Now for the first time he felt some assurance. The possibility that he could at last put it all behind him. After all the guilt and self-doubt, the wasted years, he saw a chance for a new beginning. His only fear was that Sunny would not be able to accept what he had not yet told her: the truth about himself and his past.

After Rhys left, Sunny could not settle down. Dandy seemed restless, too. Rhys' visit had probably been unsettling for him as well. Rhys' male scent had reminded the dog of his missing master. He prowled around, pacing back and forth on the porch, making small whining sounds in his throat. Taking pity on him, Sunny sat down on the top step and caressed his head. The dog's eyes revealed his loneliness, his bewilderment, and Sunny responded, saying, "You miss Webb, don't you, fella? Well, I do, too."

Her feelings about Webb were perplexing. She remembered how much she had disliked him at first, but since then . . . He had reached out to her in many surprising ways. She couldn't figure him out. He certainly wasn't someone you could count on. Here today, gone tomorrow. Even his showing up that awful day when those men had come had been by happenstance. Hadn't it? She was never sure. Still, a girl would be crazy to fall in love with anyone as undependable as Webb Chandler. Fall in love? What made her even *think* of that?

Sunny spent a sleepless night. In the morning she still couldn't get answers for any of the questions that had kept her awake. The simplest chore seemed almost too much to concentrate on, and soon she gave up trying. Her mind was in turmoil. Webb Chandler's absence and Rhys Graham's proposal were all she could think of.

Sunny had come to think of Rhys Graham as a benefactor. He had thrown her a lifeline when she was drowning, given her a job and then a place to live. But marriage! She had never thought that. She remembered how she had dismissed Verna's comments as nonsense. Now it made sense. Little things came back to her, small kindnesses, thoughtful gestures, that all added up to something more than friendship. But *marriage*?

Suddenly the Express station felt confining. She needed to get out. She needed someone to talk to, someone to confide in, someone she could trust to help her sift through her mixed-up feelings, find the truth. Verna. *Of course* Verna.

Sunny checked the bread she had rising on the table, tucked the cloth back over it. She fed the ponies and turned all of them but Bramble out in the corral. Then, snatching up her sunbonnet, she hitched him to the wagon and drove to the Ardley home.

Verna was putting up pickles and looked surprised when Sunny knocked at the kitchen door, then walked in.

"Hope I'm not barging in at a bad time?" Sunny asked

rather sheepishly. Looking around the kitchen, she realized at once that Verna was busy as usual.

"Not so I couldn't stand some company," was the tart reply. "I'm puttin' up my bread and butter pickles, but I'm most ways through."

"Can I do anything to help?" Sunny asked vaguely.

Watching Sunny aimlessly circle the room a couple of times, Verna concluded, *Something's up.* But she decided to wait until Sunny was ready to tell her the real reason she'd come.

"I got to go on here with what I'm doing. I'm jest now mixing the brine. I got more cucumbers in my garden this year than I know what to do with, and I'll have plenty to give away. Why don't you light somewhere while I finish up?"

Sunny nodded but remained where she stood, twisting her bonnet strings nervously.

Verna gave her a sharp look. *Something is sure enough wrong with the girl.* Making another try, she pointed to the rocker. "Pull up that chair and you can watch me. Mebbe you'd like to have this recipe for yourself."

Sunny did as Verna suggested but was too distracted to pay much attention as Verna resumed working, talking all the while.

"This recipe's been handed down in my family for goodness knows how long. Won prizes at county fairs many a time," Verna said as her hands moved deftly, measuring out the chopped onions, chunks of bell peppers, half a cup of salt, five cups of vinegar, five cups of sugar, teaspoons of clove, turmeric, mustard and celery seed, combining them in a bowl, then putting the mixture in a large pan and setting it on the stove to boil. "Now all's left to do is pour it into the packed jars," Verna said with satisfaction. But when she turned around and looked at Sunny, she realized Sunny would never be able to duplicate the pickle recipe.

What on earth was troubling the girl? "How would you like some fresh, sweet cider to have while we visit?"

Sunny glanced at Verna as one coming out of a trance, as if she had not even heard Verna's question, then announced solemnly, "Verna, you were right. About Rhys Graham."

Verna didn't need further explanation. She nodded. "Didn't I tell you he was plumb loco about you?"

"He's asked me to marry him."

Verna pursed her lips, then asked, "And what did you say? Did you accept?"

"Not yet. I told him that—well, that I'd have to think about it."

"Hmmm."

Sunny flashed her a look. "What does that 'hmmm' mean, Verna?"

Verna raised her eyebrows slightly. "Just hmmm." She gave her head a shake. "I'm thinkin' how many gals hereabouts would swoon clear away at such a proposal, give their eyeteeth for such a chance. Fine-looking man with a thriving business, no question of his being able to provide for a wife—"

"I *know* that he's considered a good catch." Sunny looked thoughtful. "But is that enough? There's love—isn't there?"

"You must be wanderin' around with your head in the clouds." Verna looked scandalized. "Most women out here don't have that luxury, child. A strong, healthy man, sober, God fearin', a good provider—that's what most are looking for, hoping for, and can't find."

Abruptly and disconcertingly that ended the conversation.

But Sunny found it wasn't the end of Verna's uncanny discernment. A few days later Verna came out to the Express station. After plunking down a batch of raisin bread and two baskets of freshly picked blackberries on the kitchen table, she said, "These are the last of the season.

Better find some use for them right away iffen you don't plan to make jelly. They don't keep very good; they soften." Then she folded her arms, pierced Sunny with her direct gaze, and demanded, "It's Webb, isn't it?"

Startled, Sunny blinked and immediately denied it. "No, of course not."

"You sure?"

"What makes you think such a thing?"

"Oh, I dunno. Just something about the way you two look at each other when you think no one else is. The way you spar all the time, spittin' and scratchin' like two cats in a gunnysack." Verna sniffed with mock impatience.

"Webb Chandler! I declare, Verna, where in the world you got such an idea I'll never know."

Verna pressed her mouth into a straight line. For a full minute she was silent, then she said, "Well, I guess I do give you credit for better sense than that. Don't get me wrong. I love Webb like he was my own son. My *prodigal* one. And if I had a daughter, I'd tell her to keep away from him. Not that he don't have his good qualities. He's honest as the day's long, loyal to his friends, braver than he's got any right to be, but"—and here Verna paused significantly—"you know what they say, 'A rolling stone gathers no moss.'"

Sunny absorbed this but then said slowly, "However, Verna, he did hint that he was about through. Tired of taking people to California and then turning around and coming right back. Sounded like he might be getting ready to stay here and settle down—or move out west and homestead."

Verna threw up her hands. "If that just don't sound like something a fella like Webb *would* say. I doubt it seriously. He's been scouting ever since I've known him, and—"

"People can change, though, don't you think?"

Verna speared her with a skeptical look. "Can a leopard change his spots? Not very likely. Not in my experience. Folks stay pretty much the same. *Unless*—" She paused.

"Unless somethin' nobody could account for happens to 'em."

After Verna left, Sunny mulled over her pithy comments. She had to admit the older woman was wiser than anyone she had ever known. Maybe she should pay attention to what she said. Could Verna be right?

*Nothing happens by chance.* She'd heard that somewhere. *"Man proposes, God disposes."* Did God have anything to do with their being here in Missouri instead of California? Was she meant to meet Rhys Graham? Or was it Webb Chandler?

# Chapter 18

*R*hys' proposal weighed heavily on Sunny. She was torn between feeling flattered and burdened by it. He had said, "You might learn to love me. I would do everything I could to make you happy." Sunny knew this was true. A man of Rhys' honor and integrity would be true to his word. But she had never thought of him romantically, and the idea of marriage without mutual love her conscience would not even consider. There was no one she could really confide in. Verna's advice was practical but born of the frontier way of thinking. In Verna's mind Rhys Graham was a godsend, meeting all the requirements of protection and provision a woman needed. Sunny would be a fool to turn him down. Sunny knew she could never make Verna understand the deeper need inside her that such a marriage would not fulfill.

In a way, she felt guilty not telling Tracy, but her brother had his own secrets. Until she knew what was going on with him, she did not want to say anything that might influence him one way or the other.

Rhys came out to the Express station more frequently, and never empty-handed, even if it was simply a bouquet of flowers. Sunny could not help being touched by his desire to please her, his carrying on an old-fashioned courtship. She already admired and respected him and now was more aware of his nobility of character, his sense of honor. He kept his promise never to mention his proposal of marriage again. Although she could not give him the answer he longed for, the appeal she saw in his eyes moved her. Intuitively she knew he had been deeply hurt by something—or someone. A terrible loss of some kind? Yet there was no bitterness in his expression, more a forlorn weariness and loneliness. Whatever it was, Sunny wished she could help or heal in some way. It wasn't as simple as "learning to love." Searching her heart for the right answer, Sunny knew that before she could be free to try to do that, she would have to do something else: forget Webb Chandler.

The longer he was gone, the more she had to admit she missed him, regretted some of her past actions. Her anger at the scene she had inadvertently witnessed at the harvest dance really seemed childish and foolish now. Wasn't it possible that the same easygoing charm that she herself found attractive about him would be irresistible to other women—even one as experienced as Juanita? Maybe she had overreacted, imagined something that didn't exist, that had been just a playful, flirtatious moment.

On the other hand, was she making excuses for him? She did not want to believe there was anything more going on between Webb and the dance hall girl. Was it so important because she wanted to believe Webb genuinely cared about *her*? Hadn't he been concerned enough for her safety to teach her to shoot, to bring his own dog for her protection? He *had* to have some special feeling to do all that. *She* had felt something real between them. It had not been her imagination!

As long as that was there, how could she consider Rhys Graham's proposal seriously?

But as Verna, who loved him like a son, pointed out,

what kind of husband would a man like Webb make? She had called him a rolling stone.

The argument went on in Sunny's mind endlessly, day after day. What was she looking for anyhow? In her girlhood dreams, she had imagined that one day she would meet a man who would match her own adventurous spirit. That is, once she got to California!

Now that she had a taste of what rough frontier life demanded, Sunny realized her dream had changed. Now she wanted not only someone to share her dream but a man who would recognize her independence, her ability, her strength, treat her as an equal partner. Or was that an impossible dream?

Weeks passed and Rhys remained outwardly patient. When he came on Express station business, he maintained a businesslike manner. Only the tenderness in his eyes betrayed the fact that he regarded her as more than an employee.

Although Sunny was sure Verna had not violated her confidence, somehow the word seemed to have got around on the notorious "small-town grapevine." Every time she went into town, she saw it in people's faces: the curious looks she got at the general store, the watchful eyes, the sly smiles, the knowing glances, on the street or in church when people greeted her. Rhys Graham was well thought of by everyone; therefore there was a natural interest in anything that concerned him.

Sunny did not know what to do to stem the tide of gossip. She was helpless to put an end to all the speculation. She knew people would talk no matter how small the grain of truth. In the meantime the tension building between Tracy and her reached a crisis.

With October weather arriving, each morning was colder and colder. Sometimes Tracy now had to wear a sheepskin-lined coat, leather chaps, and a wool scarf when he went out on his route. He talked of running into snow in the narrow passes, of winds whistling down the mountain canyons, of the pony's breath coming in icy puffs as he braved it along the frozen trails. This one particular morning Sunny awakened thinking mournfully about Christmas back home. Maybe it was the weather, which was bleak, overcast with heavy, gray clouds. As she went about the dark kitchen banging the stove door, getting a fire started, clattering the coffeepot when she set it on to boil, she grew increasingly wretched.

When Tracy came out, he seemed to be in just the opposite kind of mood. Sunny threw him a wary glance. Why was he looking so happy? Didn't he miss the same things she missed? No, probably not. Too cow-eyed over Miss Betty Brownlee, she thought irritably, plunking down his plate of flapjacks in front of him.

"What're you in a pucker about, Sis?" he asked as he poured molasses over the stack.

"I'm not in a pucker!" she retorted indignantly.

"Sure actin' mighty ornery," he said placidly, taking a large forkful.

"I am not."

"Well, could have fooled me."

"Don't talk with your mouth full!"

Tracy started to laugh.

Sunny turned her back and began pouring more batter into the pan. She knew Tracy was right. But somehow she couldn't get over feeling put upon, unhappy. She didn't respond and nothing more was said. She could hear him scrape his plate, then slide back in his chair. He came over, bringing his plate to the sink, then refilled his mug with coffee.

"Sorry if I made you mad, Sis."

She turned around. "I'm sorry, too, Tracy. I don't know what's got into me lately—"

"Maybe this will help," he said and dug in his jacket pocket and brought out a small leather pouch and set it on the table. It made a clinking sound. "Mr. Graham gave us fellas a bonus for takin' extra rides when Fergus broke his arm last month. I want you to use it and buy yourself somethin' pretty at the store. I know how hard you've been workin', Sunny. And I know ladies need to have some fancy doodads to make them happy."

"And where did you learn that piece of feminine wisdom? From Betty Brownlee?" Sunny's voice was edged with sarcasm. Tracy blushed a deep pink, and instantly she was sorry. She hurried to make amends. "I'm sorry," she said, but it was too late. Tracy was really angry.

"Doggone it, Sunny—"

"I didn't mean it—"

"Yes, you did. You can't stand for anyone else to be happy when you're miserable, can you?"

His words hit her hard. That's how it probably seemed to Tracy. Lately when he'd been coming or going to see Betty, Sunny had never failed to make some caustic comment. She was ashamed.

"Oh, Tracy, I really *am* sorry." She picked up the little money bag, opened it, and gasped when she saw what was inside. "Why, these are gold pieces, Tracy. My goodness! That was generous of Mr. Graham."

"He said we deserved it," Tracy said sullenly.

"He's right, of course. You *do* deserve it. And I don't deserve having such a kind brother! Forgive me, Tracy. But I can't spend it on myself. This will go a long way to fattening our nest egg!" She was excited. "Why, with this we could buy most of the equipment we'll need to go west by next spring."

Tracy turned away from her.

"What's the matter?" she asked, puzzled.

"That's not what it's meant for. I wanted you to use it for something nice, for yourself."

A cold certainty gripped Sunny. The unbidden thought came. *He's going to tell me he's changed his mind about going to California.* She clutched the little leather pouch in tight hands, waiting.

Tracy's voice was muffled. "You still set on going, then?"

"Yes, of course. Aren't you?" she demanded. "*Are* you?"

Slowly Tracy turned around. "Dunno. I kinda like it here."

"*Here?*"

"It's a nice town, nice folks . . ."

"You're certainly not thinking of—"

"Well, Mr. Brownlee's offered me a job on his ranch if I ever quit riding. 'Course, I'm not about to do *that*—leastways, not yet!"

Sunny swallowed. "You're not—you *can't* be thinkin' of getting married, are you, Tracy?"

"Well, we've talked about it, me and Betty—"

Something in Sunny exploded. "Are you out of your mind? You're not old enough to get married, for heaven's sake! And you can't get married without my permission. You're not even legally of age!"

Tracy's hands balled into fists. His face flushed and angry, he confronted her. "Doggone it, Sunny, you alyus gotta control everything, everybody, don't you? You gotta run the show. Mebbe I ain't old enough 'cording to the law. But I'm sure old enough to know my own mind. What I want to do and what I don't. I'm doin' a man's job right now. You've got no idea what it's like to ride the mail route—no notion what I face out there each time I go out. Mr. Graham knows, and he thinks I'm old enough. So does Mr. Brownlee. If you weren't so set in your own ways, you'd see I've grown up. I'm not the little brother you can boss around anymore."

With that Tracy grabbed his hat and jacket off the peg by the door and slammed out.

Sunny sank down on one of the kitchen chairs. She felt as if she'd been beaten by Tracy's words. Was that how he really saw her? Was that how she really was?

Salty tears ran unchecked down her cheeks, and Sunny began to sob bitterly.

What would Christmas be like here in this desolate place? Sunny stared out the window, watching rain send rivulets steadily down the pane. A tide of nostalgia for past holidays washed over her.

Christmas was snow, sleigh bells ringing in the frosty air, sledding down the snow-covered slopes on starry nights, bonfires blazing, hot cranberry punch and spiced apple cider, carols and church chimes, tiny candles sparkling on gilt-and-tinsel-trimmed cedar trees.

How could she celebrate Christmas here?

She had to do something to make up to Tracy, to let him know how sorry she was to have quarreled. She would make him his favorite cake, walnut with brown sugar icing. That meant an extra trip to Ardley's General Store to get all the ingredients, but it would be worth it.

Quickly Sunny got her cape and bonnet, her grocery basket, then hitched up the Express wagon and rode into town, imagining her brother's grin when he saw his special dessert. As simple a gesture as it was, it might be just the thing to break the ice between them.

As luck would have it, she met Rhys as she was coming out, her arms full of packages.

"Here, let me," he said and started taking the bags.

"That's not necessary. My wagon is right over there. I'm going right home."

"Well, at least let me carry this across the street for you," he said.

She hesitated a split second, then relinquished her bundle.

As Rhys took the packages he said, "Actually, I was think-ing about you just now. Not that you aren't often in my thoughts these days." He smiled at her fondly. "As a matter of fact, I intended to drive out this afternoon to see you. If that's all right with you. May I?"

Sunny hesitated. She could hardly refuse without seem-ing ungracious. Besides, Rhys *was* her employer. He had a legitimate reason to check things at the station. "Of course."

He helped her into her wagon. "I'll follow you," he said and crossed the road to get into his own buggy.

On the way out to the Express station, Sunny felt nervous. Perhaps Rhys had decided he'd waited long enough for an answer to his proposal. In spite of his pledge not to pressure her, Sunny felt her position was becoming increasingly uncomfortable. If they only had enough money to plan seri-ously to leave on one of the wagon trains this spring, it would be so much easier to explain her refusal. Tracy hadn't actually given her a firm answer when she confronted him about still wanting to go to California. Until she knew that, how could she plan her own future?

Rhys was right behind her when she turned into the sta-tion gate. He was out of his buggy and at the side of her wagon before she had braked. When Rhys took her hands to help her down, he exclaimed, "Your hands are like ice! I didn't realize it was so cold. Let's go inside. I'll make a fire. I guess winter's really on its way."

Sunny unlocked the door and they went inside.

"Keep your cape on until I get this going," Rhys said and knelt to open the stove and ram some crumpled newspaper into it, along with some sticks of kindling. Soon the room glowed with soft light and warmth. Rhys got to his feet and came over to where she stood and helped her off with her cape. He moved away from her as if afraid it would be too difficult to remain so near and not touch her.

As the silence stretched Sunny felt the need to break the invisible tension. "Did you want to check the ledgers? The account books?"

He dismissed the suggestion, saying slowly, "No. . . . In fact, I've come for a personal reason." He paused and, frowning, said, "I'm afraid I may have put you into an awkward position. Perhaps I have taken too much for granted. My feelings for you are so . . . so deep that I've expected you to respond in a different way, a way you have not—perhaps cannot. There is, after all, a difference between love and friendship."

"Rhys, I value your friendship. I admire you very much. You have been more than generous to me and Tracy. We are so grateful—"

"I don't want your gratitude, Sunny." He made an impatient gesture. "Nor do I want your friendship. I want your love."

His expression of expectation and hope twisted Sunny's heart. She *did* admire him so much. He had all the qualities most women looked for and wanted in a husband and seldom found all in one man, but—

As if reading her mind, he said, "But you don't love me. That's it, isn't it, Sunny?"

"Rhys, I—"

"Is there any possibility, given time, you *could*?" he persisted. There was such longing in his eyes that Sunny hesitated.

"I don't know, Rhys. It's just that I never thought of you that way . . . before . . . until . . ."

Hope lit his eyes. "Do you mean you are *now*? Oh, Sunny, if I thought there was a chance . . . I'll wait. However long it takes, however much time you need."

"I can't promise anything, Rhys, I—"

"Of course not. I understand that."

He glanced at the stove, where the fire was now snapping

and burning brightly. "That should keep you warm through the rest of the day." Then, picking up his hat, he started toward the door. Sunny followed him. His hand on the latch, he turned and said, "I won't bother you with this again, Sunny. Let me know if and when you want to see me." He lingered a moment longer as if he would say more, then decided not to and left.

Sunny turned back into the room. The only sound in the room was the thrum and crackle as the fire burned, snapping once in a while. After a while she got out a bowl and sat down at the kitchen table and began shelling the walnuts she'd bought.

Uncertainty filled her with troubling thoughts and doubts. Why couldn't she love a man such as Rhys Graham, who had everything to offer her: steadfastness, security, devotion?

If only . . . Her thoughts drifted. If only what? What did she really want? Whose love would satisfy that empty place in her heart?

# Chapter 19

*D*ecember brought none of the snow Sunny longed for to give her a sense of Christmas. Back home in Ohio there had always been white Christmases, skating on the pond near their farm, sledding on the hillside back of the barn. This December was gray, heavy with clouds, and brought a cold, raw wind. It had also brought Webb Chandler back.

Or at least that's what she'd *heard*! Sunny lifted the heated flatiron off the stove and angrily plunked it down on the trivet on the end of her ironing board. She was as angry as she could ever remember being. Most of all, she was angry with herself for *being* so angry.

It was so silly. It had all started when Tracy said he ran into Webb Chandler at Ardley's General Store that morning. Her brother had mentioned it offhandedly as she packed his saddlebag lunch before he left on his mail route. Webb was back in town.

She'd been too surprised at the news to find out more. Besides, she hadn't wanted Tracy to see how eager for details she was. So Tracy rode off and Sunny was left with all sorts of unanswered questions. How long had Webb been back? Days? Weeks? No matter. It was odd he hadn't come out to the Express station, at least to check on Dandy!

She glanced at the sleeping dog curled up contentedly in front of the stove, Shadow beside him, and thought indignantly, *How about that? Your master not even bothering to see if we're alive or dead? You'd think that is the least he could do.*

Of course, that wasn't the only thing bothering Sunny. She and Tracy had not regained their easy, comfortable relationship since their quarrel. She felt that her brother was being secretive, keeping his real feelings and true thoughts from her. She couldn't blame him. After all, when he had tried to express them, she had lost her temper. And at the idea he was even *considering* marriage, she'd flown at him in a rage! Even that he was courting that little piece of fluff, Betty Brownlee, was bad enough! Imagining her as a sister-in-law was too much to contemplate. What about all their dreams, hopes, and plans? Had Tracy totally forgotten those?

Sunny banged the iron down over the starched sleeve of Tracy's shirt. The hot iron made a hissing sound as she slid it back and forth. He was wearing these more now that he spent his evenings at the Brownlee ranch. Guess *she* wouldn't stand over an ironing board doing his shirts as his sister did!

Sunny took another of Tracy's shirts from the basket of damp laundry, unrolled it, and shook it out. Carrying on a furious mental conversation, she smoothed it onto the board, reached for the flatiron, and set it down. It stuck! The iron made a sizzling sound as it hit the cloth. The smell of scorch rose into her nostrils. Quickly she removed the iron, but it was too late. There was already a V-shaped burn on the back of the collar. Slamming the iron down, she snatched the shirt off the board and went over to the kitchen pump, where she held the mark under the sloshing water, then rubbed the cloth vigorously. This was about the last straw of a day that had got off to a bad start. Absurdly, tears spurted into her eyes. *Sometimes it all seems too much,* she sniffled as she scrubbed at the stubborn burn. It was futile. Giving up, she flung the shirt onto the floor in frustration.

"Hello there, little lady."

At the sound of the familiar teasing voice, Sunny looked up, startled. Webb! She had been too preoccupied to notice Dandy's ears pricking up or the skittering of his paws on the wooden floor as he made a dash for the door. Neither had she heard a knock or the door open. But there he was, leaning against the door frame, hands in his pockets, regarding her as if he'd just "happened by to pass the time of day"—three months later.

Seeing him like this, so unexpectedly and with no warning, Sunny's heart gave a leap. In the flash of a second, she realized how much she had missed him, how empty the weeks had seemed since he left. At the same time, she felt caught unawares. As a result, she was flustered.

While Dandy made half-strangled sounds of recognition and bounded across the room, barking madly, Sunny tried to get her breath and gather her scattered thoughts. She made some ineffectual swipes at her hair and smoothed her apron, telling herself she must look dreadful. As for Webb, she quickly observed, he looked better than ever. Taller, leaner, and handsomer than she remembered. Weeks out on the plains had deepened his tan, making his eyes blue as prairie skies. It was all she could do to hide her pleasurable shock at his appearance.

Dandy was dancing around Webb in a paroxysm of joy, leaping up frantically. Webb went down on one knee and embraced him, looking over the dog's head at Sunny.

"What are you doing here?" was all she could manage to say.

"Aren't you supposed to say somethin' like, 'You're a sight for sore eyes'?" he laughed. He got to his feet and started toward her, with Dandy prancing at his side. "Or better still, 'Welcome back'?" His gaze met hers, and at its impact she flushed.

Quickly she transferred her attention to Dandy.

"I suppose you came for your dog." Her voice sounded sharper than she intended. She felt a little stab of jealousy at seeing how happy Dandy was to have his master back. She tried not to show it. After all, he *was* Webb's dog. However, during the past few weeks, Dandy had seemed to become *her* dog. At least Sunny felt he had, but the dog now seemed to have immediately reverted to his true allegiance. Watching them reminded Sunny poignantly of how alone she was. Self-pity suddenly overcame good sense. Betraying tears sprang up in her eyes, and to hide her irrational hurt she turned quickly away from the scene of affectionate reunion. She replaced her flatiron on the stove. Behind her the room was very still.

Without looking at Webb again, Sunny turned around and smoothed out another shirt to iron. For a moment the only sound was the iron moving against the fabric. Then Webb spoke slowly.

"That isn't all I came for."

"I can't imagine what else you would come for," Sunny said petulantly, knowing she must sound ridiculous but being unable to help it.

"Can't you?" he asked, then drawled, "And I thought you were bright as well as pretty."

She went on ironing, not daring to look up at him, wondering what he was going to say next.

"Well then, if you can't, I reckon the rumors I've been hearing around town are true," he said.

She stiffened but still didn't look up. "What kind of rumors?" She thought he might have heard something about Tracy and Betty Brownlee and that her brother was thinking of buying land. That alarmed her. If Webb, being just back in town, had heard it, it could be true. But that wasn't it.

"About you and Rhys Graham."

Sunny nearly dropped her iron. Oh, my! Her cheeks flamed and she felt as if the breath had been knocked out of her. She hadn't expected *that*. Webb was regarding her with unusual intensity, as if he really wanted to get an answer. She swallowed and tossed her head and retorted, "You listen to small-town gossip?"

"As they say, 'Where there's smoke, there's fire.'"

"Why do you always have to use something out of the farmers' almanac to say what you mean?"

"They're as good as anything and mostly true." Webb shrugged. "Anyway, it looks like I hit the nail on the head."

Sunny started to say, "What business is it of yours?" But instead she burst out, "Why did you go away? Really?" She was thinking that if he hadn't gone, Rhys might have noticed the attraction between *them* (after all, Verna had) and never proposed, and she wouldn't have been in this awkward situation. If Webb had ever given her so much as a hint that he was interested in her—well, *romantically*—maybe things would be different. How she wasn't sure, just *different*. Now she just felt angry, confused.

"Why? You mean the real reason. If I'd told you then, you wouldn't have believed it. Now there's no use to tell you."

"What do you mean?"

"It's too late, from what I hear. A smart gambler knows when to fold."

Sunny knew little about gambling but recognized the term Webb was using. It meant when things look hopeless, you don't keep playing; you cut your losses and pull out of the game.

What did he mean? That he felt he had no chance against someone like Rhys? That Rhys held all the winning cards? That's what it sounded like.

The flatiron steamed on the stove burner. Sunny grabbed a pot holder and picked it up, slid it back onto the ironing board. Pretending to concentrate on the shirtsleeves she was pressing, she did not look up. She could not bring herself to meet Webb's questioning look. Conscious that Webb was moving toward the door, her hand tightened on the handle of the iron. She wanted to stop him, ask him to stay, tell him it wasn't too late, she hadn't promised Rhys anything. She tried to think of something to keep him from leaving. Anything! Then she heard the sound of Dandy's anxious whine. He was afraid he'd be left behind again.

Webb spoke softly to the dog. "Well, I guess there's no use us hanging around here any longer, old fella. Looks like we've worn out our welcome."

She panicked. How to stop him? How to keep him from leaving? The first thing that wildly came to mind was, of course, the wrong thing.

"I guess I get no thanks for keeping your dog all these weeks. Not that I expected any." Even to her own ears, her words sounded waspish. She knew they were perverse and wrongheaded and utterly untrue. It was *she* who should have thanked *Webb* for bringing Dandy to her!

"Thanks." There was undisguised sarcasm in Webb's voice. To Dandy he said, "Come on, fella."

Oh, why hadn't she bitten her tongue before saying that? Sunny kept on ironing. Then the door closed with a final click.

What a fool she was! Why did she behave that way? All the time Webb had been gone, she had thought about him. In fact, she had not been able to stop thinking about him. She had relived encounters, conversations, especially that pivotal night at the harvest dance. She had rehearsed what she would say, if she had a chance, to undo some of the misunderstandings, the tiffs they'd had. Then today she had ruined any possibility—

But why had her knees weakened, her pulse raced, when he walked in? The truth was, Verna was right: she was in love with him!

Why then had she not asked him to stay? Sadly, Sunny knew the answer. She was afraid. Afraid that if she let him know, he would break her heart. Better that he thought she was engaged to Rhys Graham. Safer.

Sunny put down the iron and ran to the window just in time to see Webb climb into a small buckboard, Dandy leap up on the seat beside him. Miserably she watched Webb ride away, too proud to call him back.

To her dismay, just as he reached the gate, Rhys Graham's small, shiny buggy rounded the bend. They passed each other at the entrance. Sunny's heart sank. Now Webb would be sure those rumors were true.

# Chapter 20

That evening a kind of hopelessness set in on Sunny's usually determined optimism.

Even the fact that her walnut cake had turned out perfectly, the brown sugar icing spread in luscious swirls and peaks, didn't make her feel any better. Somehow Tracy hadn't seemed to enjoy it as much as he used to. She supposed it was too much to expect a mere cake to heal the growing gulf between them.

Was she really as bossy, self-centered, and stubborn as he had called her? If she was, why would someone like Rhys Graham want to marry her? Or why, as Verna believed, had Webb Chandler been attracted to her? Well, there was no use even thinking about Webb anymore. She had finished any hope of his returning under any circumstances.

Webb's showing up as he did had upset her. Rhys' unexpected visit had also been upsetting. He was going to St. Louis on business, he told her, and would be gone about a week. Rhys lingered awhile as if trying to find reason to stay longer. It was as if he wanted to say something personal or hoped she had something to say to him. Sunny kept very busy, moving about, straightening the ledger books, tidying the mail. She could tell Rhys wanted to kiss her good-bye, but she knew that would only encourage his hopes. Finally Rhys accepted her unspoken no with his usual graciousness, yet she could see the deep disappointment in his eyes as he bid her farewell.

After Rhys left and she was alone again, Sunny was plagued with indecision about everything. Just a few months ago her vision had been so clear, California her goal—right there beyond the horizon, like a distant dawn awaiting her coming. If Tracy had now lost interest in going, had found another direction he wanted to travel to find happiness, what then for her?

Of all the words Tracy had hurled at her in anger, what had hurt most was that he'd accused her of not wanting anyone else to be happy. She *did* want her brother to be happy. His welfare had always been her primary concern. All his life she had cared for and looked out for him, dreamed for him—but maybe now he had his own dreams, and they didn't include her.

Sunny had always prided herself on being honest. Now she had to be scrupulously honest, face the facts of her situation. *I'm at a crossroads, that's all,* she thought. *I've just got to figure out which one to take.*

No amount of soul-searching, however, calmed Sunny's unquiet spirit that evening. She felt restless and worried. She thought about what Verna had said when she told her about Rhys' proposal: *Whenever I don't know which way to go, I rely on the Good Book. That's my map.*

Sunny felt conscience stricken. Lately she hadn't been faithful about reading her Bible. Her prayers had usually been haphazard and fleeting. She hadn't even attended church regularly. She was always so busy. With Tracy often gone over the weekends, she didn't feel she could leave the station unattended. Payrolls, money orders, cash enclosed in personal letters, valuables in small packages, were kept in the safe. The ponies always had to be taken care of, fed, curried.

Not that any of this was an excuse to neglect private daily devotions. Convicted, Sunny got down her Bible from the shelf. Ashamed at the dust collected on it, she wiped it carefully, opened it, turned over the pages randomly. What should she read? Where would she find *her* map?

*The Lord is always faithful,* she remembered Verna saying. *I've never asked him for help in vain.*

Sunny tried not to worry that her negligence might cause the Lord not to be disposed to answer her, help her. She would trust Verna's faith. Wisdom is what she needed. Proverbs, she decided. But somehow she turned to Jeremiah instead. Her fingers slid down the thin pages, her eyes searching. Then she saw a verse that seemed to spring up from the print. Jeremiah 6:16: "Stand at the crossroads and look; ask for the ancient paths, ask where the good way is, and walk in it."

The word "crossroads" struck her. Coincidence or guidance? Sunny wasn't familiar enough with the interpretation to be sure. But she did remember one verse of Scripture she'd learned in childhood: "Ask and ye shall receive, seek and ye shall find, knock and it shall be opened unto you." That's all she could do—ask to be shown *her* path.

A dreary succession of days followed, then a week went by. At the end of it Rhys came out to the Express station. He seemed quieter than usual and did not bring up the subject of his proposal, for which Sunny was grateful. With Tracy's plans still not disclosed and her own future uncertain, she did not feel ready to discuss it. They handled the Express matters that needed to be attended to, and then Rhys said his business in St. Louis had not been satisfactorily completed and he would have to make another trip before the first of the year.

"Since I may not be here for Christmas, I brought you

an early present." He handed her a package. When she opened it, Sunny drew out a light, fringed, paisley shawl.

"Oh, Rhys, it's beautiful! But I haven't a present for *you!*"

"I didn't expect one. You know the only thing I want from you, Sunny." He smiled but his eyes looked sad. "I really wanted to give you something else—an engagement ring. I even looked at some at a jewelry store, but then I was afraid it would be presumptuous." He looked at Sunny almost shyly. "I suppose that's too much to ask or even hope for?"

"Oh, Rhys, I wish I could say what you want me to say, but—"

He held up his hand to halt her. "No, Sunny. I didn't mean to press you. I said I was willing to wait, and I am."

After he left, Sunny thought, *I don't deserve him. I wish I could love him the way he wants me to, but I just can't. I don't know if I ever can ...*

Christmas came and went and Sunny hardly noticed. She gave Tracy the wool scarf she had knitted, then he went to spend the day with the Brownlees at their ranch. She'd been invited, too, but had declined, saying she had a scratchy throat and felt she might be coming down with a cold. She had also turned down Verna's invitation to spend Christmas with them. Verna was expecting her two sisters and their families. Much as she appreciated both invitations, Sunny wasn't up to pretending holiday cheer she just couldn't seem to muster. She had spent the day feeling sorry for herself and actually ended up nursing a fever. *Serves me right for fibbing!* she admonished herself.

The week after Christmas it rained sporadically, not helping Sunny's already low spirit. No matter the weather, Tracy had taken his route, and Sunny was left on her own. She assumed Rhys was still in St. Louis. At least, he hadn't been out to the Express station. Maybe his business trip had taken longer than he had planned.

Sunny had continued her renewed habit of Bible reading and prayer. Surely God would recognize her good intentions and give her some insight about what she should do. She memorized the passage from Jeremiah as though it were some direction that she should put to the test.

What was the "good way"? Did "ancient paths" mean the trail worn by thousands of emigrants going to California? Did that mean she and Tracy should go on with their original plan? Should she be trying to talk Tracy out of an ill-advised marriage to Betty Brownlee? The more she thought, the more confused Sunny became. Maybe she wasn't doing it right. Maybe she should talk to Verna about her method of prayer.

One evening she was alone, busy knitting some heavy wool stockings for Tracy. The weather had turned so severe, he needed several layers of warmth for his feet, as his leather boots were no real protection from the bitter cold.

Her thoughts were as tangled as the ball of yarn that had fallen out of her sewing basket and become Shadow's plaything. She still hadn't settled anything in her mind about what to do. The only accompaniment to her mental debate was the soft pattering of an icy rain on the roof, the click of her knitting needles, and the occasional snap of the fire in the stove. Then suddenly the quiet was broken by the sound of buggy wheels outside. She straightened up in alarm. Who could that be on this cold, rainy night? Instinctively her eyes moved to the shotgun Webb had given her, which was on the rack he'd nailed in place for her near the front door. She got up, heart hammering, and moved slowly across the room toward the door. Before she reached it, there was a loud, steady knock, and a familiar voice called, "Don't be frightened, Sunny. It's me, Rhys."

Surprised and relieved, Sunny hurried to slide the bolt back and open the door. At the same time, she felt some apprehension. Rhys had promised not to pressure her for an answer. What had brought him out here tonight?

She opened the door and Rhys stepped inside. His caped slicker was dripping, and she took it as he shrugged it off, then she hung it on one of the pegs.

"I had to see you, Sunny." He held up a hand. "I did not come to pressure you. In fact, over the past few weeks I've kept my distance. But now I've come, because—well, it's important. To us both. I just realized I couldn't put it off any longer."

Puzzled, Sunny said, "Why, of course, Rhys, come in," and ushered him into the kitchen. Motioning him to one of the chairs, she sat down on the rocker she had drawn up to the stove.

"This is probably an intrusion, Sunny. But I've thought of nothing else for days, and I knew I'd have no rest until I talked to you—told you." Rhys leaned forward, clasping his hands in front of him so tightly that the knuckles whitened.

What on earth could it be? Rhys' face was haggard, and there were deep circles under his eyes, evident signs of stress.

"I would give anything if what I've come to tell you had never happened. Anything if I didn't feel you must know. But since I have asked you to marry me, there can't be any secrets between us. It would be wrong." A shudder shook him. Clearing his throat, he said, "Sunny, I want you to know that when I proposed, it was because I'd met someone with whom I wanted to spend my life. Someone I love, respect, and admire with all my heart. And it is because I do that the conviction grew that I must lay my soul bare. It would've been unfair to expect you to make as serious a decision as marriage without knowing everything there is to know about me. The dark side. Things in my past."

A sudden chill went through Sunny. What terrible thing was Rhys about to confide?

"I've never told this to a single soul before. I thought I had put it behind me. I thought I could forget it." Watching his face intently, Sunny thought she saw him almost wince. "But before I tell you, I release you from any feeling of obligation to me whatsoever. Any necessity of giving me an answer is hereby dismissed. I am putting away the hopes I had, because I now realize those hopes were unfounded. Do you understand?"

Speechless, Sunny nodded.

"This will come as a bad shock to you. Or maybe you have suspected there was something I was holding back? You seem to have an uncanny way of seeing through people. But this I do not think you'd have ever guessed—" Rhys paused, obviously struggling with what he had come to say. "Sunny, I've killed a man. I'm a murderer."

Sunny's hand involuntarily flew to her mouth, stifling a gasp, and she felt the blood drain from her face. One look at his anguished expression, however, brought a swift reaction. She reached her hand out to him. "Oh, Rhys, there must have been reason—outlaws, robbers at the Express station . . ."

He shook his head. "No, it didn't happen out here. It was back east—as a matter of fact, in Philadelphia." He gave a harsh, derogatory laugh. "The City of Brotherly Love. I can tell you there wasn't much of *that* a few years ago. But first I should tell you a little about my background. My parents died when I was a small boy. I was sent to live with my grandmother"—a faraway look came into Rhys' eyes, for a moment dulling their intensity—"a saintly Quaker lady, and my Uncle Jason. I was reared in a home where conflict was always avoided, where any kind of violence was abhorred—that's what makes this all so incredible."

Rhys sighed, clenched and unclenched his hands, and went on. "Growing up I didn't realize it fully, but both of my relatives and their immediate circle of friends were deeply committed abolitionists. Against slavery as an institution, and the degradation it meant to the individual, both owner and slave. What I didn't know until I was twenty was that my uncle was very involved in the Underground Railroad, the secret group helping slaves to get out of the South and escape to safety, usually in Canada. I found out about it quite by accident. Coming home from college unexpectedly one night, I found they had three runaway slaves in the house. I was shaken. I knew the danger this put us all in. Uncle Jason did not want to tell me much. He felt the less I knew, the better. He was afraid that it would get me into trouble. He wanted me to finish my education. He wanted me to return to school, try to forget what I'd seen. Of course I couldn't forget. Nor did I want to. I was deeply affected by his bravery and the risk he was taking to help these oppressed people to freedom. I was young, idealistic, and now newly awakened to the abomination of slavery, fired up with what I felt it was doing to our country. The bitterness, the divisiveness, growing between the different regions of the country, eroding the unity of the nation."

Rhys paused and took a long breath before continuing. "I did return to college. But I began to attend meetings at which famous antislavery leaders were speaking. I believed ardently in what they were saying. It was confirmation of the Quaker teachings that I had been exposed to by my grandmother, the intrinsic value of each soul. Well, to make a very long story short, one night I was caught in a riot following an abolitionist meeting. Hired toughs broke into the building and mayhem ensued. They were using clubs, swinging them wildly, hitting everyone in sight. People panicked. I can't tell you what it was like. A man standing next to me was beaten to the floor. He was bleeding profusely, and as I knelt to help him I was hit on the back and shoulders several times. Then the police arrived and started arresting everyone they could put their hands on."

Rhys heaved a deep sigh. "I was grabbed, my arm twisted behind me, and dragged off, shoved into a vehicle, and taken to jail. We were booked for inciting a riot. We, the victims, not the perpetrators. We were thrown into a cell with drunks and worse—" He shuddered again at the memory. "No medieval dungeon could have been worse. It was beyond description. Filthy, cold, no place to lie down or even sit, twenty or more men crowded in a space meant for four."

He halted, shook his head. "I didn't know what to do. I knew they would distort the truth when we were hauled into court for trial. Right then I knew I had to find a way to escape. All I could think of was how to get out. We were there for three days and nights. No air, no sanitation. I cannot tell you the horror of it. The fourth night, we were marched out to the yard, and I saw my chance. There was only one guard on duty. Most of us were too weak from lack of food and air; some were sick. Anyway, I still had the strength and the desperate determination to act. I watched and waited, fell behind the others, then slipped up behind the guard and grabbed him by the throat. He struggled but I was stronger. I heard him choke, gasp for breath, but I pressed harder, and finally he went limp and slumped to the ground. I didn't stop to see if he was still living. I stepped over him and left him. I wasted no time. I vaulted over the brick wall and ran for my life."

Sunny went cold, felt herself tremble.

Rhys' voice roughened as he continued. "For days I hid in the woods, running at night, sick with fear. Hunger had weakened me. I didn't think I'd make it. I began to not care if I did. All I was afraid of was they'd recapture me and I'd have to go back to that hellhole and stand trial for something I didn't do, maybe spend the rest of my life in jail—"

His voice broke. He shook his head as if to rid it of the scene. "I can't tell you the desperate thoughts that went through my head. If I was going to die, I wanted to die a free man. I knew all the feelings, the emotions, of the escaping slaves my uncle had tried to help."

"What happened?"

"I knew I couldn't go home, contact my family, because they would then be implicated, and maybe their own actions would come to light. I couldn't risk that. If they were arrested, taken to prison themselves—well, I couldn't bring that upon those who loved me and whom I loved."

Rhys' voice again broke a little, but he managed to go on. "I traveled by night, finally made it to a farm, where I hid in a barn. I stole eggs from the henhouse and ate them raw, but at least it gave me some strength."

Rhys stood up, paced a few times back and forth before continuing. "It was quite an odyssey. A miracle, you might say. I got help. Providentially—I don't know any other way to say it—the farmers themselves were Quakers, and when I explained, they were sympathetic. They gave me food, a change of clothing. Still, I didn't want to get them in trouble, so I left, traveling blindly, still not knowing what to do. Soon I knew my absence at school would be noted; perhaps they would notify my uncle. I didn't know which way to turn. A few miles farther along I saw a "Wanted" poster . . . and knew I was now a fugitive. I started traveling farther, to the West. I thought I could lose myself, change my identity. I knew if I went back, somehow it would be known that I killed that guard, and I'd be hung. I was sick, sick of everything. Worst of all, I knew I couldn't go home."

Rhys turned to face Sunny, his face etched in agony. "I had murdered a man. I could never get that off my conscience. It haunted me day and night. I dreamed about him—that faceless man I'd grabbed from behind, choked, *killed*. He began to have a face! I thought about him all the time. Was he married? Did he have a wife, children? Perhaps by now people who loved him were grieving for him—his widow, orphans, aging parents! I nearly drove myself insane. I kept moving farther and farther west."

Rhys sat down again, buried his face in his hands. His shoulders shook under the fine wool coat. Sunny put out her hand in a spontaneous gesture of comfort, then drew it back. It didn't seem the right thing to do. Somehow she understood that her letting him pour out his soul was what he needed now.

When Rhys began to speak again, his voice was husky. "Some men might be able to forget—probably most, excusing the act because of the extraordinary circumstances. They'd call it self-preservation, tell themselves it was acceptable. But I couldn't. For me it was different." His voice broke. "I never thought I'd kill someone! Never thought I *could*. Not even in self-defense. I was supposed to be a different kind of man." He raised his head and looked at her for a long moment. "You see, Sunny, when this happened I was attending seminary, studying to become a minister."

Sunny drew in her breath. Yet this explained so much about him that had puzzled her. His aloofness, his dignity, his familiarity with the Scriptures even. Rhys went on. "For me the memory of what I'd done became a living hell." He raked his fingers through his thick hair. "I thought I could run. If I got far enough away . . ." Rhys shook his head. "But I couldn't stop mentally looking over my shoulder, expecting someone to recognize me, arrest me."

Sunny said nothing. She could think of nothing to say or do but listen to this strange tale of violence and trauma. The room was silent for a few minutes, then Rhys began to speak again, his voice calmer, steadier.

"Anyway, my original plan was to go farther west, to California. It seemed the farthest, safest place I could go. I thought it would be the ideal place for me to make a new start with a clean slate. I figured nobody out there would care where a person came from, what his past had been." His smile was ironic. "But when I got to Independence, the 'jumping-off place' for emigrants going west, I saw all sorts of opportunities no one else was taking advantage of in the rush to go to the goldfields and all that California promised. I saw these just waiting for someone with some intelligence, some vision, to develop. Like the Express business. Here. So I decided to settle here. People accepted me for what I appeared to be. I thought maybe I could make a life here, with no reminders of the past."

There was a pause and then, with another ironic smile, Rhys continued more slowly. "I had to learn that you can never lose yourself completely. Not that anyone ever *did* come to get me. I was damned by my own conscience. And when a man has that, he needs no other kind of fear." He sighed. "I tried to blot that out by drinking too much. That didn't work. Nothing worked. Until—" He looked at Sunny for a long time. "Until you, Sunny."

"*Me?*"

"Yes. You with your youth, honesty, ideals, dreams. You brought back to me all I'd left behind when I ran away. Any chance of the life I'd always planned I'd have someday, a life of purpose and meaning, shared with a woman of virtue, beauty, and character." He hesitated and then, with his voice shaking a little, he told her, "I was foolish enough to think I had paid my dues in some way." Rhys shook his head. "But now I know I can't. I was wrong to ask you to marry me, Sunny. Wrong to ask you to share a life that was dark with secrets. More than that, to share the shame of punishment that may still be in store for me if I go back east and face whatever justice my act deserves, make some kind of restitution, perhaps even go to prison."

Involuntarily Sunny gasped. Was it possible they could still convict a man for something that happened so long ago? But *murder*. She shuddered. Didn't that mean hanging? She prayed that would not be Rhys' fate.

Rhys sighed deeply and stood up. "I must go. I didn't come to beg your pity or your absolution or for you to tell me it doesn't matter. I have to figure it all out for myself. The thing that *did* matter was to tell you the truth."

"I know that," Sunny said with quick compassion.

Rhys took her hand. "Thank you, Sunny, for listening. I hope I haven't burdened you too much with what should be mine alone to bear?"

"Oh no, Rhys, please don't think that."

He kept holding her hand as though he could not relinquish it.

"Oh, Sunny, I wish to God it could have been different. I wish I could have come to you with an unsullied past, could have honestly offered you my heart with no shadows of regret. It would have been easier if you never knew. But I couldn't do that. I care too much about you." He sighed again. "Your coming into my life is a bittersweet blessing. I cannot tell you what it has meant to know you, fall in love with you. Now to have to give you up . . ."

Sunny sensed Rhys' struggle to keep a check on his emotions. She recognized it because she herself was struggling with the impulse to tell him she would stand by him, wait until he settled whatever unfinished business he had left back east. But she couldn't. She didn't love him. Not like that. Not enough. All she could be was a compassionate friend, when he wanted so much more.

"Sunny, no matter what, loving you has been the one perfect thing that's happened to me in the last six or seven years. I thank you for that." His fingers tightened around her hand, then he raised it to his lips, kissed it. She saw in his eyes the battle he was waging against passionate desire restrained by honor. He pressed her hand with both of his to his breast. She could feel his heart pounding. Finally, with an effort he said, "I really must leave."

Sunny walked to the door with him. When he opened it,

a cold wind rushed in, chilling her. She stepped back. Rhys looked at her again. This time she saw infinite tenderness in his eyes, infinite sorrow.

"Good night, Sunny. Bless you."

Sunny closed the door, stood there until the sound of Rhys' buggy wheels faded away, then she returned to the kitchen. She was shivering. Hugging her arms, she got close to the warmth of the glowing fire.

It had been an amazing evening. In the space of a few hours, so much had changed.

She wondered what Rhys would do. Go back east? Give himself up to the authorities? If he did, what would happen to the Express station, to Tracy and the other riders, to *her*?

It seemed ironic that in different ways, she had now lost the two men who had become part of her life here. Webb because he thought she was engaged to Rhys, Rhys because of his past and his conscience.

# Chapter 21

*T*wo weeks into the new year, it continued to rain off and on. Skies hung gray and heavy with clouds threatening more. Rivers were swollen; there was talk of possible floods.

One morning Sunny woke to the sound of rain pelting the window like pebbles flung by a furious hand. Groaning, she huddled into her quilt, dreading getting up. Finally she pulled herself up and out of bed, fighting the urge to dive back under the warm covers and go back to sleep. As she dressed the steady rain increased. What a morning for Tracy to have to set out on his route!

In the dim kitchen, she lit the oil lamp and set it on the drain board so she could see to make coffee. Shadow came stretching out, curling around her ankles until Sunny put down a saucer of milk for him. As she did she felt something clutch her heart. She missed Dandy, who had always greeted her with a wag of his tail, then waited patiently at the front door to be let out. She missed the dog. She missed his master too.

Determinedly Sunny thrust away the thought of Webb. What good did it do to look back in regret? He was probably not giving a thought to *her*!

She sliced bread, cheese, and ham to fix a lunch for Tracy to pack in his saddlebags. When the coffee was ready, she poured a mug, then took it in to Tracy. She bent over his bunk and shook him gently awake. A few minutes later he came into the kitchen, fully dressed but still groggy, and filled his mug again. He threw a yellow rain slicker over one of the chairs, walked over, peered out the window, and remarked, "Comin' down cats and dogs, ain't it?"

Tracy, who like everyone else had been aware of Rhys' interest in his sister, had been pleased when Sunny first told him of the proposal. When Sunny, without betraying Rhys' secret, told him that it was off by mutual agreement, he was disappointed. Since their relationship had remained stiff since their quarrel, Sunny and Tracy did not discuss it further.

Sunny had not dared bring up again the subject of going to California. She tried to think how she might revive Tracy's interest in going west. Could she persuade him to seek his fortune in California, as so many others were doing, *then* return to marry the girl he left behind?

Frying his sausage and eggs for breakfast, she wondered if this might be a good time to bring it up. Might give him time to think about it as he sloughed through the rain, wind, and mire on his route. Make him pine for sunny California. She placed his plate on the table and poured him another cup of coffee.

"You're gettin' to be some cook, Sunny," Tracy said, looking up at her with a grin.

The smile caught Sunny off guard. It was their mother's smile, the mother Tracy didn't remember. Yet there it was in his half-boy, half-man face. His thick, curly hair needed cutting, but Sunny checked her impulse to touch it tenderly. It was silky still, a child's head of hair. The gap between his two front teeth still gave him a little-boy look. Sunny felt a melting tenderness for her brother. Hadn't she practically raised him single-handedly? She felt the old protective urge. A new determination to not lose their dream of finding that distant rainbow, the two of them together, gripped Sunny. She would not let him be swayed by a temporary infatuation, not let him do something so foolish as rush into an ill-advised marriage. Impulsively she launched into the subject.

But it was the wrong moment. The words, "Tracy, I hope you haven't made any foolish promises to Betty Brownlee—" were hardly spoken when she realized she'd put the proverbial foot in her mouth. She should have talked about California first, not mentioned Betty.

Tracy gave her a furious look. His jaw jutted, his expression hard, his eyes cold, he shoved back his chair, stood up, flung his napkin down on the table beside his unfinished breakfast.

"I ain't going to discuss Betty with you, Sis. You don't like her. Without even gettin' to know her. Without even tryin' to. And this ain't a good time to talk about going to California. You don't seem to realize everything's changed." He strode over to the coatrack, grabbed his jacket, and shrugged into it. "Just because things have turned sour for you don't mean I've got to go along with your ideas, Sunny. I've quit tagging along after you like some little puppy. From now on, *I* decide what I want or don't want to do. Now I gotta go." Grabbing his hat and mail pouch, Tracy stormed out, letting the door slam after him.

For a minute she stood looking after him in shock. His shouted words and the banging of the door reverberated in her ears. At first she felt a reactive rush of anger. What had got into Tracy? Couldn't she even talk to him anymore, express an opinion, make a suggestion? Full of indignation at the way he had treated her, she snatched her shawl from the peg beside the door and stepped out onto the porch. The wind knifed through her, and she pulled the woolen shawl closer as she stomped down the steps and through the puddled yard to the barn.

Her brother was tightening a pony's girth and strapping on the saddlebags when she entered. "Tracy—," she began.

"No, don't start in on me, Sunny. I said all I mean to say on the subject. This ain't no time to discuss goin' to California. Right now I got to get on my route. The mail's got to get through—and it's gonna be a hard ride this day."

Sunny realized he was right. She couldn't have picked a worse time. Sunny said, "All right, but we will have to sometime."

"I said leave it alone, Sunny!" Tracy mumbled. He adjusted the bridle on the pony and backed him out of the stall. Sunny had to step back as he walked the pony to the open barn door.

Unwilling to let him go like this, with all this anger between them, she called, "Wait! Wait, please wait." But if he heard her, Tracy gave no sign. He swung himself up onto the pony's back, gave it a quick prod with his spurs, and without a backward look galloped out toward the station gate. He was soon lost from sight in a gray veil of rain.

She knew her brother was very angry. And it frightened her. It was her fault again. The ancient adage "Fools rush in where angels fear to tread" rebuked her. Just as her stepmother had predicted years ago: *Your tongue is your worst enemy.* Hadn't Webb Chandler said almost the very same thing to her? Truth, no matter what the source, was hard to take. This break with Tracy, further eroding the closeness they'd once had, was almost too much.

Sunny returned to the house feeling burdened and disconsolate. The sense of loss was heavy. All the things that mattered to her were slipping away. Perhaps even her dream of going to California, which had sustained her so long. Was she to lose everything? Even her brother's love?

The weather did not help. Fresh bursts of rain continued

during the long, lonely day. Late in the afternoon the storm broke with an unleashed fury. Wind slashed at the windows, sending the rain pounding against the panes. The wild sound of the storm made Sunny shudder; it was as if even nature bore a grudge against her. The walls of the Express station building seemed to close in upon her, while outside the storm raged. She tried to read and distract herself, but all she could think of was her brother on his dangerous trip in this terrible night.

Finally she went to bed, but sleep eluded her. She shivered as she lay there and listened to the wind howling, rattling the windows, and hissing down the chimney.

*Dear God, please protect Tracy. Keep him safe, Lord, and guard him as he rides.* Her prayer was repetitive, while her thoughts zigzagged from Tracy to her own dilemma. What was she to do now that Tracy no longer wanted to go west?

That same evening, Webb Chandler left Rhys Graham's office in a muddled state of mind. This was something he'd not counted on. Maybe he'd thought he could find out something just by casual conversation, a little prodding. But he sure hadn't expected the information he'd got.

Rhys Graham was selling out, going back east. Leaving Missouri. No real explanation other than he wanted to move on, do something else with his life.

Webb had been too shocked to be tactful. Jolted by the surprise of Graham's statement, Webb had stammered, "But I thought—I mean, I heard you were probably going to get married, settle down—" He flushed, realizing he was repeating gossip.

A rueful smile lifted the corner of Rhys' mouth slightly. He shook his head. "No, I'm afraid that's not so. There's no truth to whatever you've heard, Webb."

Webb also realized Rhys Graham was too much of a gentleman to discuss a lady, so the next question that sprang to his mind couldn't be asked. The fact that Rhys was pulling up stakes, giving up a lucrative business, and leaving Missouri could only mean one thing. Either he had asked Sunny and been turned down or there had never been anything to the rumors.

It gave a man pause, that's for sure. Had he got things figured all wrong? Maybe he should go out and talk to Verna and Clem. They were like the folks he'd never had—they always treated him as if he belonged to them. Maybe Verna would straighten him out on Sunny Lyndall. Webb shook his head. Women! They sure were a mysterious breed. He couldn't understand them. Used to be he could take 'em or leave 'em. Mostly he'd got along pretty well with the ones he was interested in. Not that he'd ever done any serious courting. But this was different. Webb leaned against the post of the boardwalk and surveyed the scene. Rain coming down in sheets. Main Street a river of mud. Should he ride out and face Sunny tonight, just come right out and say what was on his mind, in his heart?

A picture of her floated into his mind. Webb remembered the first time he had seen her, his first impression of her. The small, determined chin, the wide, lovely eyes that held fear she was trying too hard to hide, the soft, pretty mouth, its lower lip trembling a little—still, even then he had recognized grit, courage, spirit. Something he admired greatly in a man, a horse, *or* a woman. Something he hadn't seen a lot of in any of these. But Sunny had it. He remembered thinking at the time that she was feisty, though, like an unbroken colt.

Of course, he felt and thought much differently about her now. He saw so much more in her than that first male admiration of a pretty woman. He saw a strength more than beauty, a character honed by hardship, a stubbornness refined to a determination to endure.

She still looked fragile somehow, as if in spite of everything she needed taking care of. The question was, would she let anyone, would she let *him*? He knew he would have to choose his words carefully. Not tread on her new independence, her confidence gained by what she had done. Yet he wanted to let her know how much he cared, how much he wanted her.

Still, it might not be a good idea to ride out there tonight. Might frighten her if he came out like that in the middle of a storm. Might take her by surprise, get her dander up, like other times he'd come unannounced.

No, he'd wait until tomorrow. Think of some reason to ride out. What he didn't know. He'd think of something. Doggone it. Why did the idea seem so—well, so uncomfortable? All she could do was turn him down, say no.

Webb moved on to the small house he had rented since his return. He walked past the hotel, from which he could hear the sounds of the tinny piano. He imagined the smoky scene inside, the loud voices, the clink of glasses, and the smell of tobacco. That didn't interest him anymore somehow. Not that it ever did much. He'd just gone there out of loneliness mostly. He thought of the kitchen at the Express station. Sunny had sure fixed it up bright and cozy, with the walls whitewashed and the little flowered curtains. Something in Webb pictured what it might be like to have a home of his own, to be sitting with his feet up on the stove's fender, looking over at Sunny, the lamplight sending little sparks of light through her hair and onto the sweet curve of her cheek as she worked on some sewing, maybe mending some socks—*his* socks!

Man! If *that* wasn't wishful thinking. More than likely the truer picture would be Sunny riding beside him or galloping on ahead, looking back over her shoulder, laughing at him, daring him to catch her. The possibility of losing what he'd never had made Webb feel as though a steel band were tightening around his chest.

# Chapter 22

*U*nable to sleep, Sunny got up toward dawn and peered out into the darkness. The rain had become a steady downpour whipped by a ferocious wind. She shuddered. Soon she would have to brave the gale to go out to the barn and feed the ponies. Drawing her shawl close around her shivering shoulders, she went out to the kitchen, stoked the fire, put the kettle on the stove. Where was Tracy out in all this? Had he reached the next station safely?

Prayer for her brother came as naturally as measuring coffee into the pot. *Lord, please be with him as he rides, protect him*—The words of the psalmist, memorized in childhood, sprang spontaneously into her mind: *O God, our refuge and our strength, a very present help in trouble*—

Trouble, danger, peril of all kinds, were a rider's constant companions on the trail. Although Tracy had been lucky so far, other riders had had accidents. Sunny felt a sharp twinge of fear but quickly thrust it away. *It's just me*, she told herself. *My own uncertainties, anxieties*—

She poured herself a steaming cup of coffee, held it in both hands to warm them, and brought it to her mouth. If only they hadn't quarreled before Tracy left. If anything happened to him ... Sunny felt a hollow sensation. A premonition? She gave herself a mental shake. That was simply superstitious. She was feeling guilty, that was all. She'd make it up to him when he got back, tell him she was sorry.

Trying to escape from these dark thoughts, she got on with her chores. But a strange restlessness kept her uneasy. For some reason she kept going to the window, looking out into the gray, misted landscape. Once in a while she glanced at the clock. Tracy should be safe at the other station by now, she thought. Probably sound asleep. Not worrying about her or their quarrel. Her strange apprehensions were all just her overwrought imagination.

Then, on one of these seemingly pointless trips to the window, she saw a figure stumbling through the Express yard gate. As she watched he staggered forward, grabbed one of the corral posts, clung to it. For a moment she could not move. Then she recognized the yellow poncho. The man was one of the Express riders! Her next thought was, *Tracy?* With a horrified gasp Sunny whirled from the window and bolted out of the building. Outside she ran, slipping and sliding on rain-slick mud, toward the man slumped against the rails of the corral. Reaching him, she saw her worst fear realized. It *was* Tracy. His face was blood-streaked and swollen, one eye nearly closed. He had kept himself from falling completely only by holding with one hand to one of the rails; his other arm hung uselessly at his side.

"Tracy! My God, what happened?"

One eyelid opened with effort. A glint of recognition flickered briefly. "Ambushed. Attacked. . . . Looked like Injuns," he mumbled hoarsely.

On her knees in the mud beside him, Sunny placed her arm around his shoulders to help him stand. He let out an agonized groan. "No! Don't touch me. . . . I think some ribs are broke—my arm's been shot, too. Tried to fight 'em off, but there were three of them. . . . They beat me up pretty bad, and—"

"Never mind that now. You can tell me later. First we've got to get you inside. Here, hold on to me—I'll try to be careful."

Sunny was weeping, her tears mixing with the rain that fell steadily and soaked her hair and dress. "It's a wonder you weren't killed."

"I played dead, or they would have finished me off," moaned Tracy. "I managed to lie on top of one of the mailbags. They got off with everything else."

"Where's the pony?"

"Spooked—run off. They were shootin' and hollerin'. It's a wonder it was only my arm they hit."

Sunny used all her strength pushing and pulling Tracy to his feet amid his heart-wrenching moans, telling him, "Hold on to the corral railing as long as you can, then lean on me, and I think we can make it up to the porch."

Tracy's breathing was shallow. Sunny knew he was close to the end of his endurance. How far must he have come from his attack? His clothes were sodden. He might have been unconscious, lying out in the rain for hours. Through her anguish at her brother's condition, Sunny prayed. *Dear God, help us, please. Give me the strength to get him inside. Please, please.*

Afterward Sunny wasn't sure how they managed to drag themselves up the steps and into the building. Her tears streamed helplessly as she got him onto the bed in her room, which was the closest. The leather mailbag Tracy had concealed and then stashed in the large inner pocket of his rain slicker dropped to the floor, and she kicked it out of the way while she attended to her brother. His hat, with its dripping brim, had fallen off as Tracy collapsed, a dead weight, onto the bed. She removed his soaked boots, then covered him with a blanket.

Looking down at him, Sunny stifled a sob. Gently she brushed back the thick hair that was plastered to his forehead by the rain and blood. His face was ashen. Both eyes were nearly shut, and she realized he was slipping into unconsciousness. He was probably in shock from loss of blood and the stabbing pain of his arm and broken ribs.

What to do? Should she leave him? Ride into town, get the doctor? Sunny stood by the bedside, looking down at her wounded brother in a confusion of indecision. The slightest move caused him agony. She could see his arm was in pretty bad shape. She would have no idea how deep the gash on his head was until she washed away the dirt and blood. It probably needed to be stitched. *Oh, dear Lord, what shall I do?*

The old adage "First things first" activated her. Disregarding her own wet clothes, Sunny hurried into the kitchen and put water on to boil. She filled a basin with hot water and carried it back into the bedroom. Tracy was moving his head from side to side on the pillow, mumbling incoherently. Sunny put her hand against his cheek, and it was burning: he had a fever.

"I'm here, Tracy. I'm going to take care of you," she murmured soothingly. As gently as possible, she lifted his arm, biting her lip as Tracy let out a groan. With her sewing scissors, she cut through the leather jacket and flannel shirt. It took some doing, but she finally was able to examine the wound. It seemed the bullet had torn the flesh but not lodged in or shattered the bone. However, the wound bled profusely. She staunched the blood temporarily with the wadded material from his shirt. Then she ran to get some of the cotton batting Verna had given her to use as underpadding for the quilt top she had started. This she folded, and with strips she tore off one of her clean petticoats, she wrapped and tied it securely for a bandage on the jagged wound. Tracy might need stitches later, but for now this would keep him from losing too much blood.

That done, Sunny looked at his forehead. Her hand

trembled as she took a folded cloth, dipped it in the water, and began to remove the crusted blood from his forehead. Tracy flinched and she withdrew it quickly. Fresh blood began to trickle out of the cut. His eyes opened and they were glazed. For a second they focused, and then he recognized her.

"Sunny, you gotta saddle up one of the ponies. I gotta get back on the trail, carry the mail through. Fred Miller's waiting for me—" He tried to struggle into a sitting position, but the pain was too severe, and he fell back against the pillows with a spontaneous cry.

Sunny knew he meant that the rider at the next station depended on receiving the mail from this one so he could carry it on to the next. But she knew what Tracy in his delirium didn't. He was in no possible condition to ride now—or anytime in the near future. She also knew she had to keep Tracy calm, or he would do something more to injure himself. A sudden move would put him in danger of one of the broken ribs piercing his lungs. Then there would be no hope. At all costs, she had to keep him still.

The only medicines they had on hand were bicarbonate of soda, iodine, eucalyptus oil, and a tiny bottle of tincture of opium, which the doctor in Cartersville had once given Tracy when he went there with a toothache. She wasn't sure whether it had cured his toothache, but it *had* put him sound asleep for a number of hours. Maybe that was what she should give him.

She went to get it, measured several drops into a small tumbler of water, then took it in to Tracy. Raising his head gently, she pressed the glass between his lips, forcing the liquid into his mouth. He sputtered, coughed, then swallowed at least part of the dosage.

Exhausted from all the effort, Sunny started out of the room. She wanted to get out of her wet clothes, which clung to her chillingly. As she was about to leave Tracy mumbled something. She went back over to the bed. Seeing him so battered, bruised, filled her with tenderness. This was her little brother, but he was a man—a brave one who had courageously battled the band of ruthless Indians and outwitted them. At least he had salvaged part of the mail he'd sworn to protect. He had lived up to his responsibility.

As she leaned over him Tracy licked his dry, parched lips, lifted his head and tried to say something. Sunny knelt down beside the bed, bending close to hear what he was saying.

"The mail . . . gotta get through—"

She eased him back onto the pillow. "Hush, hush. Don't worry." A wild thought entered her mind. "It's taken care of." Even as she spoke the words Sunny knew what she had to do.

In the months she had worked at the Express station, Sunny had learned and understood the importance of the mail getting through on time. Payrolls, telegrams, mail, medicines that people were waiting for, cash, even jewelry—a wedding ring for an anxious bride and a nervous bridegroom, as well as less sentimental things. Everyone relied on the intrepid riders to come through the rain, sleet, or snow. . . . Tracy, a true Pony Express rider, had risked his very life to protect the mail.

Everything combined to argue Sunny out of the idea that had come and burrowed into her mind: the weather outside worsened with every passing minute, and she worried about leaving Tracy alone and unattended. Still, the idea lodged ruthlessly in her brain. Why not? It was only ten miles. Ten *hard* miles, in a terrible downpour, she reminded herself. But hadn't she ridden six miles each way to school every day for years, with Tracy behind her on the saddle when he got old enough to go? Hadn't their father always declared she could ride as well as any boy? Her stepmother had wailed over the fact that she rode astride. And until Matilda put a stop to it, she'd ridden bareback whenever she had a chance. Hadn't she taken care of the ponies all these months? They knew her; she could handle any of them, especially Jericho.

It seemed the right thing to do, the *only* thing. If she rode into town and told Rhys that he would have to find a relief rider, time would be lost. Riding over to the Ardleys to ask Verna to come would waste precious moments.

Sunny changed the cloth on Tracy's burning brow. Wringing out a new one in cool water and placing it on his fevered forehead, she heard herself saying, "It's all right, Tracy. Someone's taking it. It'll get there."

Leaving him, she quickly unbuttoned her dress, stepped out of it, unfastened her petticoats, and let them drop to the floor. She grabbed a pair of Tracy's jeans that had been hanging on the drying rack near the stove and pulled them on. Next she put on a flannel shirt and dragged on her boots.

Just to be certain he would sleep until she returned, Sunny measured out a few more drops of the opium tincture, mixed it with water, and returned to the bedroom. She tilted Tracy's head up a little, forced open his mouth enough to get the rest down. That surely would keep him asleep for a couple of hours. She hated leaving him, but she had to get started before the rain turned to sleet.

If only there were someone she could depend on. If only someone would come to help. But there was no one. She only had herself to rely on. And God. She would have to trust that she was doing the right thing and that God would take care of Tracy and her. If, after she delivered the mail to the next station, she turned around and came right back, she still would not get back before noon tomorrow. She would have to trust God to protect them both.

Hastily she twisted her hair up into a knot, then jammed a woolen stocking cap over her head and ears and put Tracy's suede slouch hat on over it, drawing the leather thongs tight under her chin. Then she went to the bedroom door to take a last look at her brother. His breathing came heavily but regularly. *He'll be all right. Please, God.* No matter her anxiety, she couldn't linger. To make up for the lost time, she had to leave now.

She picked up the mailbag and went back to the kitchen just as there was a loud, insistent banging on the front door. A tremor of fear passed through her. Had those savages followed Tracy back to the station, bent on getting more loot? She hesitated there a minute while the banging continued. She realized she hadn't bolted the door. She glanced over to where the shotgun hung on the wall. Did she have a chance to get to it before they broke in? There wasn't time. The door, caught by the strong wind, swung open and banged against the wall. There on the threshold stood Webb Chandler.

Relief exploded through Sunny. "Oh, thank God, Webb! You're an answer to prayer!"

At this unexpected greeting he look stunned. A smile tugged at his mouth, and he started to say something comical in response, when his startled gaze took in her altered appearance. "Why in the world are you git up like *that*? You look like a dadgum *boy!*"

"I don't have time to explain," she said. "Tracy's been hurt on his route."

"What do you mean, hurt? How?"

"He was attacked by Indians. He fought them off, saved a mailbag—but a bullet got him in the arm, I'm afraid. Anyway, Webb, will you ride over and get Verna? Then get Doctor Hayes?"

"Well sure, but—" Webb frowned. His puzzled gaze swept over her again. Sunny looked slim as a young boy in the well-worn jeans, and the old, gray felt hat that was pulled down over her ears concealed the sunshine gold hair. "What the blazes are you doing in that getup?"

Sunny was sure that he would object to her plan, but she had no time to argue. The situation was too desperate.

"I'm going to take Tracy's route, get the mail through."

"You out of your mind? You can't do that!"

"No?" She turned away and drew on leather gloves, saying, "Just watch me!"

"You little fool! You can't. That's no job for a woman."

In a few quick strides Webb crossed the room. He grabbed her arm, swinging her around. His grip was so tight it hurt, and she reacted. Her other hand swept up and smacked his face. As her fingers felt the sting of the slap Sunny gasped. She had never struck anyone in her life before. Instantly she felt sick and ashamed. Immediately something snapped. The built-up tension of the past twenty-four hours—the quarrel with Tracy, her remorse, followed by the shock of his return—suddenly broke loose like a cracked damn. She burst into tears.

For a single second Webb's grip on her arms tightened, then his hands loosened and he drew her into his arms, holding her securely. He cradled her gently, rocking her a little against him. For a moment she sobbed, then pulled away and looked up at him.

"I've got to do it, Webb. The other riders are waiting—it's what Tracy would want. You *know* I can ride."

"That's not it. It's too dangerous. Those Indians, they may still be out there somewhere. No, Sunny. *I'll* go."

She shook her head, stepping back out of his arms. "You can't. You aren't an Express company employee. I am."

"I won't let you go." His mouth tightened. "Besides, Graham would have me strung up if I did."

The mention of Rhys brought a flush into Sunny's pale face.

"I'm going with you and that's it," Webb said stubbornly.

"All right. But first couldn't you get Verna? Tell her what's happened, see if she'll stay here with Tracy? I've given him a heavy dose of laudanum. He'll sleep for hours."

"Right. Clem can go for the doctor. OK. I'll make it as fast as I can." He gave her a little shake, his eyes riveted on hers. "Promise me you won't leave until I get back?"

"Yes, I promise," Sunny nodded, then as Webb turned to leave she said, "Webb, I'm sorry about slapping you."

He gave her a small salute. "I understand."

After Webb left, Sunny went back to the bedroom to check on Tracy. He hadn't moved an inch. He was breathing evenly. She drew the covers higher over his chest and shoulders. "Dear God, watch over him, please," she whispered. "And thank you for bringing Webb."

She hurried back to the kitchen, put on Tracy's heavy jacket, and went out to the barn to saddle Jericho. It had stopped raining momentarily, but the sky was still dark with clouds.

Sunny led the pony out of his stall, slipped the bridle and bit on him, threw the folded blanket over him. She was tightening his girth, securing the saddle, when she heard the sound of hooves. A minute later Webb entered the barn. "Verna's on her way in her buggy. Clem'll ride into town for Doc Hayes," he told her. "Can I ride one of the other ponies? I rode my own horse pretty hard; he's probably not good for the long trail to the next station."

Quickly Sunny got Plato out of his stall, and together they got him saddled and ready to ride. After buckling the mail-bag under her saddle, Sunny swung up onto her pony's back. Webb led both ponies out of the barn and shoved the doors closed. Webb and Sunny were both silent with tension.

"All set?" Webb asked. "Then good luck and God bless!" he said between clenched teeth.

"You too," she said and gave her pony a slap on the flanks, a kick in the ribs with her boot, then she and Webb galloped forward.

They had not gone far when they ran into heavy rain. Sunny dug her spurs in and hunched over the pony's neck. Wind and rain stung her eyes. The trail was rougher than she had figured. Once or twice Jericho seemed to stumble and slide on the muddy ground. Maybe Webb was right. Maybe what she was doing was foolhardy. Maybe it would have been wiser to go into town, get one of the regular riders. But all that would have taken too much time. Tracy was sworn to the duty of making his schedules—no matter what. She would try not to let her brother down.

They rode for miles over the rugged terrain, Sunny in front, Webb following closely. The sound of his pony's hoofbeats back there made her feel safer somehow. But ahead loomed darkness and uncertainty.

The trail seemed to go on forever, and Sunny was beginning to search anxiously for signs of the station. Suddenly she heard Webb shout behind her. She tugged on her reins to slow Jericho down as he came riding alongside her.

"You ride on ahead, Sunny. I'm going to double back. I saw something suspicious I want to check out."

Before she could ask what it was, Webb whirled his pony around and soon was lost in the rain that now came down in sheets, obscuring her view. Her heart pumped wildly. Had he seen the marauding Indians who attacked Tracy? Maybe they should have alerted the sheriff about the mail robbery. Then he could have rounded up deputies to form a posse to go after them. She hadn't thought of that. Now Webb was putting himself in danger. Not for the Express company but for *her*. She'd misjudged him, all right. Even tonight. There had been something in the set of his jaw, in his eyes, even after she slapped him, that her heart instinctively recognized. When this night was over, she'd have a lot to make up for to that man. But after what she'd done, would Webb Chandler forgive her? She couldn't think about all this now. All that was important was making these next miles ahead.

As she rode through the lonely night Sunny knew fear in all its starkness. She was so scared that she could hear her blood pounding in her ears. Hostile Indians might be lurking anywhere along the trail. Everyone knew the Pony Express mail route. They could be waiting around the next bend. Her lungs pushed the breath up and out through her mouth as she leaned over the pony's neck. Riding astride on a saddle contoured for a man was difficult; she'd always preferred riding bareback. The reins cut into her palms even through the worn leather gloves.

The wind whipped her hair into her eyes, and the rain plastered it to her forehead. Was there no end to this? Every breath she took burned her lungs, and her face felt raw from the sting of the wind. She had not ridden this long or this far in years. Every muscle ached. Her wrists were growing weak, and she had to grit her teeth to keep some strength in her hands. Her fingers cramped as she clung to the reins, urging the tiring pony onward.

Where was Webb? Had anything happened to him? Had the Indians lain in wait for the next rider, planning to attack again? She strained to hear the comforting sound of Plato's hooves behind her. She longed to feel the assurance that Webb was back on the trail again. But all she heard was the whistle of the wind in her ears. She prayed, "Oh, God, an ever present help—" The words were carried away in the wind.

Finally she saw a faint light far ahead. Peering through the darkness and the rain, she saw the outline of a building. Jericho, exhausted now from being ridden so hard, tripped and almost stumbled. She jerked his head up with a sharp pull of the reins. She knew that must be the Express station. She halted the pony and slid off, grabbing the reins in one half-frozen hand. She staggered forward, dragging the pony with her. The wind-driven rain almost blinded her. Then she saw a lantern swinging in front of her. With extreme effort she took a few more slogging steps. The wind was behind her now, pushing her, thrusting her forward.

"Hello!" a voice called.

"Hello!" she shouted back with her remaining strength. "I'm here! Rider with the mail!"

# Chapter 23

*S*unny opened heavy-lidded eyes and for a moment did not know where she was. The room into which she awakened was dark. A narrow wedge of light shone through a ragged canvas cloth, a makeshift curtain pulled over a window high in the wall opposite where she was lying. She lay there for a second, dull with sleep and confusion. Then she remembered. She had made it! Barely able to walk, she had staggered into the Cartersville Express station, where the rider was ready, his pony saddled to take the mail on to the next station.

She had been almost too tired to do more than take a few scalding sips from the mug of bitter coffee someone thrust at her. Then Sunny took the blanket he handed her and went into the riders' sleeping quarters. A jerk of the station manager's thumb indicated the way. Without bothering to remove her hat or boots, she wrapped the blanket around herself and slumped onto the lower bunk. Her last thought before falling into a dense slumber was the desperate hope that Webb was all right.

That was also her thought as she lay awake now. All the events of last night rushed into her consciousness. Webb. Tracy. Feeling uncomfortable from having slept in clothes and rain-stiffened leather boots, Sunny began to raise herself up on her elbows, when she heard two men's voices coming from the other room.

"Nah, our rider got off—a little late, but with this kind of weather all along the Missouri border, they know down the line we might be slower than usual getting through."

"That was some attack, but they weren't Indians after all. They was rigged up like Indians—headbands, feathers—to give that idea. Three no-good outlaws. All of 'em got a price on their heads. Lookin' for gold they'd heard was in the mail."

"Is the kid they ambushed all right?"

"He'll be out of commission for a spell. But nuthin' too serious."

"Could have been killed, that's for sure."

"Could've been worse, and that's a fact."

"The mail got through, though."

"Durned brave youngster that did it."

"Very brave."

"Not many young fellas would do that—storm and all."

Slowly Sunny swung her legs over the edge of the bunk. Holding on to the splintery post of the bunk bed, she pulled herself into a standing position. Every muscle cried out in protest. Her whole body was sore. Taking careful steps, she moved to the door, hoping she could better hear what else was being said in the other room. The squeaking floorboards made her miss the next part of the conversation. What she *did* hear was an astonished exclamation.

"A *girl*? You say that was a *girl* come in here last night?"

"A very brave young woman," a new voice said. Sunny was startled. That was *Rhys'* voice! "It's her brother who was hurt. She rode for him. That's the main reason I drove over here this morning. To take her back to our station."

Sunny drew a long breath, then held it. So Rhys had driven over to get her himself? Where was Webb? And what

215

had happened? Curiosity banished any thought of her appearance. Sunny pushed back the flimsy canvas curtain that separated the riders' sleeping quarters from the office. At her entrance all three men turned to look at her. Two of the faces wore expressions of amazement, as though the men did not quite believe what they saw. Only Rhys' face was unreadable. What was it she saw there? Before she could say anything, he crossed the room.

Speaking in a low voice so the others might not hear, he said, "Sunny, you shouldn't have—it was much too dangerous, too much of a risk. You should have sent for me. I'd have found another rider." Then he spoke more loudly. "You and your brother are both a credit to the Express company. We shall certainly see that you are rewarded for your bravery."

"And Webb?" Sunny asked through dry lips. "Webb Chandler? Is he all right?"

"Another brave one. When he had seen you safely to almost within sight of this station, he went back to check something strange he'd noticed a little off the trail. He came upon the three men who attacked Tracy. They were camped in a makeshift shelter, out of the storm. They'd built a fire, and Webb had seen its glimmer and suspected it might lead to something. He got off his horse and crept up on them. They were huddled together, passing a bottle around. They all were half drunk. It looked as if they might have been planning to wait for the next rider—who knows what they were up to?"

"Was Webb—I mean, he wasn't hurt or anything?"

"He's fine." At her anxious question, something curious flickered in Rhys' eyes. "He says in their condition he didn't have too much trouble getting their firearms, then trussin' them up and bringing all three back to jail. Webb found headbands and feathers at the camp—they'd tried to pass themselves off as Indians. The sheriff said they've all got warrants out on them. They're in custody now. So all's well that ends well." He smiled slightly. "Now, I'm sure you want to get home, see your brother, and—"

Suddenly Sunny was conscious of her straggly, uncombed hair, the fact that she was still dressed in Tracy's jeans and shirt. Standing beside Rhys, who was, as usual, impeccably groomed and immaculate, made her feel even worse. But there was nothing she could do about it. After bidding the two still-astounded Express station employees an awkward good-bye, she left with Rhys.

Outside Rhys helped Sunny up into the seat beside him in the buggy. She felt self-conscious with no skirts to spread over her knees and felt ridiculous as she folded her hands demurely in her jean-clad lap. Before Rhys picked up the reins and urged his horse to start, he glanced over at her and said softly, "Thank God you weren't hurt, Sunny. When I think what could have happened, what those rene-gades might have done if they had caught up with you . . . I don't know what I would have done—" He didn't finish his thought. He gave the horse a flick with the reins, and they moved forward.

The first person Sunny saw when she walked into the Express station was Verna Ardley. She might not have looked like an angel to anyone else, but to Sunny she certainly did. Good smells were wafting through the place from whatever Verna was cooking. Tracy, pale but on his feet, his arm in a sling, was grinning from ear to ear.

Sunny felt tears gather in her eyes at the sight of her brother, but when she rushed toward him, he backed away, holding up his one good arm.

"Whoa! No hugs! I gotta couple of cracked ribs!"

That brought laughter and more tears, and even Verna joined in, wiping her eyes on her apron. She soon took charge. "I've got water on boiling so's you kin have a nice, hot bath and git out of them clothes," she told Sunny.

"Not that I *need* it!" Sunny laughed, only too glad to obey.

Using his good arm, Tracy helped Verna drag the tin bathtub into Sunny's bedroom. Then he carried in a bucket of hot water to fill it. Verna followed with a kettle of boiling water to add to it for the right temperature. "There now," she said with satisfaction. "Go to it. We'll have supper on the table when you finish."

Never had a warm bath and soap been so welcome or felt so good. Resting her head on the edge of the tub, Sunny closed her eyes. The sensation of comfort and safety was mingled with the feeling of accomplishment, of having overcome fear, flouted danger, pushed herself beyond expectation. Perhaps for the first time she *really* understood Tracy's pride in being a Pony Express rider.

Dressed in fresh clothes and feeling herself again except for some lingering stiffness and soreness, Sunny went back out into the kitchen. Clem Ardley had arrived, and he added his hearty congratulations to the others Sunny had received, declaring, "It was the durndest thing for a little slip of a girl to do I'd ever heard tell of."

While she basked in his admiration Sunny noticed with a small twinge that Rhys was gone. In all the confusion he must have slipped out. Hadn't anyone thought to ask him to stay for supper? She didn't have long to dwell on the omission, because Verna, turning from the stove, announced, "Come on, sit down, folks, or else everything'll get cold."

They all gathered at the table, and Verna said a heartfelt grace. "Heavenly Father, we do thank you tonight for the safe return of loved ones, for your gracious protection, and for your bountiful provision of this food which we are about to partake." She said her "amen" like a question, and everyone echoed it enthusiastically.

While they consumed a savory stew and cornbread, followed by sweet potato pie and apple cake, Sunny picked up all the missing pieces of the harrowing story of her brother's attack. Then she told a rapt audience of her own part of the episode. She was sure all the details of the Lyndalls' adventure would be repeated and discussed around the potbellied stove at the store for weeks to come. When the Ardleys finally left, Sunny was barely able to keep her eyes open and hardly remembered climbing into her own clean, sheeted bed.

The following morning Sunny woke up early. She lay there relishing the fact that she was safe and sound, then she wondered about Webb. Why hadn't he ridden out to see her? To find out how she had weathered her wild ride? There had been something so caring, so protective, in the way he had treated her the other night—even after she'd slapped him! It was as if he'd really understood. There had been no condescension in his attitude. He had accepted her decision to ride and given her due respect, acknowledging that she was capable of doing it. That meant more than he'd ever know. She also remembered how she felt when he held her, how she was tempted to remain there, secure, sheltered, and then how knowing he was riding with her had given her courage.

After what they had gone through together, she would have thought that he—but then, she had never been able to figure out Webb Chandler. What he thought or how he felt. Would Webb Chandler always be an unanswered question in her heart? Sunny dared not explore her feelings for him too closely. She feared having her heart broken. It was better not to think of what might have been. Better to burn her bridges behind her when she and Tracy left here. *If* she and Tracy went on to California, she amended. She still wasn't sure about her brother's plans.

Even though it was early, she couldn't go back to sleep. She looked in on Tracy, who was still sleeping like a baby, then tiptoed past his room. Grinding coffee in the kitchen, she still couldn't seem to stop thinking about Webb. Then suddenly she heard the clatter of hooves outside. Hope leaped up in her heart, and she rushed to open the door. When she saw it was not Webb but Rhys Graham, she quickly hid her disappointment. He came up the steps, smiled, and handed her a bouquet of early tulips and jonquils.

"For a very special lady," he said. "May I come in? I have something important to say to you and your brother."

"Tracy's still asleep."

"In that case, don't disturb him, please. Anyway, I have some things I'd like to discuss privately with you."

"Come in then. I've just made fresh coffee," she invited.

"I can't stay long," he said, following her through the office into the kitchen. "First I want to extend the Express company's gratitude to both of you for your loyal, brave actions in protecting the mail and, at great risk, carrying it through to the next station." He placed a small leather bag on the table. "That is only a small token in comparison to the fact that you both put your lives on the line. If anything had happened to you—to *either* of you—I would have never forgiven myself." He paused. "Of course, I have enough to forgive myself for as it is—as *you* already know."

With a slight shake of her head and a dismissing gesture, Sunny indicated that he need say no more. She poured him a mug of coffee. But Rhys made no movement to take it. Instead he went on seriously.

"Since we talked, since I told you about … everything, I've made a decision, the *only* decision I could make. I've at last come to the conclusion that although nothing will erase what I did, my only salvation will be to make something out of all this pain. I can't give that man back his life, but I *can* do something with the rest of mine. Something better, more worthwhile, than making money and trying to forget the past." He drew a long breath. "So I've decided to go back east, back to the seminary, finish my training, then spend what life I have left doing whatever the Lord purposes, wherever he sends me. I don't mean to sound pretentious—" He broke off as if embarrassed.

"It doesn't sound pretentious, Rhys. It sounds humble—and very sincere."

He looked at her fondly. "Thank you, Sunny. You always seem to know the right thing to say."

She had the grace to blush. "Oh no, not always! In fact, I know other people who would take quite the opposite view of that," she said lightly.

Rhys smiled, too. "Well anyway, besides bringing you the reward money, I've come to say good-bye. I've sold the Express station, and I'm taking the noon train. There was no use to delay once I'd made up my mind."

All at once Sunny felt a lump rise in her throat. She felt an unexpected sorrow, a regret that she had not been able to love this man—at least, not enough. She realized that Rhys Graham had come to mean a great deal to her and that she would never forget him.

They stood for a moment looking at each other. Then, as with immense effort, Rhys moved toward the door. Sunny went with him. There his eyes moved over her, almost as if he were memorizing her face, and he said, "I want you to know how much knowing you has meant to me, Sunny. You were, without knowing, God's instrument in my life." He opened the door and stepped out onto the porch, then turned and spoke quietly, unable to keep the sadness out of his voice. "I wish you all good things in whatever lies ahead for you and your brother."

This was, they both knew, farewell. They would probably never see each other again.

That night, Sunny and Tracy sat up talking long into the night. Drinking mug after mug of coffee, they shared the way brother and sister had never done before.

When they had counted the award money, the amount stunned them both. It felt like finding the pot of gold at the end of the proverbial rainbow. It doubled the money Sunny had put in their nest egg.

Tracy's eyes regarded Sunny with new respect. "I still can't get over your doing what you did, Sunny. If it hadn't been for you—well, none of this would be happenin'." He lowered his head and, looking embarrassed, said, "And I want you to know I'm really sorry about—you know—giving you a hard time. I can't go back to riding for quite a spell, Doc Hayes says, and besides, I've been thinkin' a lot about what you said. I really ain't ready to take on a wife and family. I mean Betty's a nice girl and all, but—well, I been thinkin', and I think we should go on with our plans. Go to California."

"Really, Tracy? That's what you *really* want to do?"

"Yep, I sure do, Sunny." He grinned. "Cross my heart and hope to die."

"Well, with the reward money, we'll certainly have enough for everything . . . ," she said slowly. "If that's what you want to do."

"I heard Lucas Flynt is getting a wagon train come spring," Tracy said.

*"Lucas Flynt?"* Sunny exclaimed, horrified. The image of the red-mustached, poker-playing, cigar-smoking, hard-as-nails wagon master who had heartlessly turned down her pleas to allow them to work their way to California came back into Sunny's mind. "After what he did to us?"

"Ah, Sunny, let bygones be bygones, right? Besides, *this* time we ain't greenhorns, Sis!" He laughed boisterously, slapping his knee at his joke.

"No, we're certainly not that," she agreed grimly. What she didn't say was that the mention of the name Lucas Flynt also brought up the name of his scout. She *had* to stop thinking about Webb Chandler. He was as much out of her life as Rhys Graham was now.

The important thing was that the reward bonus would

222

enable them to buy the wagon, mules, and equipment necessary for their westward journey. But why didn't her enthusiasm match her brother's excitement? It had all been *her* idea from the very first, hadn't it?

Again. They were on their way again. Going to California to find—what? For a moment Sunny's eagerness drained away completely. The whole plan struck a hollow note. Something was missing. Her joyous anticipation, the adventure of it, the challenge, all seemed somehow pointless. How could she have lost what kept her going all these dismal months?

It was probably just that she was tired. Worn out from the unusual physical exertion of the last few days, the fear and tension she'd been under. She was exhausted emotionally. Surely now everything would fall into place. They were free to pick up their dreams and follow them again. To look forward to the overland journey, to homesteading. This had only been a detour on the way to the new life that awaited them in California.

However, Tracy was so fired up after their conversation, he didn't seem to notice *her* lack of enthusiasm. He started shopping for the best bargains in the equipment they would need. Even with his arm still in a sling, he managed to ride around getting things lined up. When he learned that Lucas Flynt's wagon train was getting filled up, he made reservations for them to ensure they would be among the ones heading out from Independence the second week in April.

Sunny was still managing the station, sorting and packing the mailbags and taking care of the ponies, while two other riders were alternating taking Tracy's route.

In the meantime she had been doing some packing for their trip. From what Rhys had told her, it would only be a matter of months until all the Pony Express stations would be closing. The nearly completed transcontinental railroad would take over the transportation of mail across the country. Soon the gallant riders, and the little stations dotted all through the western territories, would be forgotten. But Sunny knew she would never forget her own experience nor the people she had met, the friends she had made. She knew that when it came time to leave, she would of course miss Verna and Clem. Rhys had already left. The person she knew she would find it hardest to forget was Webb. She didn't even know if she'd get a chance to say good-bye to him.

Sunny felt a stab of resentment but mostly frustration. If he really cared, if he was at all interested, if what she thought she had glimpsed in his eyes had any truth—then why hadn't he come to see her? Surely he couldn't still believe that gossip about her and Rhys. Not when Rhys had sold out and left town.

There was no use worrying about it. She should know better than to expect Webb to behave in any normal way. A man with his own code—unpredictable, undependable, irresponsible. A "rolling stone," Verna had called him. And yet not easy to forget.

"I'm just not going to think about him anymore," she told herself resolutely. She had other things on her mind to do. More important things. Making lists, for one thing. She tried to remember all the necessities that the scoundrel Faraday had told her they had to have to complete their equipment and supplies for the journey west. Ironically Sunny recalled how meticulously she had written everything down, with the estimated cost beside each item, and then so naively counted out to him the money with which to purchase it all for them. Even though they had been swindled and had never seen a penny of the amount she had given him to pay for it all, Sunny still knew the list almost by heart. Now she went over her notes in order to better advise Tracy when they shopped for the best equipment. Naturally she had planned to go with Tracy to make the final decisions. That's why she was surprised and more than a little miffed when he came in one day, his eyes lighted with excitement, and told her, "Sis, I've got us a rip-roarin' deal. Mr. Ardley told me to go out to the rendezvous place, that he'd heard tell of a fully equipped wagon for sale, all outfitted and ready to go. Seems like the man who bought it was fixin' to go west with the wagon train. Well, at the last minute his plans changed—his wife decided she wouldn't go or some such fracas—and he wants to get at least some of his money out of it."

Sunny blinked. It seemed too good to be true. "And you went out to see it?"

"I sure did. And it's just like Clem said. It's a good, sturdy wagon, already has boxes and shelves built inside, plenty of storage space—"

"Mules to go with it?"

"No, he'd already sold the livestock he was taking. Anyways, the fella who showed it to me said it's better to take oxen. Oxen's the most durable for the long trip. Don't require much care, are strong, easily driven. We'd need at least four to spell them pulling the wagon in case one got lame or they got sore necks. But they're cheaper than mules and we can sell them for four times as much when we get to California." Tracy halted only long enough to catch his breath, then rattled on. "And we should have a milk cow but Clem said he'd sell us one of his and—"

"Wait a minute, Tracy, wait! Are you *sure* this is all as it's supposed to be? I mean we're not being taken again?"

Tracy assumed a pained expression. "Come on, Sunny! Don't you think I remembered we was hornswoggled once? I've smartened up some since then. Besides—" He started to say something else, then stopped. "Get your bonnet and shawl and come see for yourself. Seein's believin'."

Reluctant to admit she resented her younger brother having taken on so much on his own without consulting her, Sunny hid her feelings and kept herself from saying more. Instead she did as he suggested. A few minutes later they were in their small wagon, riding out to Oakmont, the gathering place for the wagons forming the Flynt train.

On the way out there, Sunny took herself firmly in hand. If they were going to make this long, hazardous journey together, she would have to remember that Tracy was no longer a boy. In the past several months, her brother had come a long way from being the boy with whom she had left Ohio. He had become a young man, having proved himself capable of handling responsibility, exercising good judgment, and showing courage.

When they pulled to a stop at the edge of the circle of wagons, Tracy jumped out and ran around, ready to help her. Sunny straightened her bonnet, adjusted her shawl, then put out her hand and got down, asking, "So where do we go? Where is the wagon you want me to see?"

"Over there." Tracy pointed.

Just as she turned around to look in that direction, she saw Webb Chandler sauntering toward them.

"Miss Lyndall," he said as casually as though it had been only yesterday they had seen each other. As though they had not ridden through a stormy night, risking danger and ambush. As though he had never held her so close in his arms that she had heard his heart beating as wildly as her own . . .

Sunny just watched him coming, unable to move or respond to his greeting.

"Mornin', Webb," Tracy hailed him and stuck out his hand to grasp the other man's in a friendly shake.

Like two men on equal terms, Sunny thought. Although she was impressed with her brother's display of new maturity, seeing Webb was disconcerting. She was determined not to reveal the hurt she felt that he had obviously been avoiding her since the night of her wild ride. Acting cool as

226

the proverbial cucumber, he was. As if nothing had passed between them! Well, two could play at this game, Sunny decided.

"You've come to look at my wagon?" Webb spoke to Tracy, but his eyes moved to Sunny.

"*Your* wagon?" surprise made Sunny blurt out. She turned an accusing glance on her brother. "You didn't tell me *that!*"

Tracy looked just as surprised. "I didn't know. How come, Webb?"

"Well, I kinda felt sorry for the poor fella—," he drawled. Then, as if he didn't want to be presumed softhearted, Webb quickly amended the statement. "He would have been taken by grafters, he was so desperate. The main thing is, it's a good rig, one of the best I've seen. Besides, I've been thinking for a while now of mebbe"—he paused, pushed the brim of his hat back off his forehead with his thumb— "staying out west this time. Homesteadin'." He glanced at Sunny, then went on. "I could let you have it for half of what I paid for it. Then when we get to California, we could sell it and split whatever we got for it. Sound fair?"

Tracy looked at Sunny. When she didn't say anything, he answered. "Sounds fair to me."

Sending Tracy an insinuating glance, Sunny found her voice and said primly, "*Before* we make any commitment, I'd like to see the wagon."

Webb looked amused. "Sure enough, Miss Lyndall. Let's take a look."

The wagon was everything Tracy had said. Sturdily built, its twelve-foot-by-four-foot frame covered by yards of oiled canvas stretched over arched supports, its wheels rimmed with iron. Webb held out his hand to assist Sunny's climb into the wagon by means of pull-down steps at the back. There was a split-second hesitation before she placed her hand in his. Something within her both wanted and dreaded the contact. But not to do so would have seemed rude. His fingers grasped hers firmly. She stepped up and inside the wagon, the vehicle that—if they purchased it—would be their home for months to come.

The interior was as well ordered and constructed as the exterior was. Wooden storage bins had been built on either side, pockets for extra storage had been sewn on the inside between the wooden hoops holding the canvas ceiling, space had been provided for a small cookstove, cooking pots, and utensils, and shelves had been made for supplies.

"Well, what do you say, Sunny?" Tracy asked eagerly. "Isn't this a jim-dandy outfit?"

There was no question of that. Again, coming into such a fine wagon, already outfitted and supplied, seemed like some kind of miracle. Was it happenstance? Or was there more to it than that? One of those old adages she'd accused Webb of employing now flashed into her own mind: "Don't look a gift horse in the mouth." Not that it was exactly a gift. But it was certainly a good price for such a windfall. And they still had to buy oxen.

"You'll want time to discuss this together and decide," Webb said after they were all standing outside the wagon. "I've got some things to tend to. Let me know if you want it." With that he walked back into the circle of wagons, leaving brother and sister alone.

"How does Webb figure in all this?" Sunny asked Tracy.

"He's Flynt's scout on this trip. I guess he was in on the whole thing when the man who had signed up to go west come to Flynt and told him about his wife getting sick or whatever the reason was that he'd decided not to go. Guess Webb wanted to help out."

Sunny's reaction to the fact that Webb would be the scout on this trip was mixed. Would it be a daily struggle not to show her changed feelings toward him? Or would they all be too busy to let personal feelings interfere? She had the suspicion that being around Webb now would be like a hurting splinter in the soft regions of her heart. But the outfit for sale was too good a deal to pass up. She couldn't let Webb Chandler's effect on her keep them from the best bargain they would ever find on an outfit to go west. She would just have to deal with it. She was going to California and that was it! Nothing was going to stop her this time.

When a triumphant Tracy came back after closing the deal with Webb, Sunny asked, "Did you sign something?"

"Nope. Just a handshake."

"Was that wise? I mean—"

Tracy shot his sister a withering glance. "We trust each other, Sunny." He picked up the reins and turned the wagon around, headed back to town. "Webb's as sterling as silver. I heard Mr. Graham say so. That oughta be enough for *you*."

That silenced Sunny. It wasn't the deal of buying the wagon. It was the months ahead that worried her. Maybe she could trust Webb in a business transaction. It was with her heart she was unsure.

Determined to put her own feelings aside, Sunny smiled at her brother and gaily repeated the words on the signs she'd seen proudly posted on some of the wagons. "Then it's 'Ho for California!'"

A few days later Tracy went with Mr. Brownlee to select the oxen they would hitch to their wagon. Sunny was alone at the Express station, doing her final packing. As she gave the living quarters a final sweeping look, searching for additional things to take with them, her gaze rested on Webb's shotgun. She'd forgotten she had it, that it belonged to him. How could she get it back to him?

As if beckoned by her thoughts, to her amazement Webb rode through the gates of the Express yard less than an hour later.

Flustered and trying not to show it, Sunny opened the door to his knock. He tipped his hat brim. "Mornin', Miss Lyndall. Wondered if I could have a few minutes of your time."

*Why the sudden formality?* Sunny thought as she stepped back so he could enter. "Why, sure. Come in. Matter of fact, I was just thinking about you . . ."

"You *were*?" He looked wary.

"About your shotgun, actually," Sunny said hastily. "How I'd get it back to you."

"Has Tracy got one for the trip? Every wagon should have a rifle or a shotgun—in case of Indians. Not that I'm looking for that to happen. Flynt's pretty savvy with Indians, knows how to deal with them. S'long as I've been scouting for him, he never run into any trouble with Indians. So if your brother hasn't got one yet, you might as well keep that one."

"Well, if you're sure . . ." Sunny sounded hesitant.

"I'm sure." Webb stood looking around, twisting the hat he'd removed upon entering. He shifted from one foot to the other uneasily, brushed back an unruly strand of hair from his forehead before saying, "It weren't 'bout the shotgun I come." He cleared his throat. "Well, what I come for was to say—to be truthful, I had something else in mind when I bought that wagon off the fella I told you about."

"Oh, you don't want to sell it to us after all?"

"No. I *do*. I mean it was *you* I had in mind when I bought it."

*"Me?"* she repeated softly, conscious of—as she often was in Webb's presence—her heart beating very fast and hard.

"Yes, ma'am. You."

Suddenly the room seemed very quiet. Webb was looking at her steadily. Sunny's knees began to tremble. She moved behind one of the kitchen chairs, steadied herself by holding on to the back.

"I don't know exactly how to put this," Webb began

230

slowly. "For quite a while I've had in mind making this my last trip to California. I've had a hankerin' to settle down, put down some roots, homestead. Guess that comes from seeing some of the men who come west on the trains I've been scout on prosper once they get there, make a good life for themselves and their families. I'm about done crossing the prairie and the mountains, then turning right around and coming back." He paused and looked directly at Sunny and said in a softer tone, "The trip's a lot harder than folks tell you or want to believe. But then at the end there's California. And it's just as pretty as they say it is, even better maybe. It's a great place to build a home, raise a family—"

Sunny heard Webb's words but wasn't sure she quite understood where they were leading. Stiltedly she echoed his words. "Build a home, raise a family? Homestead? *That's* what you plan to do?"

"That's sure what I'd *like* to do." Webb paused. "But a man can't do that alone." He put his hat on the kitchen table and took a few steps toward her. Sunny did not move. Gently prying her fingers from their grip on the chair, he moved the chair out of the way. Now they stood only a breath apart, looking into each other's eyes. Sunny saw in his what she had longed all her life to see in a man's eyes. He reached for her hands, and the minute he touched her, she felt a strong current pass between them. She had felt the same thing the very first time they met. Or something like it. Then she had thought it was antagonism. This was even stronger. She quivered as if electricity were coursing through her entire body. She felt both weak and excited, frightened yet happy.

Webb dropped her hands and took her face between both his hands, looking at her as if searching for something. His question was asked and an answer given without a word being spoken. With a little sigh Sunny closed her eyes as Webb leaned forward to kiss her. It was a kiss both had long dreamed of, and now they experienced it in all its tenderness and promise. He gathered her to him, holding her against his heart, and whispered, "I love you, Sunny."

The strength of his sheltering arms was familiar and comforting, and she whispered back, "I love you, Webb," knowing it was true.

Sunny almost laughed. For joy. How could she have been so blind? Had she not known it before this? Had she not seen that Webb Chandler was the kind of man she had always secretly wanted?

All the misunderstandings, the misgivings, of their prickly past relationship faded away in this newfound certainty.

This was a man she could trust, knowing that he loved her in spite of what she seemed to be. Here was a man with whom she would never have to pretend. With whom she was free to be who she really was. He knew her weaknesses, admired her strengths, shared her faults of being opinionated and quick-tempered and her good qualities of loyalty and honesty.

Perhaps this is what it had all been for, the swindling, the delay, the time of waiting "in the desert." It had all been for a purpose. She had grown, matured. The girl she had been when they arrived had changed. That girl was almost a stranger to the woman she had become. Sunny rejoiced in the thought that what the Scripture said was true: "Everything works together for good." *Maybe even the things we think we don't want, things that are hard and difficult, that seem to thwart our desires, in the end prove to be the best. Maybe this is what I came west for, what I've been hoping to find all this time.*

"So when we get to California, will you consider marrying me?" Webb sounded anxious.

"Oh yes, Webb, I will." Her voice rang with happy conviction. Webb kissed her again, caught her up in his arms, and swung her around, singing out, "Then it's 'Ho for California!'"

Sunny had planned to conquer the trail to California on her own. Now she knew that if she accepted Webb's proposal, she would never look back, there would be no regrets. Loving Webb and agreeing to be his wife would be the beginning of the greatest adventure of all. It might take a long time for two such stubborn people to really get to know, understand, and accept each other. But it was a long way to California, and they still would have the journey of a lifetime before them to learn all the lessons love teaches.